ARMS OF THE TOWN OF OAKHAM, RUTLANDSHIRE, ENGLAND.

[From an Old Engraving.]

THE

MAGIC OF THE HORSE-SHOE

With Other Folk-Lore Notes

BY

ROBERT MEANS LAWRENCE, M. D.

Fredonia Books
Amsterdam, The Netherlands

The Magic of the Horse-Shoe:
With other Folk-Lore Notes

by
Robert Means Lawrence

ISBN: 1-4101-0050-2

Copyright © 2002 by Fredonia Books

Reprinted from the 1898 edition

Fredonia Books
Amsterdam, The Netherlands
http://www.fredoniabooks.com

In order to make original editions of historical works
available to scholars at an economical price, this
facsimile of the original edition of 1898 is
reproduced from the best available copy and has
been digitally enhanced to improve legibility, but the
text remains unaltered to retain historical
authenticity.

PREFACE

THE study of the origin and history of popular customs and beliefs affords an insight, otherwise unattainable, into the operations of the human mind in early times. Superstitions, however trivial in themselves, relics of paganism though they be, and oftentimes comparable to baneful weeds, are now considered proper subjects for scientific research. While the ignorant savage is a slave to many superstitious fancies which dominate his every action, the educated man strives to be free from such a bondage, yet recognizes as profitable the study of those same beliefs. The heterogeneous character of the material drawn from so many sources has rendered it difficult, if not impossible, to follow any distinctly systematic treatment of the subject. However, the development in recent years of a widespread interest in all branches of folk-lore warrants the hope that any volume devoted to this subject, and representing somewhat diligent research, may have a certain value, in spite of its imperfections. The expert folk-lorist may find much to criticise; but this book, treating of popular beliefs, is intended for popular reading. It has been the writer's aim to make the chapter on the Horse-Shoe as exhaustive as possible, as this attractive symbol of superstition does not appear to have received hitherto the attention which it merits. This chapter is the outgrowth of a paper read at the seventh annual meeting of the American Folk-Lore Society, at Philadelphia, December 28, 1895, an abstract of which appeared in the Society's Journal for December, 1896.

Extended quotations are indicated by smaller type.

R. M. L.

BOSTON, September 1, 1898.

CONTENTS

THE MAGIC OF THE HORSE-SHOE

And still o'er many a neighboring door
She saw the horse-shoe's curvèd charm.
WHITTIER, *The Witch's Daughter*.

Happy art thou, as if every day thou hadst picked up a horse-shoe.
LONGFELLOW, *Evangeline*.

I. HISTORY OF THE HORSE-SHOE

THE evolution of the modern horse-shoe from the primitive foot-gear for draught animals used in ancient times furnishes an interesting subject for investigation. Xenophon and other historians recommended various processes for hardening and strengthening the hoofs of horses and mules,[1] and from this negative evidence some writers have inferred that the ancients were ignorant of farriery. It seems indeed certain that the practice of protecting the feet of horses was not universal among the Greeks and Romans. Fabretti, an Italian antiquary, examined with care the representations of horses on many ancient columns and marbles, and found but one instance in which the horse appeared

[1] *New Cabinet Cyclopædia*.

to be shod;[1] and in most specimens of ancient art the iron horse-shoe is conspicuous by its absence. But in the mosaic portraying the battle of Issus, which was unearthed at Pompeii in 1831, and which is now in the Naples Museum, is the figure of a horse whose feet appear to be shod with iron shoes similar to those in modern use;[2] and in an ancient Finnish incantation against the plague, quoted in Lenormant's "Chaldean Magic and Sorcery," occur these lines:—

O Scourge depart; Plague, take thy flight. . . . I will give thee a horse with which to escape, whose shoes shall not slide on ice, nor whose feet slip on the rocks.

No allusion to the horse-shoe is made by early writers on veterinary topics. But, on the other hand, there is abundant testimony that the ancients did sometimes protect the feet of their beasts of burden. Winckelmann, the Prussian art historian, describes an antique engraved stone representing a man holding up a horse's foot, while an assistant, kneeling, fastens on a shoe.[3] In the works of the Roman poet Catullus occurs the simile of the iron shoe of a mule sticking in the mire.[4] Contemporary historians relate that the Emperor Nero caused his mules to be shod with silver,[5] while golden

---

[1] *Archæologia*, vol. iii. 1775.
[2] John Kitto, D. D., *Cyclopædia of Biblical Art.*
[3] John Beckman, *A History of Inventions.*
[4] Carmen XVIII. 26.
[5] Suetonius: "Soleis mularum argenteis."

shoes adorned the feet of the mules belonging to the
notorious Empress Poppæa.[1] Mention of an iron horse-
shoe is made by Appian,[2] a writer not indeed remarkable for accuracy; but the phrase "brasen-footed
steeds," which occurs in Homer's Iliad, is regarded by
commentators as a metaphorical expression for strength
and endurance. Wrappings of plaited fibre, as hemp
or broom, were used by the ancients to protect the feet
of horses.[3] But the most common form of foot covering for animals appears to have been a kind of leathern
sock or sandal, which was sometimes provided with an
iron sole. This covering was fastened around the fet-
locks by means of thongs, and could be easily removed.[4]

Iron horse-shoes of peculiar form, which have been
exhumed in Great Britain of recent years, have been
objects of much interest to archæologists. In 1878 a
number of such relics shaped for the hoof and pierced
for nails were found at a place called Cæsar's Camp,
near Folkstone, England.[5] In the south of Scotland,
also, ancient horse-shoes have been found, consisting of
a solid piece of iron made to cover the whole hoof and
very heavy. In the year 1653 a piece of iron resem-
bling a horse-shoe, and having nine nail-holes, was

[1] Pliny : "Jumentis suis soleas ex auro induere."
[2] Fosbroke, *Dictionary of Antiquities.*
[3] *Knight's Mechanical Dictionary.*
[4] Alexander Adam, LL. D., *Roman Antiquities.*
[5] *Archæologia*, vol. xlvii.

found in the grave of Childeric I., king of the Franks, who died A. D. 481. Professor N. S. Shaler believes that the iron horse-shoe was invented in the fourth century, and from the fact that it was first called *selene*, the moon, from its somewhat crescent-like shape, he concludes that it originated in Greece.[1] But even in the ninth century, in France, horses were shod with iron on special occasions only,[2] and the early Britons, Saxons, and Danes do not appear to have had much knowledge of farriery. The modern art of shoeing horses is thought to have been generally introduced in England by the Normans under William the Conqueror.[3] Henry de Ferrars, who accompanied that monarch, is believed to have received his surname because he was intrusted with the inspection of the farriers; and the coat-of-arms of his descendants still bears six horse-shoes.[4]

On the gate of Oakham Castle, an ancient Norman mansion in Rutlandshire, built by Wakelin de Ferrars, son of the first earl of that name, were formerly to be seen a number of horse-shoes of different patterns.

The estate is famous on account of the tenure of the barons occupying it. Every nobleman who journeyed

[1] *Scribner's Magazine*, November, 1894.
[2] John Beckman, *A History of Inventions.*
[3] Fosbroke, *Archæologia*, vol. iii.
[4] *Notes and Queries*, series 3, vol. v. 1864.

through its precincts was obliged as an act of homage to forfeit a shoe of the horse whereon he rode, or else to redeem it with a sum of money ; and the horse-shoes thus obtained were nailed upon the gate, but are now within on the walls of the castle.

These walls are covered by memorials of royal personages and peers, who have thus paid tribute to the custom of the county.[1]

Queen Elizabeth was thought to have initiated this practice, though this opinion is incorrect. According to tradition she was once journeying on a visit to her lord high treasurer, William Cecil, the well-known Lord Burleigh, at his residence near Stamford. While passing through Oakham her horse is said to have cast a shoe, and in memory of the mishap the queen ordered a large iron shoe to be made and hung up in the castle, and that every nobleman traveling through the town should follow her example.

A similar usage prevails to-day, new shoes being provided of shapes and sizes chosen by the donors.[2]

While John of Gaunt (1339–99), son of Edward III. of England, was riding through the town of Lancaster, his horse cast a shoe, which was kept as a souvenir by the townspeople, and fastened in the middle of the street. And in accordance with a time-

[1] *Leicestershire and Rutland Notes and Queries*, vol. i. 1889–91.
[2] Margaret G. Finch, *The History of Oakham Castle*. Oakham, 1897.

honored custom a new shoe is placed in the same spot
every seven years by the residents of Horse-Shoe
Corner.[1]

The practical value of the horse-shoe is tersely expressed in the old German saying, "A nail preserves a
country;" for the nail keeps in place the horse-shoe,
the shoe protects the foot of the horse, the horse carries the knight, the knight holds the castle, and the
castle defends the country.

The following story from Grimm's "Household Tales"
(vol. ii. p. 303) may be appropriate in this place, as
illustrating the same idea, besides pointing a moral.

The Nail.

A merchant had done a good business at the fair; he had
sold his wares and lined his money-bags with gold and silver.
Then he wanted to travel homeward and be in his house before nightfall. So he packed his trunk with the money on
his horse and rode away. At noon he rested in a town, and
when he wanted to go farther the stable-boy brought out his
horse and said: "A nail is wanting, sir, in the shoe of its left
hind foot." "Let it be wanting," answered the merchant;
"the shoe will certainly stay on for the six miles I have still
to go; I am in a hurry." In the afternoon, when he once
more alighted and had his horse fed, the stable-boy went to
him and said, "Sir, a shoe is missing from your horse's left
hind foot; shall I take him to the blacksmith?" "Let it
still be wanting," answered the man, "the horse can very well

hold out for the couple of miles which remain; I am in haste." He rode forth, but before long the horse began to limp. It had not limped long before it began to stumble, and it had not stumbled long before it fell down and broke its leg. The merchant was forced to leave the horse where it was, and unbuckle the trunk, take it on his back, and go home on foot. And there he did not arrive until quite late at night. "And that unlucky nail," said he to himself, "has caused all this disaster." Hasten slowly.

II. THE HORSE-SHOE AS A SAFEGUARD

Your wife's a witch, man; you should nail a horse-shoe on your chamber-door. — SIR WALTER SCOTT, *Redgauntlet*.

As a practical device for the protection of horses' feet, the utility of the iron horse-shoe has long been generally recognized; and for centuries, in countries widely separated, it has also been popularly used as a talisman for the preservation of buildings or premises from the wiles of witches and fiends.

To the student of folk-lore, a superstition like this, which has exerted so wide an influence over men's minds in the past, and which is also universally prevalent in our own times, must have a peculiar interest. What, then, were the reasons for the general adoption of the horse-shoe as a talisman? It is our purpose to consider the various theories *seriatim*.

Among the Romans there prevailed a custom of driving nails into cottage walls as an antidote against the plague. Both this practice and the later one of nailing up horse-shoes have been thought by some to originate from the rite of the Passover. The blood sprinkled upon the doorposts and lintel at the time of the great Jewish feast formed the chief points of an arch, and it may be that with this in mind people adopted the horse-shoe as an arch-shaped talisman, and it thus became generally emblematic of good luck.

The same thought may underlie the practice of the peasants in the west of Scotland, who train the boughs of the rowan or mountain-ash tree in the form of an arch over a farmyard gate to protect their cattle from evil.

III. HORNS AND OTHER TWO-PRONGED OBJECTS

The supernatural qualities of the horse-shoe as a preservative against imaginary demons have been supposed to be due to its bifurcated shape, as any object having two prongs or forks was formerly thought to be effective for this purpose. As with the crescent, the source of this belief is doubtless the appearance of the moon in certain of its phases.

Hence, according to some authorities, is derived the alleged efficacy as amulets of horse-shoes, the horns and tusks of animals, the talons of birds, and the claws of wild beasts, lobsters, and crabs. Hence, too,

the significance of the oft-quoted lines from Robert
Herrick's "Hesperides : " —

> Hang up hooks and sheers to scare
> Hence, the hag that rides the mare.

The horn of the fabulous unicorn, in reality none
other than that of the rhinoceros, is much valued as
an amulet, and in west Africa, where the horns of
wild animals are greatly esteemed as fiend-scarers, a
large horn filled with mud and having three small
horns attached to its lower end is used as a safeguard
to prevent slaves from running away.[1]

In the vicinity of Mirzapur in central Hindostan the
Horwas tie on the necks of their children the roots
of jungle plants as protective charms; their efficacy
being thought to depend on their resemblance to the
horns of certain wild beasts.

The Mohammedans of northern India use a complex amulet, composed in part of a tiger's claw and two
claws of the large-horned owl with the tips facing outward,[2] while in southern Europe we find the necks of
mules ornamented with two boar's tusks or with the
horns of an antelope.

Amulets fashioned in the shape of horns and
crescents are very popular among the Neapolitans.[3]

---

[1] Cameron's *Across Africa*.
[2] W. Crooke, B. A., *North Indian Folk-Lore*.
[3] Clara Erskine Clement, *Naples*.

Elworthy quotes at some length from the "Mimica degli antichi" of Andrea de Jorio (Napoli, 1832), in illustration of this fact. From this source we learn that the horns of Sicilian oxen and of bullocks are in favor with the nobility and aristocracy as evil-eye protectives, and are frequently seen on their houses and in their gardens; stag's antlers are the favorites with grocers and chemists, while the lower classes are content with the horns of rams and goats. The Sicilians are wont to tie pieces of red ribbon to the little horns which they wear as charms, and this is supposed vastly to increase their efficiency.

In southern Spain, particularly in Andalusia, the stag's horn is a very favorite talisman. The native children wear a silver-tipped horn suspended from the neck by a braided cord made from the hair of a black mare's tail. It is believed that an evil glance directed at the child is received by the horn, which thereupon breaks asunder, and the malevolent influence is thus dissipated.[1]

Among the Arabs the horn amulet is believed to render inert the malign glance of an enemy, and in the oases of the desert the horned heads of cattle are to be seen over the doors of the Arab dwellings as talismans.[2]

[1] George Borrow, *The Zincali*.
[2] A. Certeux and E. Henry Carnoy, *L'Algérie traditionnelle*, tome i. p. 159.

In Lesbos the skulls of oxen or other horned creatures are fixed upon trees or sticks to avert the evil eye from the crops and fruits.[1]

In Mongolia the horns of antelopes are prized on account of their alleged magical properties; fortune-tellers and diviners affect to derive a knowledge of futurity by observation of the rings which encircle them. The Mongols set a high value upon whip-handles made from these horns, and aver that their use by horsemen promotes endurance in their steeds.[2]

Inasmuch as the horns of animals serve as weapons both for attack and defense, they were early associated in men's minds with the idea of power. Thus in ancient times the corners of altars were fashioned in the shape of horns, doubtless in order to symbolize the majesty and power of the Being in whose honor sacrifices were offered.[3]

Apropos of horns as symbols of strength, the peasants of Bannú, a district of the Punjab, believe that God placed the newly created world upon a cow's horn, the cow on a fish's back, and the fish on a stone; but what the stone rests upon, they do not venture to surmise. According to their theory, whenever the cow shakes her head, an earthquake naturally results.[4]

[1] *Folk-Lore*, June, 1896, p. 148.
[2] Lieutenant-Colonel N. Prejevalsky, *Mongolia*, vol. ii. p. 207.
[3] William M. Thomson, D. D., *The Land and the Book*.
[4] S. S. Thorburn, *Bannú*.

The Siamese attribute therapeutic qualities to the horns and tusks of certain animals, and their pharmacopœia contains a somewhat complex prescription used as a febrifuge, whose principal ingredients are the powdered horns of a rhinoceros, bison, and stag, the tusks of an elephant and tiger, and the teeth of a bear and crocodile. These are mixed together with water, and half of the resulting compound is to be swallowed, the remainder to be rubbed upon the body.[1]

The *mano cornuta* or anti-witch gesture is used very generally in southern and central Italy. Its antiquity is vouched for by its representation in ancient paintings unearthed at Pompeii.[2] It consists in flexing the two middle fingers, while the others are extended in imitation of horns. When the hand in this position is pointed at an obnoxious individual, the malignity of his glance is believed to be rendered inert.[3]

In F. Marion Crawford's novel, "Pietro Ghisleri," one of the characters, Laura Arden, was regarded in Roman society as a *jettatrice,* that is, one having the evil eye. Such a reputation once fastened on a person involves social ostracism. In the presence of the unfortunate individual every hand was hidden to make

[1] Sir John Bowring, F. R. S., *The Kingdom and People of Siam,* vol. i. p. 145.
[2] Clara Erskine Clement, *Naples.*
[3] Elworthy, *Evil Eye,* p. 261.

the talismanic gesture, and at the mere mention of her name all Rome "made horns." No one ever accosted her without having the fingers flexed in the approved fashion, unless, indeed, they had about them some potent amulet.

It is a curious fact that the possession of the evil eye may be imputed to any one, regardless of character or position. Pope Pius IX. was believed to have this malevolent power, and many devout Christians, while on their knees awaiting his benediction, were accustomed slyly to extend a hand toward him in the abovementioned position.[1]

In an article on "Asiatic Symbolism" in the "Indian Antiquary" (vol. xv. 1886), Mr. H. G. M. Murray-Aynsley says, in regard to Neapolitan evil-eye amulets, that they were probably introduced in southern Italy by Greek colonists of Asiatic ancestry, who settled at Cumæ and other places in that neighborhood. Whether fashioned in the shape of horns or crescents, they are survivals of an ancient Chaldean symbol. It has been said that nothing, unless perhaps a superstitious belief, is more easily transmissible than a symbol; and the people of antiquity were wont to attribute to every symbol a talismanic value.[2]

The modern Greeks, as well as the Italians, wear

[1] *Popular Science Monthly*, November, 1896.
[2] Goblet D'Alviella, *La migration des symboles*, p. 25.

little charms representing the hand as making this gesture.[1]

But not alone in the south of Europe exists the belief in the peculiar virtues of two-pronged objects, for in Norway reindeer-horns are placed over the doors of farm-buildings to drive off demons;[2] and the fine antlers which grace the homes of successful hunters in our own country are doubtless often regarded by their owners as of more value than mere trophies of the chase, inasmuch as traditional fancy invests them with such extraordinary virtues.

In France a piece of stag-horn is thought to be a preservative against witchcraft and disease, while in Portugal ox-horns fastened on poles are placed in melon-patches to protect the fruit from withering glances.

Among the Ossetes, a tribe of the Caucasus, the women arrange their hair in the shape of a chamois-horn, curving forwards over the brow, thus forming a talismanic coiffure; and when a Moslem takes his child on a journey he paints a crescent between its eyes, or tattooes the same device on its body. The modern Greek, too, adopts the precaution of attaching a crab's claw to the child's head.[3] In northern Africa the horns of animals are very generally used as amulets,

---

[1] Rennell Rodd, *The Customs and Lore of Modern Greece*. 1892.
[2] *Revue des traditions populaires*, tome viii. 1892.
[3] *Mélusine*, tome viii. No. 4. 1896.

the prevailing idea being everywhere the same, namely, that pronged objects repel demons and evil glances.

Horns are used in eastern countries as ornaments to head-dresses, and serve, moreover, as symbols of rank. They are often made of precious metals, sometimes of wood. The *tantura*, worn by the Druses of Mount Lebanon in Syria, has this shape.[1]

In the Bulgarian villages of Macedonia and Thrace the so-called wise woman, who combines the professions of witch and midwife, is an important character. Immediately upon the birth of a child this personage places a reaping-hook in a corner of the room to keep away unfriendly spirits; the efficacy of the talisman being doubtless due partly to its shape, which bears considerable resemblance to a horse-shoe.

And in Albania, a sickle, with which straw has just been cut, is placed for a few seconds on the stomach of a newly born child to prevent the demons who cause colic from exercising their functions.[2]

The mystic virtue of the forked shape is not, however, restricted to its faculty of averting the glance of an evil eye or other malign influences, for the Divining Rod is believed to derive from this same peculiarity of form its magical power of detecting the presence of water or metals when wielded by an experienced hand.

---

[1] M'Clintock and Strong's *Cyclopædia*, art. "Head-Dress."
[2] Lucy M. J. Garnett, *The Christian Women of Turkey*.

IV. THE SYMBOL OF THE OPEN HAND

It is worthy of note that the symbol of an open hand with extended fingers was a favorite talisman in former ages, and was to be seen, for example, at the entrances of dwellings in ancient Carthage. It is also found on Lybian and Phœnician tombs, as well as on Celtic monuments in French Brittany.[1] Dr. H. C. Trumbull quotes evidence from various writers showing that this symbol is in common use at the present time in several Eastern lands. In the region of ancient Babylonia the figure of a red outstretched hand is still displayed on houses and animals; and in Jerusalem the same token is frequently placed above the door or on the lintel on account of its reputed virtues in averting evil glances. The Spanish Jews of Jerusalem draw the figure of a hand in red upon the doors of their houses; and they also place upon their children's heads silver hand-shaped charms, which they believe to be specially obnoxious to unfriendly individuals desirous of bringing evil either upon the children themselves, or upon other members of the household.

In different parts of Palestine the open-hand symbol appears alike on the houses of Christians, Jews, and Moslems, usually painted in blue on or above the door.[2]

[1] L'Algérie traditionnelle, tome i. p. 159. 1884.
[2] H. Clay Trumbull, The Threshold Covenant, p. 74.

Claude Reignier Conder, R. E., in "Heth and Moab," remarks on the antiquity of this pagan emblem, which appears on Roman standards and on the sceptre of Siva in India. He is of the opinion that the figure of the red hand, whether sculptured on Irish crosses, displayed in Indian temples, or on Mexican buildings, is always an example of the same original idea, — that of a protective symbol.

A white hand-print is commonly seen upon the doors and shutters of Jewish and Moslem houses in Beyrout and other Syrian towns; and even the Christian residents of these towns sometimes mark windows and flour-boxes with this emblem, after dipping the hand in whitewash, in order to "avert chilling February winds from old people and to bring luck to the bin." [1]

In Germany a rude amulet having the form of an open hand is fashioned out of the stems of coarse plants, and is deemed an ample safeguard against divers misfortunes and sorceries. It is called "the hand of Saint John," or "the hand of Fortune."

The Jewish matrons of Algeria fasten little golden hands to their children's caps, or to their glass-bead necklaces, and they themselves carry about similar luck tokens.

In northwestern Scotland whoever enters a house where butter is being made is expected to lay his hand

[1] *Folk-Lore*, March, 1898, p. 10.

upon the churn, thereby signifying that he has no evil designs against the butter-maker, and dissipating any possible effects of an evil eye.[1]

As a charm against malevolent influences, the Arabs of Algeria make use of rude drawings representing an open hand, placed either above the entrances of their habitations or within doors, — a symbolical translation of the well-known Arabic imprecation, "Five fingers in thine eye!" Oftentimes the same meaning is conveyed by five lines, one shorter than the others to indicate the thumb, thus ☰.[2]

V. CRESCENTS AND HALF-MOON-SHAPED AMULETS

The alleged predominant influence of the moon's wax and wane over the growth and welfare of vegetation was formerly generally recognized. Thus in an almanac of the year 1661 it is stated that: —

If any corn, seed, or plant be either set or sown within six hours either before or after the full Moon in Summer, or before the new Moon in Winter, having joined with the cosmical rising of Arcturus and Orion, the Hædi and the Siculi, it is subject to blasting and canker.[3]

Timber was always cut during the wane of the moon, and so firmly rooted was this superstition that

[1] *Mélusine*, tome viii. No. 3. 1896.
[2] *L'Algérie traditionelle*, tome i. p. 159. 1884.
[3] Richard Folkard, Jr., *Plant-Lore*.

directions were given accordingly in the Forest Code of France.

An early English almanac advised farmers to kill hogs when the moon was growing, as thus " the bacon would prove the better in boiling."

Even at the present time a host of credulities regarding the moon is prevalent among the ignorant classes of different lands. Thus, for example, the negroes in the vicinity of Washington, D. C., believe that potatoes should be planted before the new moon in order to thrive, and among the negroes and Indians of the State of Missouri, the proper time for weaning a baby or calf is determined by the lunar phases.

Moon-worship was one of the most ancient forms of idolatry, and still exists among some Eastern nations. A relic of the practice is seen in some parts of Great Britain in the custom of bowing to the new moon.

Astrologers regarded the moon as exerting a powerful influence over the health and fortunes of human beings, according to her aspect and position at the time of their birth. Thus in a "Manual of Astrology" by Raphael (London, 1828), she is described as a "cold, moist, watery, phlegmatic planet, and partaking of good or evil as she is aspected by good or evil stars." [1]

The growing horned moon was thought to exert a mysterious beneficent influence not only over many

[1] Rev. Timothy Harley, *Moon-Lore*, p. 192.

of the operations of agriculture, but over the affairs of every-day life as well. Hence doubtless arose the belief in the value of crescent-shaped and cornute objects as amulets and charms; of these the horse-shoe is the one most commonly available, and therefore the one most generally used.

In astrology the moon has indeed always been considered the most influential of the heavenly bodies by reason of her rapid motion and nearness to the earth; and the astrologers of old, whether in forecasting future events or in giving advice as to proper times and seasons for the transaction of business affairs, first ascertained whether or not the moon were well aspected. This was also a cardinal point with the shrewd magicians of later centuries. And should any one require proof of the existence of a modern belief in lunar influences, let him consult Zadkiel's Almanac for the year 1898. Therein he will find it stated that when the sun is in benefic aspect with the moon, it is a suitable day for asking favors, seeking employment, and traveling for health.

Venus in benefic aspect with the moon is favorable for courting, marrying, visiting friends, engaging maidservants, and seeking amusement.

Mars, for consulting surgeons and dealing with engineers and soldiers.

Jupiter, for opening offices and places of business, and for beginning new enterprises.

Saturn, for having to do with farmers, miners, and elderly people, for buying real estate and for planting and sowing.

For, says the oracle of the almanac, astrologers have found by experience that if the above instructions are followed, human affairs proceed smoothly.

In his work entitled "The Evil-Eye" (London, 1895), Mr. Frederick Thomas Elworthy calls attention to the fact that the half-moon was often placed on the heads of certain of the most powerful Egyptian deities, and therefore when worn became a symbol of their worship. Indeed, the crescent is common in the religious symbolism not only of ancient Egypt, but also of Assyria and India. The Hebrew maidens in the time of the prophet Isaiah wore crescent-shaped ornaments on their heads.[1]

The crescent is the well-known symbol of the Turkish religion. According to tradition, Philip of Macedon (B. C. 382–336), the father of Alexander the Great, attempted to undermine the walls of Byzantium during a siege of the city, but the attempt was revealed to the inhabitants by the light of a crescent moon. Whereupon they erected a statue to Diana, and adopted the crescent as their symbol.

When the Byzantine empire was overthrown by Mohammed II., in 1453, the Turks regarded the

[1] Isaiah iii. 18.

crescent, which was everywhere to be seen, as of favorable import. They therefore made it their own emblem, and it has since continued to be a distinctively Mohammedan token.

In the Mussulman mind the new moon is intimately associated with devotional acts. Its appearance is eagerly watched for and

The moment the eye lights on the slight thread of silver in the western twilight, it remains fixed there, whilst prayers of thanksgiving and praise are offered, the hands being held up by the face, the palms upward and open, and afterwards passed three times over the visage, the gaze still remaining immovable.[1]

Golden crescents of various sizes were among the most primitive forms of money. Ancient coins frequently bore the likenesses of popular deities or their symbols, and of the latter the crescent appears to have been the one most commonly employed.[2] It was the usual mint-mark of the coins of Thespia in the early part of the fourth century B. C.;[3] is seen on the coins of the reigns of Augustus, Nero, and other Roman emperors; and on the silver pieces of the time of Hadrian is found the *Luna crescens* with seven stars.[4]

A crescent adorned the head of the goddess Diana

[1] *Cornhill*, March, 1877.
[2] Thomas Inman, M. D., *Ancient Faiths embodied in Ancient Names.*
[3] Barclay V. Head, *Historia Numorum.* Oxford, 1887.
[4] *A Dictionary of Roman Coins.* London, 1889.

in her character of Hecate, or ruler of the infernal regions.

Hecate was supposed to preside over enchantments, and was also the special guardian and protectress of houses and doors.[1] The Greeks not only wore amulets in the shape of the half moon, but placed them on the walls of their houses as talismans;[2] and the Romans used *phalëræ*, metallic disks and crescents, to decorate the foreheads and breasts of their horses.

Such ornaments are to be seen on the caparisons of the horses on Trajan's Column and on other ancient monuments, in the collection of Roman antiquities in the British Museum, and in mediæval paintings and tapestries.[3]

In the portrayals of combats between the Romans and Dacians on the Arch of Constantine, the trappings of the horses of both armies are decorated with these emblems,[4] as are also the bridle reins of a horse shown in a French manuscript of the fifteenth century representing " gentlefolk meeting on horseback." [5]

Charms of similar shape, made of wolves' teeth and

[1] *Gentleman's Magazine*, vol. 84. 1814.
[2] *Popular Science Monthly*, November, 1895.
[3] *Journal of the Anthropological Institute of Great Britain and Ireland*, vol. 19. 1890.
[4] Bernard de Montfaucon, *L'antiquité expliquée.*
[5] Ph. Charles Berjean, *The Horses of Antiquity, Middle Ages, and Renaissance.* London. 1864.

boars' tusks, have been found in tumuli in different parts of Great Britain.

A sepulchral stone, which is preserved among other Gallo-Roman relics within the château of Chinon, France, bears the effigy of a man standing upright and clad in a large tunic with wide sleeves. Above the figure is a crescent-shaped talisman, a symbol frequently found in monuments of that period.[1]

But the use of these symbols, although so ancient, is by no means obsolete; the brass crescent, an avowed charm against the evil eye, is very commonly attached to the elaborately decorated harnesses of Neapolitan draught-horses, and is used in the East to embellish the trappings of elephants. It is also still employed in like manner in various parts of Europe and in the England of to-day. In Germany small half-moon-shaped amulets similar to the ancient μηνίσκοι or lunulæ are still used against the evil eye.

In Sweden and Frisia, bridal ornaments for the head and neck often represent the moon's disk in its first quarter; and it is customary to call out after a newly married pair, "Increase, O Moon."[2]

Elworthy remarks that the horse-shoe, wherever used as an amulet, is the handy conventional representative of the crescent, and that the Buddhist crescent

[1] Theodore Andrea Cook, B. A., *Old Touraine.*
[2] Professor C. H. Rochholz, *Alt-Deutsches Bürgerleben.*

emblem is a horse-shoe with the curve pointed like a Gothic arch.

The English fern called moonwort (*Botrychium lunaria*) is thought to owe its reputed magical powers to the crescent form of the segments of its frond. Some writers regard it as identical with the martagon, an herb formerly much used by sorcerers; and also with the Italian *sferracavallo*.

According to the famous astrologer and herbalist, Nicholas Culpepper, moonwort possessed certain occult virtues, and was endowed with extraordinary attributes, chief among them being its power of undoing locks and of unshoeing horses. The same writer remarked that, while some people of intelligence regarded these notions with scorn, the popular name for moonwort among the countryfolk was "unshoe-the-horse."[1]

Du Bartas, in his "Divine Weekes," says in reference to this plant: —

Horses that, feeding on the grassy hills, tread upon moonwort with their hollow heels, though lately shod, at night go barefoot home, their maister musing where their shoes become. O moonwort! tell me where thou hid'st the smith, hammer and pinchers, thou unshodd'st them with.

The horse-shoe has sometimes been identified with the cross, and has been supposed to derive its amuletic power from a fancied resemblance to the sacred Chris-

[1] Richard Folkard, Jr., *Plant-Lore*.

tian symbol. But inasmuch as it is difficult to find
any marked similarity in form between the crescent
and the cross, this theory does not appear to warrant
serious consideration.

VI. IRON AS A PROTECTIVE CHARM

Some writers have maintained that the luck associated with the horse-shoe is due chiefly to the metal,
irrespective of its shape, as iron and steel are traditional charms against malevolent spirits and goblins.
In their view, a horse-shoe is simply a piece of iron of
graceful shape and convenient form, commonly pierced
with seven nail-holes (a mystic number), and therefore
an altogether suitable talisman to be affixed to the door
of dwelling or stable in conformity with a venerable
custom sanctioned by centuries of usage. Of the
antiquity of the belief in the supernatural properties
of iron there can be no doubt.

Among the ancient Gauls this metal was thought to
be consecrated to the Evil Principle, and, according to
a fragment of the writings of the Egyptian historian
Manetho (about 275 B. C.), iron was called in Egypt
the bone of Typhon, or Devil's bone, for Typhon in the
Egyptian mythology was the personification of evil.[1]

Pliny, in his "Natural History," states that iron

---

[1] Laisnel de la Salle, *Croyances et legendes du centre de la France.*
Paris, 1875.

coffin-nails affixed to the lintel of the door render the inmates of the dwelling secure from the visitations of nocturnal prowling spirits.

According to the same author, iron has valuable attributes as a preservative against harmful witchcrafts and sorceries, and may thus be used with advantage both by adults and children. For this purpose it was only necessary to trace a circle about one's self with a piece of the metal, or thrice to swing a sword around one's body. Moreover, gentle proddings with a sword wherewith a man has been wounded were reputed to alleviate divers aches and pains, and even iron-rust had its own healing powers : —

If a horse be shod with shoes made from a sword wherewith a man has been slain, he will be most swift and fleet, and never, though never so hard rode, tire.[1]

The time-honored belief in the magical power of iron and steel is shown in many traditions of the North.

A young herdswoman was once tending cattle in a forest of Vermaland in Sweden ; and the weather being cold and wet, she carried along her tinder-box with flint and steel, as is customary in that country. Presently along came a giantess carrying a casket, which she asked the girl to keep while she went away to invite some friends to attend her daughter's marriage.

[1] Merlin, *Book of Charms.*

Quite thoughtlessly the girl laid her fire-steel on the casket, and when the giantess returned for the property she could not touch it, for steel is repellant to trolls, both great and small. So the herdswoman carried home the treasure-box, which was found to contain a golden crown and other valuables.[1]

The heathen Northmen believed in the existence of a race of dwarfish artisans, who were skilled in the working of metals, and who fashioned implements of warfare in their subterranean workshops. These dwarfs were also thought to inhabit isolated rocks; and according to a popular notion, if a man chanced to encounter one of them, and quickly threw a piece of steel between him and his habitation, he could thereby prevent the dwarf from returning home, and could exact of him whatever he desired.[2]

Among French Canadians, fireflies are viewed with superstitious eyes as luminous imps of evil, and iron and steel are the most potent safeguards against them; a knife or needle stuck into the nearest fence is thought to amply protect the belated wayfarer against these insects, for they will either do themselves injury upon the former, or will become so exhausted in endeavoring to pass through the needle's eye as to render them temporarily harmless.[3] Such waifs and strays of popular

---

[1] William A. Craigie, M. A., *Scandinavian Folk-Lore*, p. 396.
[2] Rudolph Keyser, *The Religion of the Northmen*, p. 299.
[3] *Popular Science Monthly*, vol. 44. 1894.

credulity may seem most trivial, yet they serve to illustrate the ancient and widely diffused belief in the traditional qualities ascribed to certain metals.

One widely prevalent theory ascribed to iron a meteoric origin, but the different nations of antiquity were wont to attribute its discovery or invention to some favorite deity or mythological personage; Osiris was thus honored by the Egyptians, Vulcan by the Romans, and Wodan or Odin by the Teutons.

In early times the employment of iron in the arts was much restricted by reason of its dull exterior and brittleness. There existed, moreover, among the Romans a certain religious prejudice against the metal, whose use in many ceremonies was wholly proscribed. This prejudice appears to have been due to the fact that iron weapons were held jointly responsible with those who wielded them for the shedding of human blood; inasmuch as swords, knives, battle-axes, lance and spear points, and other implements of war were made of iron.[1]

Those mythical demons of Oriental lands known as the *Jinn* are believed to be exorcised by the mere name of iron;[2] and Arabs when overtaken by a simoom in the desert endeavor to charm away these spirits of evil by crying, "Iron, iron!"[3]

---

[1] Dr. Karl Sittl, *Archäologie der Kunst*, p. 210. 1895.
[2] Edward B. Tylor, LL. D., *Primitive Culture*.
[3] William S. Walsh, *Handy Book of Literary Curiosities*.

The *Jinn* being legendary creatures of the Stone Age, the comparatively modern metal is supposed to be obnoxious to them. In Scandinavia and in northern countries generally, iron is a historic charm against the wiles of sorcerers.

The Chinese sometimes wear outside of their clothing a piece of an old iron plough-point as a charm;[1] and they have also a custom of driving long iron nails in certain kinds of trees to exorcise some particularly dangerous female demons which haunt them.[2] The ancient Irish were wont to hang crooked horse-shoe nails about the necks of their children as charms;[3] and in Teutonic folk-lore we find the venerable superstition that a horse-shoe nail found by chance and driven into the fireplace will effect the restoration of stolen property to the owner. In Ireland, at the present time, iron is held to be a sacred and luck-bringing metal which thieves hesitate to steal.[4]

A Celtic legend says that the name *Iron-land* or *Ireland* originated as follows: The Emerald Isle was formerly altogether submerged, except during a brief period every seventh year, and at such times repeated attempts were made by foreigners to land on its soil,

[1] Rev. Justus Doolittle, *Social Life of the Chinese.*
[2] *Rennell Rodd*, p. 165.
[3] William George Black, *Folk-Medicine.* London, 1883.
[4] J. B. Friedrich, *Die Symbolik und Mythologie der Natur.*

but without success, as the advancing waves always swallowed up the bold invaders. Finally a heavenly revelation declared that the island could only be rescued from the sea by throwing a piece of iron upon it during its brief appearance above the waters. Profiting by the information thus vouchsafed, a daring adventurer cast his sword upon the land at the time indicated, thereby dissolving the spell, and Ireland has ever since remained above the water. On account of this tradition the finding of iron is always accounted lucky by the Irish; and when the treasure-trove has the form of a horse-shoe, it is nailed up over the house door. Thus iron is believed to have reclaimed Ireland from the sea, and the talismanic symbol of its reclamation is the iron horse-shoe.[1]

Once upon a time — so runs a tradition of the Ukraine, the border region between Russia and Poland — some men found a piece of iron. After having in vain attempted to eat it, they tried to soften it by boiling it in water; then they roasted it, and afterwards beat it with stones. While thus engaged, the Devil, who had been watching them, inquired, "What are you making there?" and the men replied, "A hammer with which to beat the Devil." Thereupon Satan asked where they had obtained the requisite sand; and

---

[1] F. Nork, *Mythologie der Volkssagen und Volksmärchen*. Stuttgart, 1848.

from that time men understood that sand was essential for the use of iron-workers; and thus began the manufacture of iron implements.[1]

Among the Scotch fishermen also iron is invested with magical attributes. Thus if, when plying their vocation, one of their number chance to indulge in profanity, the others at once call out, "Cauld airn!" and each grasps a handy piece of the metal as a counter influence to the misfortune which would else pursue them throughout the day. Even nowadays in England, in default of a horse-shoe, the iron plates of the heavy shoes worn by farm laborers are occasionally to be seen fastened at the doors of their cottages.[2]

When in former times a belief in the existence of mischievous elves was current in the Highland districts of Scotland, iron and steel were in high repute as popular safeguards against the visits of these fairy-folk; for they were sometimes bold enough to carry off young mothers, whom they compelled to act as wet-nurses for their own offspring. One evening many years ago a farmer named Ewen Macdonald, of Duldreggan, left his wife and young infant indoors while he went out on an errand; and tradition has it that while crossing a brook, thereafter called in the Gaelic tongue "the

[1] Paul Sebillot, *Légendes et curiosités des métiers.*

[2] *The Folk-Lore Journal,* vol. vii. 1889.

[3] Jacob Larwood and John C. Hotten, *The History of Signboards.*

streamlet of the knife," he heard a strange rushing sound accompanied with a sigh, and realized at once that fairies were carrying off his wife. Instantly throwing a knife into the air in the name of the Trinity, the fairies' power was annulled, and his wife dropped down before him.[1]

In Scandinavian and Scottish folk-lore, there is a marked affinity between iron and flint. The elf-bolt or flint arrowhead was formerly in great repute as a charm against divers evil influences, whether carried around as an amulet, used as a magical purifier of drinking-water for cattle, or to avert fairy spite. It seems possible that iron and steel in superseding flint, which was so useful a material in the rude arts of primitive peoples, inherited its ancient magical qualities.

In the Hebrides a popular charm against the wiles of sorcerers consisted in placing pieces of flint and untempered steel in the milk of cows alleged to have been bewitched. The milk was then boiled, and this process was thought to foil the machinations of the witch or enchantress.[2] The fairies of the Scottish lowlands were supposed to use arrows tipped with white flint, wherewith they shot the cattle of persons obnoxious to them, the wounds thus inflicted being invisible except to certain personages gifted with supernatural sight.[3]

[1] William Mackay, *Urquhart and Glenmoriston*, p. 434.
[2] Daniel Wilson, *The Archæology and Prehistoric Annals of Scotland*.
[3] Thomas Keightley, *The Fairy Mythology*, p. 352.

According to a Cornish belief, iron is potent to control the water-fiends, and when thrown overboard enables mariners to land on a rocky coast with safety even in a rough sea.[1] A similar superstition exists in the Orkney Islands with reference to a certain rock on the coast of Westray. It is thought that when any one with a piece of iron about him steps upon this rock, the sea at once becomes turbulent and does not subside until the magical substance is thrown into the water.[2]

The inhabitants of the rocky island of Timor, in the Indian Archipelago, carry about them scraps of iron to preserve themselves from all kinds of mishaps, even as the London cockney cherishes with care his lucky penny, crooked sixpence, or perforated shilling; while in Hindostan iron nails are frequently driven in over a door, or into the legs of a bedstead, as protectives. It was a mediæval wedding custom in France to place on the bride's finger a ring made from a horse-shoe nail,[3] a superstitious bid, as it were, for happy auspices.

In Sicily, iron amulets are popularly used against the evil eye; indeed iron in any form, especially the horse-shoe, is thought to be effective, and in fact talismanic properties are ascribed to all metals. When, therefore,

[1] F. S. Bassett, *Sea Phantoms.*
[2] James W. Mackinlay, *Folk-Lore of Scottish Lochs and Springs*, p. 6.
[3] William Jones. *Credulities Past and Present.*

a Sicilian feels that he is being " overlooked," he instantly touches the first available metallic object, such
as his watch-chain, keys, or coins.[1] In ancient Babylon
and Assyria it was believed that invisible demons might
enter the body during the acts of eating and drinking
and thus originate disease, and the doctrine of demoniacal possession as the cause of illness is still widely
prevalent in uncivilized communities at the present day.
Wherever, therefore, such notions exist, talismans are
naturally employed to render inert the machinations of
these little demons ; and of all these safeguards, iron
and steel are perhaps the most potent. Quite commonly
in Germany, among the lower classes, such articles as
knives, hatchets, and cutting instruments generally, as
well as fire-irons, harrows, keys, and needles, are considered protectives against disease if placed near or about
the sick person.[2]

In Morocco it is customary to place a dagger under
the patient's pillow,[3] and in Greece a black-handled
knife is similarly used to keep away the nightmare.

In Germany iron implements laid crosswise are considered to be powerful anti-witch safeguards for infants;
and in Switzerland two knives, or a knife and fork, are
placed in the cradle under the pillow. In Bohemia a

---

[1] Giuseppe Pitré, *Usi e costumi, credenze, e pregiudizi del popolo Siciliano.* Palermo, 1889.

[2] A. Wuttke, *Der deutsche Volksaberglaube*, p. 92.

[3] *Cornhill.* N. S. vol. xix. 1892.

knife on which a cross is marked, and in Bavaria a pair
of opened scissors, are similarly used. In Westphalia an
axe and a broom are laid crosswise on the threshold,
the child's nurse being expected to step over these articles on entering the room.[1]

The therapeutic value of iron and its use as a medi-
cament do not properly belong to our subject; and,
indeed, neither the iron horse-shoe nor its counterfeit
symbol have usually been much employed in folk-medicine. Professor Sepp, in his work on the religion of the
early Germans, mentions, however, a popular cure for
whooping-cough, which consisted in having the patient
eat off of a wooden platter branded with the figure of
a horse-shoe.

In France, also, a favorite panacea for children's diseases consists in laying on the child an accidentally
found horse-shoe, with the nails remaining in it; and
in Mecklenburg gastric affections are thought to be
successfully treated by drinking beer which has been
poured upon a red-hot horse-shoe.[2]

Pliny ascribed healing power to a cast-off horse-shoe
found on the road. The finder was recommended carefully to preserve such a horse-shoe; and should he at
any future time be afflicted with the hiccoughs, the
mere recollection of the exact spot where the shoe had

---

[1] Dr. H. Ploss, *Das Kind in Brauch und Sitte der Volker*, p. 122.
[2] A. Wuttke, *Der deutsche Volksaberglaube*, p. 336.

been placed would serve as a remedy for that sometimes obstinate affection.[1]

In Bavaria a popular alleged cure for hernia in children is as follows : From a horse-shoe wherein all the
nails remain, and which has been cast by a horse, a nail
is taken ; and when next a new moon comes on a Friday, one must go into a field or orchard before sunrise
and drive the nail by three blows into an oak-tree or
pear-tree, according to the sex of the child, and thrice
invoke the name of Christ; after which one must kneel
on the ground in front of the tree and repeat a *Paternoster*. This is an example of a kind of therapeutic
measure not uncommon among peasants in different
parts of Germany, a blending of the use of a superstitious charm with religious exercises.[2]

An ingenious theory ascribes the origin of the belief
in the magical properties of iron to the early employment of the actual cautery, and to the use of the lancet
in surgery.[3]   In either case the healing effects of the
metal, whether hot or in the form of a knife, have been
attributed by superstitious minds to magical properties
in the instruments, whereby the demons who caused the
disease were put to flight. In northern India the
natives believe that evil spirits are so simple-minded as

---

[1] *Natural History*, book xxviii. ch. 81.
[2] Dr. G. Lammert, *Volksmedizin in Bayern*, p. 120.
[3] Campbell.

to run against the sharp edge of a knife and thus do
themselves injury; and they also make use of iron rings
as demon-scarers, such talismans having the double efficacy of the iron and of the sacred circle.[1]

In Bombay, when a child is born, the natives place an
iron bar along the threshold of the room of confinement
as a guard against the entrance of demons.[2]   This practice is derived from the Hindoo superstition that evil
spirits keep aloof from iron; and even to-day pieces of
horse-shoes are to be seen nailed to the bottom sills
of the doors of native houses.[3]   In east Bothnia, when
the cows leave their winter quarters for the first time,
an iron bar is laid before the threshold of the door
through which the animals must pass, and the farmers
believe that, if this precaution were omitted, the cows
would prove troublesome throughout the summer.[4]   So,
too, in the region of Saalfield, in central Germany, it is
customary to place axes, saws, and other iron and steel
implements outside the stable door to keep the cattle
from bewitchment.

The Scandinavian peasants, when they venture upon
the water, are wont to protect themselves against the
power of the *Neck*, or river-spirit, by placing a knife
in the bottom of the boat, or by fixing an iron nail in

[1] W. Crooke, B. A., *Popular Religion and Folk-Lore of Northern India.*
[2] Letter to the writer from H. Clay Trumbull.
[3] *The Folk-Lore Journal,* vol. vi. p. 77.
[4] Jones and Kropf, *Folk-Tales of the Magyars,* p. 410, note.

a reed. The following is the translation of a charm used in Norway for this purpose : —

Neck, Neck, nail in water, the Virgin Mary casteth steel in water. Do you sink, I flit.

In Finland there is an evil fairy known as the Alp Nightmare. Its name in the vernacular is *Painajainen*, which means in English " Presser." This unpleasant being makes people scream, and causes young children to squint; and the popular safeguard is steel, or a broom placed beneath the pillow.[1]

Friedrich remarks that the Moslems look upon iron as a divine gift, and that the Finlanders have their tutelary gods of this metal.

Among the Jews there prevails a popular belief that one should never make use of a knife or other steel instrument for the purpose of more readily following with the eye the pages of the Bible, the Talmud, or other sacred book. Iron should never be permitted to touch any book treating of religion, for the two are incompatible by nature, the one destroying human life and the other prolonging it.[2] The Highlanders of Scotland have a time-honored custom of taking an oath upon cold iron or steel. The dirk, which was formerly an indispensable adjunct to the Highland costume, is a

---

[1] Thomas Keightley, *The Fairy Mythology*, p. 148.
[2] Moise Schuhl, *Superstitions et coutumes populaires du Judaisme.*

favorite and handy object for the purpose. The faith in the magical power of steel and iron against evil-disposed fairies and ghosts was universal, and this form of oath was more solemn and binding than any other.[1]

Among the Bavarian peasants nails and needles have a reputation the reverse of that of the horse-shoe. A horse-shoe nail stuck into the front door of a house will give the owner a serious illness. A needle, when given to a friend, is sure to prick to death existing friendship, even as such friendship is severed by the gift of a knife or pair of scissors. Such an untoward result may be averted, however, if the recipient smile pleasantly when the gift is made. A curious superstition about iron locks prevails in Styria and Tyrol. If you procure from a locksmith a brand-new lock and carry it to church at the time of a wedding ceremony, and if, while the benediction is being said, you fasten the lock by a turn of the key, then the young couple's love and happiness is destroyed. Mutual aversion will supplant affection until you open the lock again.[2]

VII. BLACKSMITHS CREDITED WITH SUPERNATURAL ATTRIBUTES

Vulcan, the Roman god of fire, the Hephæstus of Grecian mythology, was also the patron of blacksmiths

---

[1] John Gregorson Campbell, *The Fians*, p. 52.
[2] Fräulein Helene Raff.

and workers in metals.   He was the great artisan of the
universe, and at his workshop in Olympus he fashioned
armor for the warriors of the heroic age.   On earth
volcanoes were his forges, and his favorite residence
was the island of Lemnos in the Ægean Sea.   Beneath
Ætna, with the aid of those famed artisans, the Cyclops, he forged the thunderbolts of Jove ; and there
also, according to tradition, were made the trident of
Neptune, Pluto's helmet, and the shield of Hercules.
Hephæstus was thus a controller and master of fire.

The Cyclops were believed by the ancients to have
invented the art of forging ; and the discovery of the
peculiar qualities of iron was attributed to certain mythical beings called the Dactyls, who dwelt in Phrygia,
and who were thought to have acquired this knowledge
from observation of the fusion of metals at the fabulous
burning of Mount Ida.   The Dactyls had the reputation of being wizards, whose very names possessed a
mysterious protective power when pronounced by persons exposed to sudden dangers.

Certain semi-fabulous tribes of central Asia, workers
in metals, kept secret the mysteries of their craft, and
were wont to indulge in wild orgies and festivities, which
served to inspire with awe the uninitiated.   At such
times they danced until frenzied with excitement, to the
accompaniment of cymbals and tambourines and the
clashing of weapons.   The people of neighboring tribes

feared to approach them, believing that they were possessed of a magical power which enabled them to transform one metal into another and to forge thunderbolts. They were reputed to be masters of fire and of the elements, and their forges, like Vulcan's, were volcanoes.[1]

These barbarous peoples were sometimes confounded with the Dactyls, Corybantes, Cabiri, and Curetes, traditional metallurgists endowed with supernatural skill, and therefore popularly reckoned as magicians, or even as divinities. For a long period they were supposed to be vested with the exclusive knowledge of metal-working, a knowledge shrouded in mystery.

In the "Kalevalla," or ancient epic poem of Finland, the blacksmith Ilmarinen is represented as the pioneer and most skilled of artisans, who fashioned both the implements of warfare and domestic utensils. This hero

> Came to earth to work the metal;
> He was born upon the coal-mount,
> Skilled and nurtured in the coal-fields;
> In one hand a copper hammer,
> In the other tongs of iron;
> In the night was born the blacksmith,
> In the morn he built his smithy;
> Sought with care a favored hillock,
> Where the winds might fill his bellows;
> Found a hillock in the swamp-land,
> Where the iron hid abundant,
> There he built his smelting-fnrnace.[2]

[1] *L'Initiation*, 19ᵉ volume, April, 1893.
[2] J. C. Brown, LL. D., *People of Finland in Archaic Times*, p. 112.

In the Teutonic mythology, blacksmiths were magical craftsmen; and even in the Middle Ages they were looked upon as superior to other artisans, owing to their faculty of seemingly toying with fire, rendering the dangerous element subservient to their will, and by its aid manipulating iron with ease and dexterity. In Germany their workshops were known as "Wieland's houses," in remembrance of the most cunning of smiths in the mythical lore of the North.

As in early ages the origin of metal-working was imputed to divine beings, it was natural that in popular tradition blacksmiths acquired their wondrous technical skill through the assistance of such beings, and hence were exalted above the plane of ordinary mortals because they had received supernatural instruction. . . .

The following mediæval legend serves to show that memories of the old pagan traditions lingered in the minds of the Scandinavians until long after the establishment among them of Christianity. One evening in the year 1208, a horseman rode up to the house of a blacksmith named Thord Vettir, who lived in southern Norway at Nesjar, near the town of Laurvig on the Skager-Rack, and asked for lodging overnight and shoeing for his horse. The smith assented, and early the next morning began the work, chatting meanwhile with his guest. "Where were you last night?" he inquired of the latter. "In Medaldal," was the reply.

"And where were you the night before?" asked the smith. "In Jardal," answered the stranger. "You must be a tremendous liar," said the smith, with great frankness. Then he applied himself to his task in earnest, and forged the biggest horse-shoes which he had ever seen, but which were found to fit the horse's feet perfectly. In the course of further conversation the traveler remarked that he had long dwelt in the north of Norway and was on his way to Sweden. When he was ready to continue journeying and had mounted his steed, the smith inquired his name. "Have you ever heard of Odin?" was the rejoinder. "I have heard his name," said the smith. "Then you may see him now," remarked the horseman, "and, if you do not believe what I have told you, look how I leap my horse over the fence." Thereupon he spurred the animal and rode straight at the courtyard fence, which was seven ells high. The gallant steed cleared the fence with ease, and neither he nor his rider were seen again by the worthy blacksmith.[1]

The dignity and importance of the blacksmith's art in early mediæval times in England is illustrated by the following tale from Paul Sébillot's " Légendes et Curiosités des Métiers," art. " Forgerons : " —

King Alfred the Great, who reigned in the latter part of the ninth century, on one occasion assembled

[1] W. A. Craigie, *Scandinavian Folk-Lore.*

together seven of his principal mechanics and craftsmen, and announced that he would appoint as their chief that one who could longest dispense with the assistance of the others; and he also invited them all to a banquet, on condition that each should bring with him a specimen of his handiwork and the tools wherewith it was made. At the appointed time they all appeared : the blacksmith brought his hammer and a horse-shoe; the tailor his scissors and a newly made garment ; the baker his long-handled wooden bread-shovel and a loaf of bread ; the shoemaker his awl and a pair of new shoes; the carpenter his saw and a squared plank; the butcher his chopping-knife and a large piece of meat; and the mason his trowel and a corner-stone. After careful deliberation the company decided that the tailor's work was the best, and he was accordingly chosen to be chief of the artisans.

The blacksmith was vexed at the choice, and vowed he would work no more, so long as the tailor was chief ; he therefore closed his shop and took his departure.

But his absence was speedily felt ; the king's horse lost a shoe, the six comrades one after another broke their tools, and, although the tailor continued to ply his trade longer than the others, he too was soon obliged to cease from work. Thereupon the king and his tradesmen decided to try their hands at blacksmithing, but met with ill success ; for the king's horse trod on his royal master, the tailor burnt his fingers, and the others met with various mishaps. At length they began to quarrel among themselves, even coming to blows, and in the mêlée the anvil was overturned with a crash. Just at this point Saint Clement appeared on the scene arm in arm with the blacksmith. The king saluted the newcomers respectfully, and addressed them as follows: "I have made a bad mistake, my friends, in allowing myself to be beguiled by the tailor's fine cloth and his skillful handiwork; in common fairness the blacksmith, without whose aid the other workmen can accomplish nothing, should be proclaimed chief artisan." All the tradesmen except the tailor then begged the worthy smith to make new tools for them, which he forthwith proceeded to do, even including a brand-new pair of scissors for the tailor.

Then the king reorganized the society of artisans and proclaimed as chief the blacksmith, whom all greeted with wishes for good health and happiness.

After this the king called on each one for a song, and the new chief in his turn sang one entitled "The Merry Blacksmith," which is even nowadays sometimes heard at the festivities of tradesmen's guilds in England.

Saint Clement, who figures in the above tale, was the patron saint of farriers. He was a Roman bishop, who died A. D. 100. In ecclesiastical tradition he was reckoned among the martyrs, having been bound to an anchor and thrown into the sea on November 23 of that year. His name-day was still observed in recent times by English blacksmiths, who regarded him as the originator of the art of practical farriery, and held an annual festival in his honor.

The blacksmiths' apprentices of the Woolwich dockyard were wont to form a procession on the evening of Saint Clement's Day, one of their number personating "Old Clem," with masked face, oakum wig, and long white beard.

During the festivities this worthy delivered a speech, in part as follows: —

I am the real Saint Clement, the first founder of brass, iron, and steel from the ore. I have been to Mount Ætna, where the god Vulcan first built his forge, and forged the armor and thunderbolts for the god Jupiter.[1]

Saint Eloy, or Saint Eligius, is sometimes represented as the guardian of farriers and blacksmiths. He flourished in the seventh century, and in his youth served as apprentice to a goldsmith at Limoges, where he became very proficient in the art of working the precious metals. His festival occurs on December 1.

According to a well-known legend, Saint Eloy was once shoeing a demoniac horse, which refused to stand still; he therefore cut off the animal's leg and put on

[1] T. F. Thiselton Dyer, M. A., *British Popular Customs*, p. 424.

the shoe. Then, making the sign of the cross, he replaced the leg, the horse experiencing no ill effects from the operation.

This saint is mentioned in Barnaby Googe's "Popish Kingdome," as follows : —

And Loye the smith doth looke to horse, and smithes of all degree ;
If they with iron meddle here, or if they goldsmithes bee.

In certain countries blacksmiths and farriers have always been credited with supernatural faculties, and it seems, therefore, reasonable thus to explain the origin of some portion of the alleged mystic virtues of their handiwork, the iron horse-shoe, although indeed this view does not appear to have been advanced hitherto.

Among ourselves, and in some of the principal European countries, blacksmiths are highly respectable members of society, although they do not usually deal in occult science. But in portions of the Russian empire, as in the province of Mingrelia, the Caucasus, and neighboring regions, blacksmiths do enjoy a certain reputation as magicians. Solemn oaths are taken upon the anvil instead of upon the Bible. In Abyssinia and in the Congo country all iron-workers have the reputation of sorcerers, and among the Tibbous of central Africa they are treated with great deference. When an inhabitant of the Orkney Islands wishes to obtain an amulet, he applies either to a farrier, or to his son or grandson;

and the Roumanian gypsies are mostly blacksmiths, their wives obtaining a livelihood by mendicancy, the practice of divination, and the interpretation of dreams; while both men and women are thought to have the faculty of summoning to their aid powerful spirits of the air.[1]

In Morocco, at the present day, there still exists a community of dwarfish artisans, workers in metals, magicians, and adepts in the healing art, who make little books which are used as portable amulets; and the Haratin, who inhabit the Drah valley, deem it sinful even to mention by name these dwarfs, whom they consider entitled to extraordinary respect.

Each member of this mysterious tribe of pigmy smiths is said to wear a *haik*, or outer garment, having upon the back a representation of an eye, a symbol suggestive of the Cyclops of old.[2]

There was, indeed, as we have seen, a common opinion throughout a great part of Europe that the earliest smiths were supernatural beings; for it was reasoned that the marvelous process of melting and fashioning iron could not have been conceived by man, but must have originated through magical agencies.

In Germany blacksmith's forges were often situated on highways remote from settlements, and were the

---

[1] *Mélusine*, tome iv. p. 367.
[2] R. G. Haliburton, *The Dwarfs of Mount Atlas*.

resort of travelers and teamsters, who stopped either to have a horse shod, or to obtain veterinary advice. Quite naturally these smithies, like the modern cross-roads variety stores, became little centres of sociability and gossip, and even of conviviality. Moreover, questionable characters sometimes frequented these places, and hence their reputation was not always savory. But the blacksmith himself, by virtue of his calling, was looked upon with respect, even after his craft had ceased to inspire the vulgar with mysterious awe.[1]

In south Germany and the Tyrol, when a blacksmith rests from his work on a Saturday evening, he strikes with his hammer three blows upon the anvil, thereby chaining up the Devil for the ensuing week. And so likewise, while hammering a horse-shoe into shape, he strikes the anvil instead of the shoe every fourth or fifth blow, and thus makes doubly secure the chain wherewith Satan is bound.[2]

Blacksmiths are usually clever enough to recognize the Devil, even when disguised as a gentleman.

Once upon a time the Evil One appeared at the door of a smith in the village of Gossensass, on the Brenner road, Tyrol, and wished to have his two horses shod. When the work was done, he inquired how much he should pay ; but the shrewd smith refused to take any

[1] Dr. Ludwig Beck, *Die Geschichte des Eisens*, p. 879.
[2] A. Wuttke, *Der deutsche Volksaberglaube*, p. 263.

money, and only stipulated that his customer should never enter the shop again, which the Devil promised and went away.[1]

The magicians of Hindostan, when treating cases of alleged demoniacal possession, after the performance of other mystic rites, are wont to sprinkle the patient with water from a blacksmith's shop, the water having been endowed with additional virtue by the repeated immersion of iron.[2]

In northeast Scotland a cure for rickets consists in having the child bathed by a blacksmith in the water-trough of the smithy. Then he is laid on the anvil and iron implements are passed over him, the use of each being asked, and the ceremony is followed by a second bath. To insure the efficacy of this process, three blacksmiths of the same name must take part in it.[3]

In Henderson's " Folk-Lore of the Northern Countries of England," p. 187, mention is made of a remarkable method of treatment intended for the development of sickly, puny children who are thought to be under the influence of an evil spell which retards their growth, — a notable instance of survival of the old belief in the

[1] For this legend, and for other information regarding the traditions and customs of the Bavarian and Tyrolese peasantry, the writer is indebted to Fräulein Helene Raff, of Munich.

[2] Crooke, p. 199.

[3] Gregor, *Scotch Folk-Lore*, p. 45.

blacksmith's magical powers. Very early in the morning the little patient is brought to the shop of a smith of the seventh generation, if such can be found, and laid quite naked on the anvil. The blacksmith raises his hammer thrice as if to strike a glowing horse-shoe, each time letting it gently fall on the child's body, — a simple ceremony, but vastly promotive of the child's physical welfare, in the minds of its rustic parents.

The farriers of the Arabs inhabiting the oases of the great Sahara desert are exempt from taxes and enjoy numerous privileges. Of these the most important and striking, as showing the honor accorded to the men of this craft, is the following : —

When, on the battlefield, a mounted farrier is hard pressed by enemies, he runs the risk of being killed so long as he remains upon his horse with weapons in his hand. But if he alights, kneels down, and with the corners of his hooded cloak or *burnous* imitates the movements of a pair of bellows, thus revealing his profession, his life is spared.[1]

The Baralongs of South Africa regard the art of smelting and forging as sacred, and, when the metal begins to flow, none are permitted to approach the furnaces except those who are initiated in the mysteries of the craft.[2]

---

[1] E. Daumas, *The Horses of the Sahara*, pp. 150 *et seq.*
[2] Rev. James Macdonald, *Religion and Myth*, p. 92.

In Finland, also, blacksmiths are held in profound respect, and the greatest luxuries are none too good for them. They are presented with brandy to keep them in good humor; and a Finnish proverb says, "Fine bread always for the smith, and dainty morsels for the hammerer."[1]

Among certain tribes of the west coast of equatorial Africa the blacksmith officiates also as priest or medicine-man, and is a chief personage in the community, which often embraces several adjacent villages. Indeed, there appears to be a quite general belief in different portions of Africa that metal-workers as a class are superior beings, — of higher origin than their fellow-tribesmen. When a savage people, without a knowledge of farriery, acquired by conquest a new territory, and found therein blacksmiths plying their vocation, they naturally regarded these artisans with wonder, not unmixed with fear.[2]

Moreover, the early association, in mythology and tradition, of metal-working and sorcery, appears to explain in a measure, as already suggested, the reason for the magical properties popularly ascribed to horse-shoes and to iron articles generally.

---

[1] Dr. O. Schrader, *Prehistoric Antiquities.*
[2] Richard Andree, *Ethnographische Parallelen und Vergleiche,* p. 155.

VIII. FIRE AS A SPIRIT-SCARING ELEMENT

The horse-shoe is a product of the artisan's skill by the aid of fire.

This element has in all ages been considered the great purifier, and a powerful foe to evil spirits.[1]

The Chaldeans venerated fire and esteemed it a deity, and among primitive nations everywhere it has ever been held sacred. The Persians had fire-temples, called *Pyræa*, devoted solely to the preservation of the holy fire.[2]

In the " Rig-Veda," the principal sacred book of the Hindus, the crackling of burning fagots was listened to as the voice of the gods, and the same superstition prevails still among the natives of Borneo.[3]

In a fragment of the writings of Menander Protector, a Greek historian of the sixth century, it is related that when an embassy sent by the Emperor Justin reached Sogdiana, the ancient Bokhara, it was met by a party of Turks, who proceeded to exorcise their baggage by beating drums and ringing bells over it. They then ran around the baggage, bearing aloft flaming leaves, meantime, by their gestures and movements, seeking to repel evil spirits ; after which some of the party them-

---

[1] Chambers' *Encyclopædia*.
[2] Banier, *Mythology*, vol. ii. p. 570.
[3] Brinton, *Religions of Primitive Peoples*, p. 142.

selves passed through fire as a means of purification.[1]

Fire is especially potent against nocturnal demons, and also against the evil spirits which cause disease in cattle. Hence the utility of the ancient "need-fires," produced by the friction of two pieces of wood, which were thought to be an antidote against the murrain and epizoötics generally, — a custom until recently in vogue in the Scottish Highlands, and formerly practiced in many other regions.

The midsummer fires kindled on Saint John's Eve, in accordance with an ancient British custom, were regarded as purifiers of the air. Moreover, the whole area of ground illuminated by these fires was reckoned to be freed from sorcery for a year, and, by leaping through the flames, both men and cattle were insured safety against demons for a like period.[2]

In Ireland it was customary for people to run through the streets on Saint John's Eve carrying long poles, upon which were tied flaming bundles of straw, in order to purify the air, for at that time all kinds of mischievous imps, hobgoblins, and devils were abroad, intent on working injury to human beings.[3]

Midsummer fires were still lighted in Ireland in the

---

[1] Henry Yule, *Cathay and the Way Thither.*
[2] *Gentleman's Magazine*, vol. 281, p. 514. 1896.
[3] *The Comical Pilgrim's Pilgrimage into Ireland, 1723*, p. 92.

latter half of the nineteenth century, a survival of pagan fire-worship. In many countries people gathered about the bonfires, while children leaped through the flames, and live coals were carried into the cornfields as an antidote to blight.[1]

Sometimes the remaining ashes were scattered over the neighboring fields, in order to protect the crops from ravaging vermin or insects; and in Sweden the smoke of need-fires was reputed to stimulate the growth of fruit-trees, and to impart luck to fishing-nets hung up in it.[2]

When a child is born, the Hindus light fires to frighten demons; and for the same reason lamps are swung to and fro at weddings, and fire is carried before the dead body at a funeral.[3]

Devout Brahmins keep a fire constantly burning in their houses and worship it daily, expecting thereby to secure for themselves good fortune. The origin of the respect accorded to fire among these people has been attributed to its potency in alleviating or curing certain diseases,[4] as, for example, when applied in the actual cautery, or by means of the moxa; for, wherever a belief exists in demoniacal possession as the cause of

---

[1] Dyer, *British Popular Customs*, p. 322.
[2] W. K. Kelly, *Curiosities of Indo-European Tradition and Folk-Lore*, p. 48.
[3] Campbell, p. 24.
[4] Campbell, p. 318.

bodily disorders, the cure of the latter is evidence that the malignant spirits have been put to flight.

The fire-worshiping Parsees also keep a fire continuously in the lying-in room; and when a child is ailing from any cause, they fasten to its left arm a magical charm of written words prepared by a priest, exorcising the evil spirits in the name of their chief deity, Ormuzd, and " binding them by the power and beauty of fire." [1]

On the birth of a child among the Khoikhoi of south Africa a household fire is kindled, which is maintained until the healing of the child's navel; and when a member of the tribe goes a-hunting, his wife is careful to keep a fire burning indoors; for, if it were allowed to go out, the husband would have no luck.[2]

The conception of a mediæval smith as a master and controller of fire was embodied in a group of figures modeled by the Austrian sculptor, Karl Bitter, and placed at the southern entrance of the Administration Building at the World's Fair, Chicago, in 1893. This group, which was called " Fire Controlled," consisted of a female figure, whose uplifted right hand carried a torch, while at her feet stood a brawny smith resting a sledge hammer upon the prostrate form of a fire demon.

[1] L. Maria Child, *The Progress of Religious Ideas*, vol. i. p. 276.
[2] Theophilus Hahn, Ph. D., *Tsuni-Goam*, p. 77.

Above this group stood a single figure, by the same artist, representing a blacksmith standing at his anvil, with hammer resting against it, and in his belt hung a pair of pincers. In his left hand was a horse-shoe, which he was examining.[1]

IX. THE SERPENTINE SHAPE OF THE HORSE-SHOE

The theory has been advanced that in ancient idolatrous times the horse-shoe in its primitive form was a symbol in serpent-worship, and that its superstitious use as a charm may have thus originated. This seems plausible enough, inasmuch as there is a resemblance between the horse-shoe and the arched body of the snake, when the latter is so convoluted that its head and tail correspond to the horse-shoe prongs.

Both snakes and horse-shoes were anciently engraved on stones and medals, presumably as amuletic symbols;[2] and in front of a church in Crendi, a town in the southern part of the island of Malta, there is to be seen a statue having at its feet a protective symbol in the shape of a half moon encircled by a snake.

The serpent played an important rôle in Asiatic and ancient Egyptian symbolism. This has been thought to be due partly to a belief that the sun's path through

[1] The Werner Company, *Art Treasures from the World's Fair.* Chicago, 1895.

[2] *All the Year Round.* N. S. vol. xxxix. 1887.

the heavens formed a serpentine curve, and partly because lightning, or the fertilizing fire, sometimes flashes
upon the earth in a snake-like zigzag.[1] The serpent
was endowed with the attributes of divinity on account
of its graceful and easy movements, the brightness of
its eyes, the function of discarding its skin (a process
which was regarded as emblematic of a renewal of its
youth), and its instantaneous spring upon its prey.[2]
The worship of serpents is of great antiquity, the
earliest authentic accounts of the custom being found
in Chaldean and Chinese astronomical works. It was
nearly universal among the most ancient nations of the
world, and this universality has been ascribed to the
traditionary remembrance of the serpent in Eden,[3]
and has given rise to the opinion of some writers that
snake-worship may have been the primitive religion of
the human race.[4]

On the walls of houses in Pompeii are to be seen the
figures of snakes, which are believed to have been intended as preservative symbols;[5] and we learn from Mr.
C. G. Leland's " Etruscan Roman Remains " that the
peasants of the mountainous regions in northern Italy,
known as the Romagna Toscana, have a custom of

[1] *Indian Antiquary,* vol. xv. 1886.
[2] *Cornhill Magazine,* vol. xix. 1869.
[3] E. G. Squier, A. M., *The Serpent Symbol.*
[4] Sir John Lubbock, *The Origin of Civilization.*
[5] Marc Monnier, *Les contes populaires en Italie.*

painting on the walls of their houses the figures of serpents with the heads and tails pointing upward. These are intended both as amulets to keep away witches, and as luck-bringers, and are therefore exact counterparts of the horse-shoe and the crescent as magical emblems. The more interlaced the snake's coils, the more effective the amulet; the idea being that a witch is obliged to trace out and follow with her eye the interweaving convolutions, and that in attempting to do this she becomes bewildered, and is temporarily rendered incapable of doing harm.

In ancient Roman works of art the serpent is sometimes portrayed as a protective symbol. In some bronze figures of Fortune unearthed at Herculaneum, serpents are represented either as encircling the arm of the goddess, or as entwined about her cornucopia, thus typifying, as it were, the idea of the intimate association of the snake with good luck.

The Phœnicians rendered homage to serpents, and history shows that the Lithuanians, Sarmatians, or inhabitants of ancient Poland, and other nations of central Europe, treated these reptiles with superstitious respect. In Russia, also, domestic snakes were formerly carefully nurtured, for they were thought to bring good fortune to the members of a household.[1]

The worship of serpents is still practiced in Persia,

[1] *Grosses Universal Lexicon.*

Tibet, Ceylon, and other Eastern lands. In western Africa, also, the serpent is a chief deity, and is appealed to by the natives in seasons of drought and pestilence.[1] A talisman having the form of a snake, and known as *la sirena*, is in use among the lower classes at Naples.

In the folk-lore of the south Slavonian nations the serpent is regarded as a protective genius, not only of the people, but of domestic animals and houses as well. Every human being has a snake as tutelary divinity, with which his growth and well-being are closely connected, and the killing of one of these sacred creatures was formerly deemed a grave offense. To meet with a snake has long been accounted fortunate in some countries. The south Slav peasant believes that whoever encounters one of these creatures, on first going into the woods in the spring, will be prosperous throughout the year. But on the other hand he regards it as an evil omen if he happens to catch a glimpse of his own tutelary serpent. Fortunately, however, a man never knows which particular ophidian is his special guardian.[2]

The relation of the serpent to sculptured or engraved stones reveals to us the reptile as still the object of veneration, if not of adoration, among widely remote nations. If we search

[1] Astley, *Collection of Voyages.*
[2] Dr. Friedrich S. Krauss, *Sréca, Glück und Schicksal im Volksglauben der Südslaven.* Wien, 1886.

among the tombs of Egypt, Assyria, and Etruria, we shall find innumerable signets, cylinders, and scarabei of gems engraved with serpents; these were proverbially worn as amulets, or used as insignia of authority; and, in the temples and tombs of these and other countries, serpents are engraved or sculptured or painted, either as hieroglyphics or as forming symbolical ornaments of deities or genii. In India they are sculptured twining around all the gods of the cave temples which mark the graves of kings and heroes, and the oldest of the Scandinavian runes are written within the folds of serpents engraved on stones.[1]

In ancient Mexican temples the serpent symbol is frequently seen. The approach to the temple of El Castillo, at Chichen in Yucatan, is guarded by a pair of huge serpent heads, and a second pair protect the entrance to the sanctuary. Figures of serpents also appear in the Mosaic relief designs of the façades, and within on the sanctuary walls. So, too, in the temples of Palenque and other southern Mexican towns, serpents are everywhere plentiful in the decorations and sculptures.[2]

Representations of snakes are to be seen on the walls of houses in many parts of India at the present day, and villages have their special ophite guardians.

The fifth day of the first or bright half of the lunar month S'ravana, which nearly corresponds with August,

---

[1] A. W. Buckland, *St. Paul's Magazine*, vol. i. 1874.
[2] *Amer. Antiq.*, vol. xviii. p. 141. 1896.

is celebrated by the Brahmins in honor of the naga or cobra. Some interesting details of the ceremonies on these occasions are given in Balfour's "Cyclopædia of India." We learn from this source that native women are wont at such times to join in dancing around snake-holes, and also to prostrate themselves and invoke blessings; while others bow down before living cobras at their own homes, or worship figures of serpents.

Visits from snakes are highly appreciated as auspicious events, and the reptiles are sure of a hospitable reception, because they are looked upon as tutelary divinities.

Thus the serpent was held sacred by the nations of antiquity, being a prominent feature in every mythology and symbolizing many pagan divinities.

The Vlach women of European Turkey, who inhabit villages in the mountain ranges of Thessaly and Albania, treat serpents with great respect and even with veneration. If one of the harmless white snakes which abound in the country chances to enter a cottage, it is provided with food and allowed to depart unharmed, its appearance indoors being accounted a lucky event. Such friendly treatment often results in the snake's becoming domesticated and receiving the title of "house-serpent." [1] The Carinthians, too, are wont to treat

---

[1] Lucy M. J. Garnett, *The Christian Women of Turkey.*

snakes as fondlings, for they consider that these reptiles bring good luck proportionate in degree to their bodily diameter; hence they are fed with care and provided with bowls of milk twice a day.[1]

Indeed, in many countries the serpent or dragon, originally a guardian of treasure, is considered a house-protector. The same conception is embodied in the grotesque dragon-headed gargoyles so common in mediæval architecture.[2]

Dr. Daniel G. Brinton, in speaking of the emblematic significance of the serpent among American aborigines, remarks that this symbol has ever been associated with religious mysteries.

Many derivatives from the Hebrew and Arabic words for serpent signify the practice of sorcery, consultation with familiar spirits, and intercourse with demons.[3]

It would seem, therefore, not improbable that the horse-shoe amulet has acquired some portion of the magical influences ascribed to it through its serpentine form.

The serpent-symbol has furnished a theme for many writers, and sumptuous volumes attest its deep interest.

The chief points which relate to our present subject are briefly: (1) The similarity of form between the

---

[1] *Popular Science Monthly*, vol. 35. 1889.
[2] *Mélusine*, tome viii. No. 2. 1896.
[3] *The Myths of the New World*, p. 132.

horse-shoe and a serpentine coil, and (2) the association of ideas resulting therefrom in the popular mind. The horse-shoe, when allied symbolically to the serpent, represents a creature which has ever been an object of superstition, whether as a deity, household guardian, or embodiment of evil. Hence it suggests magical power, whether good or evil, but chiefly the idea of beneficent, protective influence.

X. THE HORSE-SHOE ARCH IN ANCIENT CALEDONIAN HIEROGLYPHICS

The horse-shoe arch was a common emblem on pagan monuments, and is frequently seen in Caledonian sculptured hieroglyphics, where it is believed to have had a special significance as a protective symbol. Lieutenant-Colonel Forbes Leslie, in "The Early Races of Scotland," remarks that the horse-shoe arch was probably emblematic of the serpent as a protecting and beneficent power, because this arch closely resembles a peculiar mark or attribute of the so-called *Nagendra*, the hooded serpent-king, a chief deity in the mythical lore of Ceylon. It would appear quite unnecessary to refer to the Cingalese mythology in this connection, inasmuch as the close resemblance between the shape of the horse-shoe and the arched body of a snake has already been commented on. As illustrative of the somewhat unique theory which claims the ancient horse-shoe arch, itself a talismanic symbol, as the original source of all the superstitions associated with the modern iron horse-shoe, it may be appropriate to quote a few lines from the authority above mentioned : —

Whatever this figure (the horse-shoe arch) may have represented to our heathen ancestors, it seems very likely that from it the horse-shoe derived its supposed power of promoting the fortune of its possessor and protecting him against threatened calamities, whether designed by men or demons. Superstition clung to the symbol that was hallowed by antiquity, and even impressed this emblem of paganism on the Christianity by which it was superseded.

The historian Diodorus Siculus said that the Chaldeans imagined the earth as having the shape of a round boat turned upside down. The boats still used on the rivers Tigris and Euphrates resemble in form a beehive with a considerable bulge in the middle. Gerald Massey ("The Natural Genesis," vol. ii. p. 63) says that this conception of the earth's figure

corresponds to the Egyptian *Put-sign* with its hollow underneath. Various forms of this formation of the world are extant. The horse-shoe is one. *Hence its value as a symbol of superstition.* The head-dress of the Egyptian goddess Hathor has the shape of a horse-shoe. The letter omega (Ω) is another form of the same sign.

The Rev. C. Vernon Harcourt, in his "Doctrine of the Deluge" (vol. i. p. 141), suggests that the moon was anciently regarded as particularly sacred when in the first quarter, because at that period it resembled most closely the ark of Noah, which was crescent-shaped.

Again, the horse-shoe form is believed to be a survival of an ancient religious symbol often seen in Assyrian and Egyptian sculptures, signifying the mystical door of life.

The D of the Italic alphabets placed ◠ reveals its early picture origin, while the Greek delta (Δ) represents a tent door. The Egyptian hieroglyphic for ten was ∩. It is plain, therefore, that the horse-shoe is the mystical door reduced to its simplest possible form, and as a fetish for bringing good luck, or as a talisman to avert the evil eye, it would have no meaning except with the points downward.[1]

From a scientific standpoint, therefore, the horse-shoe, when used as a protective symbol, should be placed with its convex arch uppermost; but as a luck token, the reverse position is the proper one, else, according to a popular notion, the luck may be spilled out.

In northern Germany and Bavaria figures of horse-shoes are sometimes cut on boundary stones, as for example, on a stone which separates the hamlets Ellerbek and Wellingdorf, suburbs of Kiel; and, again, on one between the estates of Depenau and Bockhorn, in middle Holstein. In these cases the idea involved is probably that of the beneficent horse-shoe arch, impartially guarding the interests of both villages or estates.

[1] John Newton, *Notes and Queries*, 7th series, vol. iii. April, 1887.

XI. THE HORSE-SHOE AS A SYMBOL OF THE HORSE

But the efficacy of the horse-shoe as a protector of people and buildings depends not solely upon its arched shape, nor on its bifurcated form, nor yet upon its fancied resemblance to a snake. Its relation to the *horse* also gives it a talismanic value; for in legendary lore this animal was often credited with supernatural qualities. An English myth ascribes to the horse the character of a luck-bringer, and horse-worship was in vogue among the early Celts, Teutons, and Slavs.

In Hindostan, also, the horse is regarded as a lucky animal; and when an equestrian rides into a sugar-cane field in the sowing season, the event is considered auspicious. In the same region the froth from a horse's mouth is thought to repel demons, which are believed to have more fear of a horse than of any other animal. The natives of northern India also believe that the horse was originally a wingéd creature, and that the horny protuberances on his legs indicate where the wings were attached.[1]

In the Norse mythology almost every deity has his particular steed, as have most of the heroes of antiquity, for the heathen nations regarded the horse as sacred and divine.[2]

---

[1] W. Crooke, B. A., *Popular Religion and Folk-Lore of Northern India.*
[2] Jacob Grimm, *Deutsche Mythologie.*

Tradition says that when the city of Carthage was founded by Dido, the Phœnician queen, in the ninth century B. C., a priestess of Juno dug in the ground, by command of the oracle, and discovered the head of a bullock. This was considered unsatisfactory, because bullocks and oxen were servile animals under the yoke. Thereupon the priestess again turned up the soil and found a horse's head, which was reckoned auspicious, for the horse, although sometimes yoked to the plough, was also symbolic of war and martial glory. Therefore a temple of Juno was built on the spot, and the figure of a horse's head was adopted as an emblem by the Carthaginians and stamped upon their coins.[1]

Dr. Ludwig Beck, in his "History of Iron," states that in Teutonic legends the horse was sacred to Wodan or Odin, who always rode, while Thor either drove about in his chariot or went afoot. Thence it is, says this writer, that the Devil of the Middle Ages is represented with the hoofs of a horse.

The reputation of the horse as a prophetic and divinatory animal, even among Christian peoples, is shown by various German traditions, of which the following is an example. When the inhabitants of Delve, a village in the Duchy of Holstein, were about to build a church,

[1] Friedrich Creuzer, *Symbolik und Mythologie der alten Völker*, vol. iv. p. 380.

the choice of a site was determined in this manner:
An image of the Virgin was fastened upon the back of
a parti-colored mare, which was then allowed to roam
at will; and it was agreed that the church should be
erected upon the spot where the mare should be found
the next morning. This proved to be a neighboring
bramble-thicket, and the new edifice was accordingly
placed there, and dedicated to " Our beloved Lady on
the Horse." [1]

The ancient belief in the oracular powers of the
horse is well shown by a custom formerly in vogue
among the Pomeranians. On the outbreak of a war
a priest laid three spears at equal distances upon the
ground in front of the temple. Two other spears were
then leaned transversely across them, with their points
resting in the earth. After a prayer the high priest
led up a sacred horse, and if he stepped with his right
foot foremost thrice in succession over the spears without stumbling, it was accounted a good augury, otherwise not. [2]

A dragon-headed horse, emblematic of grandeur,
having on its back the civilizing book of the law, is one
of the four great mythic animals of the Chinese; and
the Tibetans have a like symbol, which they use as a
luck-bringing talisman.

[1] *Das Kloster,* vol. ix. p. 97.
[2] Friedrich, p. 454.

The association of the horse with luck is prominent in Indian myth as well : —

The jewel-horse of the universal monarch, such as Buddha was to have been had he cared for worldly grandeur, carries its rider Pegasus-like through the air in whatever direction wished for, and thus it would become associated with the idea of material wishes, and especially wealth and jewels.[1]

Among the lower classes of the Hindus of Bombay, a notion is prevalent that spirits are frightened by the sound of a horse's hoofs; and this superstition has been thought to explain the custom, in vogue among the Hindus generally, of having a bridegroom ride a horse when on his way to the bride's residence.[2]

In Bokhara, when a horse stumbles in fording a stream, and the rider thereby gets an involuntary wetting, it is considered a most fortunate occurrence instead of a mishap. In the same country it is also accounted lucky to meet an equestrian.[3]

One reason in favor of the theory which ascribes the horse-shoe's weird powers to its connection with a luck-bringing animal is the fact that various portions of the equine frame serve as amulets in different localities. Thus not only the horse-shoe but the hoof, or

[1] L. Austine Waddell, M. B., *The Buddhism of Tibet*, p. 413.
[2] Campbell, p. 457.
[3] Schuyler, *Turkistan*, p. 30.

even a single bone of the foot, may be used for this object.

In the island of Montserrat the two incisor teeth of a horse are carried about as charms.[1] The popular belief of many people credits equine hair with special virtues. "Honor abides in the manes of horses" is a saying of Mohammed, and in Turkey a horse's tail as an emblem is significant of dignity and exalted position.

In certain villages of Brandenburg every new-born boy, before his first bath, is placed upon a horse, the animal being brought into the chamber for the purpose. This is thought to impart to the child manly qualities for life. In other districts small children are allowed to ride a black foal to facilitate the cutting of their teeth; and the neighings of horses are believed to be of favorable import if listened to carefully. The popular belief on this subject is exemplified in the German saying, "He has horse-luck," in reference to a piece of extraordinary good fortune.[2]

The Irish think that the reason for the horse-shoe's magical power is because the horse and the ass were in the stable where Christ was born, and hence are evermore blessed animals.

The romantic literature of Ireland affords evidence

---

[1] *Mélusine*, tome viii. No. 1, p. 17. 1896.
[2] Max Jähns. *Ross und Reiter.* i. 371.

of the existence of a species of horse-worship in that country in former ages, and tradition says that in the olden time there were horses endowed with human faculties.[1] We learn from Tacitus, moreover, that the Teutonic peoples

used white horses, as the Romans used chickens, for purposes of augury, and divined future events from different intonations of neighings. Hence it probably is that the discovery of a horse-shoe is so universally thought lucky, some of the feelings that once attached to the animal itself still surviving around the iron of its hoof. For horses, like dogs and birds, were universally accredited with a greater insight into futurity than man himself.[2]

The horse is seen among the insignia of Kent, the first of the Anglo-Saxon kingdoms, and is displayed at the present time on the shields of the houses of Hanover and Brunswick.[3]

One of the most solemn forms of oath taken on the eve of battle required a warrior to swear "by the shoulder of a horse and the edge of a sword" that he would not flee from the enemy even if the latter should be superior in strength.[4]

At the time of the conquest of Peru, the Indian aborigines were amazed at the sight of the Spanish horse-

---

[1] *Ulster Journal of Archæology*, vol. vii. p. 69.
[2] *Cornhill Magazine*, article on "Comparative Folk-Lore," vol. lxxvi.
[3] Thomas A. Wise, M. D., *History of Paganism in Caledonia*.
[4] Mallet, *Northern Antiquities*, p. 154.

men, believing that man and horse were one creature.
And it is said that Pizarro owed his life to this superstitious belief; for on one occasion, when pursued by
the natives, he fell from his horse, and the Peruvians
who witnessed the mishap, believing that one animal
had by magic divided itself into two, gave up the pursuit in dismay.[1]

M. D. Conway, in his " Demonology and Devil-Lore,"
asserts that the Scandinavian superstition known as the
" demon-mare " is the source of the use of the horse-
shoe against witches.   In Germany there is a saying in
reference to the morbid oppression sometimes experienced during sleep or while dreaming, and which is a
symptom of indigestion, " The nightmare hath ridden
thee."

This elvish mare rides horses also, and in the morning their manes are found all tangled and dripping with
sweat.

Grimm says that the traditional idea of the Nightmare seems to waver between the ridden animal and the
riding, trampling one, precisely as the Devil is sometimes represented as riding men, and again as taking
them on his back after the manner of a horse.

According to a Bavarian popular belief, the Nightmare is a woman, who is wont to appear at the house-
door of a morning, invariably requesting the loan of

[1] *Gentleman's Magazine,* vol. 278, p. 417.   1895.

some article. In order to get rid of her at night, one should say: "Come to-morrow and receive the three white gifts." The next morning the woman comes, and is given a handful of flour, a handful of salt, and an egg.[1]

In the north of England, naturally perforated stones are hung up by the side of the manger to prevent the Night Hag from riding the horses. In a rare book of the sixteenth century, entitled "The Fower Chiefest Offices belonging to Horsemanship, by Tho. Blundenill, of Newton Flotman, in Norffolke," the following curious charm is given as a remedy for horses affected with the nightmare:—

Take a Flynt Stone that
hath a hole of hys owne
kynde, and hang it ouer
hym and wryte in a bill:

In nomine patris, etc.
Saint George our Ladyes Knight,
He walked day so did he night
Until he hir found,
He hir beate and hir bounde,
Till truely hir trouth she
him plyght
That she woulde not come
within the night.

[1] Fräulein Helene Raff.

There as Saint George
our Ladyes Knight
Named was three tymes,
Saint George.

And hang this Scripture ouer him, and let him alone.
With such proper charmes as thys is, the false Fryers in
tymes past were wont to charme the money out of the playne
folkes purses.

Drink offerings were anciently poured from vessels
made from horses' hoofs; and witches are popularly
supposed to drink with avidity the water which collects
in equine hoof-tracks. German writers on early traditions and folk-lore agree in ascribing to the horse-
shoe divers magical properties, whose origin is vaguely
connected with the ancient pagan conception of the
horse as a sacrificial animal.[1]

According to a popular poetic fancy of the ancient
Teutons, horses, Wodan's favorite and darling animals,
were endowed with the gifts of speech and prophecy
during the twelve days between Christmas and Epiphany. At this holy season they were wont to put
their heads together, and impart to each other confi-
dentially their experiences and trials of the past year;
and this communion of equine spirits was the sole pleasure vouchsafed to the noble animals, and atoned in a
measure for the hard work which was their lot.

[1] Professor Dr. Sepp, *Die Religion der alten Deutschen*, p. 340. 1890.

Even nowadays many peasants do not venture to harness their horses at Christmas time, and do not even speak of the animals by name, but make use of pet epithets and circumlocutions when they have occasion to refer to them. On Christmas night, hostlers often sleep in the manger or under it, and their dreams at such times are prophetic for the coming year, for in their sleep they can hear what the horses are saying.

In order to impart health and vigor to the animals without incurring the expense of extra fodder, the hostler walks at Epiphany season by night three times around the village church, carrying in his uplifted hands a bundle of hay, which he afterwards feeds to the horses; or on Christmas night he steals some cabbage, which is then mixed with the fodder; or, before going to the midnight Christmas Mass, he lays on the manure-heap a quantity of hay called the "Mass hay," and on his return from church this is given to the horses. Some peasants have a yet more simple method of promoting the welfare of their horses, which consists in laying the cleaning-cloth upon a hedge on the evenings of Christmas, New Year's Day, or Epiphany, and afterwards grooming the animals with the dew-laden cloth.[1]

In the popular mind horses are credited with extraordinarily keen faculties for detecting ghosts and

[1] Jähns, i. pp. 294-296.

haunted places, which they instinctively scent from afar. The Thuringian peasant does not beat his horse when the latter refuses to proceed along some gloomy forest road; for the whip is useless against spiritual obstacles, whereas a *Paternoster* devoutly repeated is usually much more effective.

It is a Bohemian superstition that a horse sees everything magnified tenfold, and that this is the reason why the noble animal submits to being led by a little child.[1]

When a Brandenburg rustic has bought a horse in a neighboring town and rides him homeward, he dismounts at the boundary line of his own village, and, gathering a handful of his native soil, he throws it backward over the line to prevent the animal's being bewitched. In Bohemia the chief signs of bewitchment in a horse are thought to be shivering, profuse sweating, and emaciation. A charm against this consists in drawing one's shirt inside out over one's head, and using it as a wherewithal to groom the animal, — a method which may be acceptable to superstitious jockeys and hostlers, but which will hardly commend itself to a fastidious horse-owner.[2]

XII. HORSES' HEADS AS TALISMANS

In early times it was customary to use horses' heads as talismans, by means of which also the ancient heathen

---

[1] Wuttke, p. 185.   [2] Wuttke, p. 423.

nations practiced various magical arts. Grimm says in
his "Teutonic Mythology" that the Scandinavians had
a custom of fastening a horse's head to a pole, with the
mouth propped open with a stick. The gaping jaws
were then turned in the direction whence an enemy
was likely to come, in order to cast over him an evil
spell. This contrivance was known as a spite-stake,
or nithing-post. In Mallet's "Northern Antiquities"
(p. 156, 1890), it is related that Eigil, a famous Icelandic
bard, on being banished from Norway in the ninth century, fixed a stake in the ground and fastened thereon
a horse's head, saying meanwhile: "I here set up a
nithing-stake, and turn this my banishment against King
Eirek and Queen Gunhilda." Then, pointing the horse's
head toward the interior of Norway, he uttered a solemn imprecation against the protecting deities of the
land, invoking evil upon them, and expressing a wish
that they might be compelled to wander about and
never find rest until they had driven forth the hated
king and queen. In these cases the horse's head was
magically employed as an instrument for working evil
upon an enemy, but later the same symbol was widely
used among northern peoples as a talisman *against*
evil.

Not alone in remote antiquity, but throughout the
Middle Ages, the old pagan device of the spite-stake
continued to be employed by the Teutonic peoples; and

even after the Reformation, as late as the year 1584, a
mare's skull placed upon a pole was a favorite means
for driving away rats and other vermin in Germany.
The principle involved appears to have been always the
same, namely, the power of averting evil supposed to
be a magical attribute of horses' heads; and this power
was not only effective against human enemies, but likewise against the spirits of evil.[1]

When the Roman general Cæcina Severus reached
the scene of Varus's defeat by the German tribes under
their chieftain Arminius, in the year 9 A. D., near the
river Weser, he saw numbers of horses' heads fastened
to the trunks of trees. These were the heads of
Roman horses which the Germans had sacrificed to
their gods.[2]

In the fifteenth century a savage tribe known as the
Wends had a practice of placing a horse's head in the
crib or manger to counteract the influence of evil spirits,
and to prevent their horses from being ridden by the
Night Hag. And in many countries analogous notions,
veritable relics of paganism, exist in full force to-day.
Thus in Mecklenburg and Holstein it is a common
usage to place the carved wooden representations of the
heads of horses on the gables of houses as safeguards,
and when fixed upon poles in the vicinity of stables they

[1] Richard Andree, *Braunschweiger Volkskunde*, p. 128.
[2] Grimm, vol. i. p. 47.

are thought to ward off epizoötics. In Mecklenburg, also, horses' heads, when placed beneath the pillows of the sick, are believed to act as febrifuges, and in Holland they are hung up over pigsties. The fore-parts of horses are to be seen on the gables of old houses in the Rhætian Alps, "carved out of the ends of the intersecting principals." [1]

The use of horses' heads as talismans is thought to have some connection with the ancient pagan sacrificial offerings of horses. Adherence to the latter custom was formerly regarded as a pledge of loyalty to heathenism, and conversely its renunciation was a sign of adopting the new religion. In the tenth century the Norwegian king Hakon Athelstan, known as "Hakon the Good," endeavored persistently to extirpate heathen idolatry in his kingdom, but without much success, owing to the vigorous opposition of his people. At one of their great Yule-tide festivals the king was urged to eat some horse's flesh as a proof of devotion to the old faith, and on his refusal to do this they wished to kill him.

On another occasion King Hakon so far yielded to the importunities of his people as to inhale the steam from a kettle of horse-broth. He also drank some Yule-beer, holding the cup in his left hand, while with his right he made the sign of the cross, which the pagan

[1] S. Baring-Gould, M. A., *Strange Survivals*.

mind conceived to be the symbol of Thor's hammer. Finally he was even induced to eat a couple of mouthfuls of horse-flesh, an act which his people accepted as a satisfactory guarantee of his orthodoxy.[1]

Among the newly converted Northern nations the use of horse-flesh as food fell into disrepute, and the practice was looked upon as a secret sacrifice to the old idols, while those indulging in it were punished as obdurate pagans.[2]

The employment of horses' heads as talismans, a custom doubtless originating in heathendom, has been thought not only to suggest the sacrificial offering of a horse, but also to symbolize the religious dedication of a building placed under the protective influence of such a symbol. For among the ancient Teutons the horse was held to be the most holy of animals, and auguries were derived from the neighings of white horses in their sacred groves. There exists, moreover, among German peasants a widespread belief that the placing of carved wooden representations of horses' heads upon house-gables is an act of homage to the Deity, whose blessing and benediction are thereby invoked upon the dwellings thus adorned, and upon the inmates as well. When, however, the heads are directed *outwards*, in order to

---

[1] J. Scheible, *Das Kloster*, Band ix. p. 101; Thomas Carlyle, *Early Kings of Norway*, p. 8.

[2] Dr. Karl Weinhold, *Altnordisches Leben*, p. 145. 1856.

ward off evil, the principle involved is evidently akin
to that of the pagan spite-stake, of which mention has
been made.

Professor Christian Petersen, of Hamburg, who inves-
tigated this subject some years ago, expressed the belief
that among the pagans every dwelling was protected by
three talismanic emblems, namely: (1) on the gable a
horse's head, or the representation of some other animal
or bird; (2) by the side of the entrance door a *broom*,
as a preservative against lightning; and (3) on the
threshold a *horse-shoe*.

The German botanist, Karl Friedrich von Ledebour,
who visited the Altai Mountains early in the present
century, wrote that among the Kalmuks, a nomadic
people inhabiting that region, he observed numerous
horses' heads and hides, relics of sacrifices, placed upon
scaffolds; and the direction of the horses' heads, pointing east or west, indicated whether the sacrificial offering was made to a good or evil deity.[1]

Formerly in some parts of Germany, especially in the
north, it was customary to place a horse's head above
the stable door; sometimes also horses were killed and
their bodies buried beneath the corner-stone of a building, in order to bring good luck. In the same region
the association of horses and horse-shoes with lucky
influences is everywhere apparent: a horse-shoe when

[1] Brand, vol. ii. p. 664.

found is either carried about as an amulet, or placed on the chamber wall or threshold; and a young girl who finds a certain number of horse-shoes in a year, or who sees a hundred white horses within the same period, will be married before the year is out.[1]

In Moldavia the head of a horse or of an ass is much esteemed on account of its reputed magical properties, and is believed to be a powerful agent not only for the production of witchcraft, but conversely as a powerful antagonist of evil.[2]   Inclosures where animals are kept are very commonly protected by one of these talismans placed upon a forked stake; and the same device is popular as a safeguard against wolves and robbers.[3]   In Roumania the skull of a horse is placed over a court-yard gate as a preservative against ghosts, and in Tuscany it is also used as a charm.[4]

The Christmas festivities at Ramsgate, in Kent, formerly included a peculiar feature called " going a-hodening." A horse's head fixed on a pole was carried through the town by a party of young people, grotesquely attired and ringing hand-bells. By pulling a string attached to the lower jaw, the horse's mouth was made to open and shut with a snapping sound. In this case the horse's head was typical of the good

[1] Fräulein Helene Raff.
[2] J. B. Friedrich, *Die Symbolik und Mythologie der Natur.*
[3] E. Rolland, *Faune populaire de la France,* tome iv.
[4] C. G. Leland, *Gypsy Sorcery.*

Demon, threatening and overcoming the powers of darkness.[1]

It appears that a modern counterpart of the ancient heathen practice of hanging equine heads upon trees, as tributes to Wodan, still exists in Sussex, where the bodies of horses are suspended by the legs from horizontal tree-branches, as a means of bringing luck to the cattle. And the evident analogy between the two customs of widely separated epochs, the sacrificial offering of horses upon trees in order to avert evil or to invoke protection, has not escaped the attention of modern writers.[2]

The Ostiaks of southern Siberia were wont to suspend horses' heads from the branches of trees, and to protect bees from witchcraft they also placed them near the hives.[3]

In Bulgaria and among the Osseten, an Asiatic tribe, the same talismans are affixed to the palings inclosing farmyards. The ancient Teuton placed a horse's head on the weather-vane of his barn, while he hung up a horse-shoe in some consecrated place, as a deprecatory offering to the god of thunder and storms;[4] and the Tartars of the Chinese province of Koukou-Nor seek to protect their bees from the "evil eye" by hanging up

[1] Gerald Massey, *A Book of Beginnings.*
[2] *Folk-Lore,* vol. iv. p. 6.   1893.
[3] *Mélusine,* tome viii. No. 1, p. 17.   1896.
[4] Professor Dr. Sepp, *Die Religion der alten Deutschen,* p. 263.   1890.

near the hives either a skull, a foot, or in fact any bone of a horse.

In Mecklenburg one remedy for the delirium of fever consists in placing a horse's skull under the bed; and in some parts of Prussia certain spinal affections of children are treated by bathing the patient in rainwater in which a horse's head has been dipped thrice daily for three successive Thursdays.[1] In a curious old work by M. Fugger (1854), the writer says that a mare's skull, fixed on a pole and placed in a garden, has a wonderful effect in promoting the growth of plants and vegetables, and, moreover, insures freedom from rats and caterpillars.[2]

The Magyar shepherds place horses' and asses' skulls as talismans about their sheepfolds to keep wolves away from their flocks, and also to prevent herbaceous animals other than their sheep from eating the grass of their pasture lands. Also when, as occasionally happens, some hill or upland region gains an unsavory reputation among the peasants as an alleged meeting-place of witches, horses' skulls are placed there in order to prevent such unseemly orgies, for, according to the popular report, where witches meet grass will not grow. Whoever has the courage to visit such a place on the midnight of Good Friday with a so-called *Luciastuhl*,

---

[1] Jähns, vol. i. p. 373.
[2] *Das Buch der ritterlichen Reutterkunst.*

a peculiar chair or stool made during Christmas week, may see the witches at their revels, and may easily disperse them by throwing a horse's skull into their midst.[1]

The gypsies inhabiting lands bordering on the eastern Danube are wont to fasten the skulls of horses and cattle upon the fence-palings which surround their farmyards, to prevent witches and evil spirits from entering the inclosures. So, too, the Transylvanian gypsies bury horses' skulls beneath the floor of the earth caverns which they occupy in winter; and the tribes of southern Hungary place similar talismans upon the graves of their kindred, that no witch may tread upon the sanctified ground.[2]

The wizards and conjurers of the Shamans pretend to be experts in sorcery, and to possess a secret knowledge which enables them to control the actions of evil spirits. They wear a long elk-skin robe adorned with many fetich objects, such as bells and pieces of iron; and to assist them in their magic rites they carry staves, whose tops are carved into the shape of horses' heads, and by means of these staves they are enabled to leap high into the air.[3]

---

[1] Heinrich von Wlislocki, *Aus dem Volksleben der Magyaren*, pp. 9, 10.

[2] Heinrich von Wlislocki, *Volksglaube und religiöser Brauch der Zigeuner*.

[3] M'Clintock and Strong's *Encyclopædia*, art. "Shamanism;" E. B. Tylor, *Primitive Culture*, vol. ii. p. 142.

XIII. THE HORSE-SHOE AS A FAVORITE ANTI-WITCH
CHARM

The *universality* of the use of the horse-shoe as a safeguard against evil spirits is indeed noteworthy.

It is the anti-witch charm *par excellence*, as well as the approved symbol of good luck, and, used for these purposes, it is to be seen throughout a large portion of the world. The horse-shoe is most commonly placed over the entrance-doors of dwellings; but stables likewise are thought to be effectually protected by it, for "witches were dreadful harriers of horse-flesh." In William Henderson's "Folk-Lore of the Northern Countries of England " we read of a Durham farmer who was convinced that one of his horses had been ridden by hags, as he had found it bathed in sweat of a morning. But after he took the precaution to nail a horse-shoe over the stable-door, and also to hang some broom above the manger, the witches had not been able to indulge in clandestine rides on his horses. While many an honest fellow in England and elsewhere is a firm believer in witches and magical horse-shoes, very few of them can give plausible reasons therefor.

The Lancashire farmer thinks that mischievous fairies not only ride horses by night, but drive cows out of the barn, steal the butter, and eat up the children's porridge; so he, too, affixes horse-shoes to his buildings.

Any one visiting the hamlets of Oxfordshire can hardly fail to notice the numerous horse-shoes affixed to the picturesque thatched-roofed cottages; and the countryfolk in this neighborhood are not always content with *one* of these popular safeguards, for two or three of them are often to be seen on the walls of a dwelling, invariably placed with the prongs downward.

In Brand's "Popular Antiquities" (vol. iii. p. 19, 1888) may be found a clipping from the Cambridge (Eng.) "Advertiser," which relates that one Bartingale, a carpenter and resident of Ely, suspected a woman named Gotobed of having bewitched him, and of being the cause of an illness which he had recently had. Thereupon, at a consultation of matrons of the neighborhood held in his chamber, it was decided that the most efficient means of protecting him from the evil influence of the suspected sorceress was to have three horse-shoes fastened to the door. A blacksmith was accordingly summoned, and

an operation to this effect was performed, much to the anger of the supposed witch, who at first complained to the Dean, but was laughed at by his reverence. She then rushed in wrath to the sick man's room, and, miraculous to tell, passed the Rubicon in spite of the horse-shoes. But this wonder ceased when it was discovered that Vulcan had substituted donkeys' shoes.

Miss Georgiana F. Jackson says, in "Shropshire Folk-

Lore," that, in the home of her childhood at Edgmond, the stable-door was decorated with three rows of horse-shoes arranged in the form of a triangle; and the grooms used to say that they were placed there to exclude witches.

In this region, too, an old horse-shoe placed above the door of a bedroom is a preventive of the night-mare.

In Shrewsbury, the ancient county town of Shrop-shire, horse-shoe talismans are to be seen not only above the house-doors, but also on the barges which navigate the river Severn.

In quite recent times a case has been reported of a poor girl of Whatfield, in Suffolk, who had experienced a long illness, during which she was visited daily by an old woman who appeared to be very solicitous as to her welfare. At length the girl's family began to suspect that this old woman was none other than a witch; they therefore caused a horse-shoe to be fastened to the sill of the outer door. The precaution was successful, so runs the tale, for the reputed witch could never there-after cross the threshold, and the girl speedily recovered her health.[1]

Aubrey, in his "Remains of Gentilisme," describes the horse-shoe as a preservative against the mischief or power of witches, attributing its magical properties to

[1] *Gentleman's Magazine.* 1867.

the astrological principle that Mars, the God of War and the War Horse, was an enemy of Saturn, who according to a mediæval idea was the liege lord of witches.[1]

During the witchcraft excitement in Scotland, one Elizabeth Bathcat was indicted for having a horse-shoe attached to the door of her house " as a devilish means of instruction from the Devil to make her goods and all her other affairs to prosper and succeed well." [2]

According to an old legend St. Dunstan, the versatile English ecclesiastic of the tenth century, who was a skilled farrier and the owner of a forge, was requested by the Devil to shoe his " single hoof." Dunstan, who recognized his customer, acceded, but during the operation he caused the Devil so much pain that the latter begged him to desist. The request was heeded on condition that the Devil should never enter a place where a horse-shoe was displayed.[3] The popular belief is that his Satanic Majesty has always faithfully kept the contract, and quite naturally all lesser evil spirits have followed his example.

In Scotland, even as late as the beginning of the nineteenth century, the peasantry believed that witches were able to draw milk from all the cattle in their

[1] Rev. T. Thiselton Dyer, *Domestic Folk-Lore.*
[2] *Museum of Foreign Literature,* vol. xxvi. 1835.
[3] The Rev. E. Cobham Brewer, LL. D., *Dictionary of Phrase and Fable.*

neighborhood, by tugging at a hair-rope in imitation of
the act of milking. Such a rope was made of hairs
from the tails of several cows, whose exact number
was indicated by knots in the rope. While tugging
at the rope the witches repeated either the following
or a similar charm : —

> Cow's milk and mare's milk,
> And every beast that bears milk,
> Between St. Johnstone's and Dundee,
> Come a' to me, come a' to me.

The only adequate protection from such mischievous
pranks as these was afforded by nailing a horse-shoe to
the byre-door and tying sprigs of rowan with a red
thread to the cow's tail. If, however, these precautions
were neglected, the guilty witch might yet be discovered by placing the " gudeman's breeks " upon the
cow's horns, a leg upon either horn ; and thereupon
the animal, being let loose, was sure to run directly to
the witch's house.[1]

In many places, certain houses continue even at the
present time to have an evil reputation as harborers of
witches and goblins. In these cases it seems probable
that the owners or occupants of such dwellings neglected to avail themselves of the immunity afforded
by horse-shoes and other safeguards. For no one, we
believe, has ever seriously maintained that evil spirits,

[1] Robert Ford. *Thistledown.*

who are once firmly domiciled, can be easily expelled.
Familiarity with their surroundings may breed a contempt for amulets. Certain it is, however, that an
ounce or two of iron by way of prevention is worth a
pound or more of cure. When a dwelling is demoni-
acally possessed, the devils must be driven out somehow,
and for this purpose recourse is had to exorcisms, and
to religious or magical ceremonies. In the words of
the poet Dryden (" Wife of Bath's Tale," i. 28) :—

> And friars that through the wealthy regions run
> Resort to farmers rich, and bless their halls,
> And exorcise the beds and cross the walls.

In "Antiquitates Vulgares," by Henry Browne
(1725), the writer gives elaborate directions as to the
proper mode of exorcising a haunted dwelling, and
says that the house which is reported to be vexed with
spirits shall be visited by a priest daily for a week, appropriate prayers and scriptural selections being read.
Sometimes magical procedures supplanted religious
exercises, and experts in sorcery were employed to rid
a mansion of its undesirable tenants. The following
advertisement from a London newspaper of 1777 may
be appropriately given here : —

HAUNTED HOUSES.—Whereas there are mansions and cas-
tles in England and Wales which for many years have been
uninhabited, and are now falling into decay, by their being
visited and haunted by evil spirits or the spirits of those who

for unknown reasons are rendered miserable, even in the grave, a gentleman who has made the tour of Europe, of a particular turn of mind, and deeply skilled in the abstruse and sacred science of exorcism, hereby offers his assistance to any owner or proprietor of such premises, and undertakes to render the same free from the visitation of such spirits, be their cause what it may, and render them tenantable and useful for the proprietors. Letters addressed to Rev. John Jones, No. 30 St. Martin's Lane, duly answered, and interview given if required.[1]

XIV. THE POSITION OF THE HORSE-SHOE AS A PRO-TECTOR OF BUILDINGS

It has been supposed that the horse-shoe is placed at the *outer* entrance to a building because of an ancient Saxon superstition that witches were unable successfully to practice their wiles upon persons in the open air.[2] The horse-shoe effectively bars the ingress of witches and evil spirits, but an entrance once obtained by these creatures, it is powerless to expel them. Therefore the horse-shoe within doors loses much of its efficacy, but is still an emblem of good luck.

Placed on the outside of the door, or above the entrance of a dwelling, or upon the threshold, the horse-shoe is easily first among the inveterate foes of witches and devils generally.

> Laugh if you will, who imps nor devils fear,
> Whom death appals not, phantoms come not near ;

[1] *Boston Transcript*, May 9, 1898.   [2] Turner's *Anglo-Saxons*.

Along whose nerves no quick vibrations dart,
As teeming twilight's shadowy offspring start ;
Not yours to feel the joy with which I flew
To snatch the rusty, worn, but lucky shoe.
Oft have I heard them chattering at my door,
The hags whose dances beat the shrinking moor;
Oft have I sprung from nightmare-haunted rest,
And gasped an *oro* from my panting breast,
As forms that vanished ere the half-shut eye
With fright could open, from their revels fly.
Henceforth, good horse-shoe, vain shall be their ride :
Their spells are baffled and their rage defied.[1]

Edward Moor, in his "Oriental Fragments" (p. 455, London, 1834), relates having once, in company with a gang of urchins, nailed a donkey-shoe under the threshold of a poor woman in Suffolk who was suspected of sorcery. He and his youthful companions endeavored thus to keep her all night within doors, as witches cannot cross iron.

An English writer [2] tells of having heard an animated discussion in the parlor of a London beer-shop as to whether it were preferable to nail a horse-shoe *behind the door* or upon *the first doorstep ;* and instances of extraordinary good luck were mentioned as the direct result of the potency of the amulet in each position.

But there are weighty reasons for the selection of the front door, or the parts immediately connected with

[1] John Brooks Felton, *The Horse-Shoe*, a Poem. Cambridge, 1849.
[2] James Napier in *Folk-Lore*.

it, as the proper place for the display of horse-shoes as household guardians.

In the earliest historic times, and in primitive communities, the entrance of a dwelling was considered a sacred place; and in the opinion of eminent scholars who have made a study of the subject, the threshold was the first family altar. A peculiar reverence for the doorway and threshold prevails to-day in many parts of the world, as is evident from the numerous ceremonial rites in vogue among widely separated savage tribes and uncivilized peoples.[1] Indeed, the custom of placing amulets and charms in and about the entrance-doors of houses, stables, and other buildings is almost universal. In Russia a cross is marked on the threshold to keep witches away. In Lithuania, when a house is being built, a wooden cross, or some article which has been handed down from past generations, is placed under the threshold. There, also, when a newly baptized child is being brought back from church, it is customary for its father to hold it for a while over the threshold, "so as to place the new member of the family under the protection of the domestic divinities." Sick children who are supposed to have been afflicted by an evil eye are washed on the threshold of their cottage, in order that with

[1] H. Clay Trumbull, *The Threshold Covenant*, chap. i.

the help of the Penates who reside there, the malady may be driven out of doors.[1]

Under the threshold of the Assyrian palaces at Nineveh were found certain images of grotesque monsters, as, for example, a human form with the head of a lynx, and a lion's body with a man's head, which were intended as tutelary deities.[2]

John Netten Radcliffe, in his "Fiends, Ghosts, and Sprites" (p. 43, London, 1854), says that the horse-shoe superstition is a remnant or relic of the worship of household guardians or divinities, — a practice still in vogue among the natives of Ashantee, and also among the Bhutas of Hindostan. In some English counties, naturally perforated stones are hung behind the door; and in Glamorganshire the walls of the houses are whitewashed in order to terrify wandering spirits of evil. Whether successful or not for this purpose, the custom is certainly effective as a destroyer of the demoniac germs of certain diseases.

The French Canadians are not the least superstitious of mankind, neither do they wholly neglect to take due precautions against the admittance to their homes of evil spirits.

They do not answer "Entrez!" when a knock is heard at the door, but call out "Ouvrez!" This custom is

---

[1] Ralston, *Songs of the Russian People*, p. 136.
[2] Bonami, *Nineveh and its Palaces*, p. 159.

said to have originated from a current tradition regarding a young woman who once answered "Entrez!" in response to a knock, whereupon the Devil promptly came in and carried her away.[1] Where such legends find open-mouthed credence, it does not appear strange that horse-shoes and other talismans should be at a premium.

In Tuscany magical medicines are taken upon the threshold, which also plays an important part in sorcery. One reason assigned for this fact is that the threshold forms the line separating the outer world, where demons are rampant, from the domestic precincts, where human beings dwell.

One writer affirms it to be a fixed law in demonology that spirits cannot cross the threshold and enter a house unless previously invited to do so, but adds that there are many exceptions to this rule.[2] The weight of evidence does not support this view, for mischievous fairies and witches are known to rudely disregard the laws of etiquette, and do not wait for an invitation to enter dwellings. This fact is, indeed, a chief *raison d'être* for the use of talismans at the entrance of habitations.

The residents of the beautiful Thuringian Forest region, in whose neighborhood these lines chanced to be

---

[1] *Popular Science Monthly*, vol. 44, p. 520. February, 1894.
[2] C. G. Leland, *Etruscan Roman Remains*, p. 282.

penned, are wont to affix horse-shoes to the thresholds of their chamber-doors, lest some rude goblin enter and disturb their slumbers. But the fastidiousness of these sylvan folk is not content with an ordinary shoe, even though found on the road and venerable with rust; in order to serve its purpose as a talisman, a Thuringian horse-shoe must have been forged by a bachelor of wholesome life and good character, on Saint John's Eve.[1]

In German households, the horse-shoe over the door is believed to afford protection against divers apparitions, as well as against the Devil, witchcraft, lightning, sickness, and evils of every sort.

The cross, symbol of the Christian faith, is the most potent of all talismans, but is seldom seen at the entrance of dwellings. In some Roman Catholic countries the crucifix is, indeed, everywhere conspicuous, not only in churches and shrines, but by the roadside, in fields, and on the outer walls of houses, but it is rarely placed at the front door. In Hungary, however, the Magyars mark with black chalk the figure of a cross upon their stable-doors, and also brand anew thereon the sacred emblem each year at Christmas time.

The respect paid by the inhabitants of Tibet to their household divinities somewhat resembles the worship of

[1] Petersen, *Hufeisen*, p. 7.

their *Lares* by the Romans of old, and finds a parallel in the honor accorded to the favorite amulet of Western civilization, the horse-shoe.

The Tibetans set up above the entrances of their houses complex talismans, composed of various mystical objects, such as a ram's skull with horns attached, having displayed along the base of the skull pieces of carved wood representing a man and woman, a house, and other symbols; the idea being to deceive the demons, and to make them believe that these objects are the real dwelling and its inmates. The Tibetans believe that the demons are thus tricked, and that the wooden images are the victims of their mischievous designs.[1]

Far away among the nomadic tribes of Turkestan, horse-shoes are occasionally seen nailed to the thresholds of dwellings in the vicinity of the ancient city of Merv; and within doors, near the entrances of these peculiar habitations, which resemble mammoth parrot cages, pieces of linen or calico, four or five inches square, are seen upon the felt wall-lining, to serve as receptacles for the free-will offerings of such wandering spirits as may pass the magic barriers of the horse-shoes.[2]

In some regions there still prevails a time-honored custom of placing over the chief entrances of dwellings

[1] Waddell, p. 484.
[2] Edmond O'Donovan, *The Merv Oasis*, vol. ii. p. 141.

inscriptions, embodying usually a religious thought or exhortation. Sometimes, however, the sentence commends the house and its occupants to the care of the goddess Fortune, thus having a significance akin to that of the horse-shoe symbol. In the year 1892 the writer copied many inscriptions found above the doors of houses in northern Italy and Switzerland, some of them being written in Latin, others in German, French, Italian, and the Romansch dialect, current in the Engadine. Here, for example, is one from a house in the Swiss village of Bergun, the original being in German : "This house is in God's hand ; May Good Luck come in, and Bad Luck stay out ! 1673."

Many of these inscriptions are Biblical verses, which are here used as talismans, just as the pious Moslem employs sentences from the Koran.

Here, again, is the translation of a German sentence over the door of a dwelling in the village of Ober-Schönberg, near Innsbruck, Tyrol, copied in 1897 : —

All persons entering this house are recommended to Divine protection. God and the Virgin Mary guard all such, even though powerful enemies threaten, and lightnings and thunder rage without !

Above the door of a house in the village of Welschnofen, near Botzen, the wayfarer may read the following sentence : "Pray for us, holy Florian, that fire may not harm our dwelling." Above the inscription an eye is painted, while below is a realistic picture of Saint Florian, the protector of buildings against fire, engaged in pouring water on a burning roof.

The Bassamese, inhabitants of the Gold Coast of Africa, west of Ashantee, use certain fetich objects for the protection of their dwellings. These amulets, which are often merely pieces of wood painted red, or fragments of pottery, are placed upon the doors of their huts, and are believed to afford ample protection against thieves.[1] Such a fetich is probably intended to exclude evil spirits as well, and is, therefore, a substitute for both the horse-shoe and the watch-dog, those guardians of the household so popular in civilized communities.

When a modern Egyptian returns from a pilgrimage to Mecca, he fastens above the entrance of his house a branch of the aloe, which is not only a proof of his religious zeal in having accomplished the holy journey, but is also reckoned a protection against objectionable spiritual intruders, and is, therefore, seen in Cairo over the doors of the houses both of Christians and Jews.

In northern Scotland, formerly, a branch of the rowan-tree was placed over a farmhouse door, after having been waved while the words " Avaunt, Satan ! " were solemnly pronounced.[2]

---

[1] A. Featherman, *Social History of Mankind*.
[2] Rev. Charles Rogers, D. D., *Social Life in Scotland*, vol. iii. p. 229.

About the year 1850 the Rev. Andrew A. Bonar, who was then assistant minister in Collace Parish, Perthshire, Scotland, found the custom of displaying horse-shoes on the doors of farm buildings so prevalent that he thought it his duty to remonstrate against a practice savoring of paganism. But his efforts in this direction, though hardly crowned with success, were yet not wholly without avail, for his superstitious parishioners removed the guardian horse-shoes from the outsides of the doors, and nailed them up on the insides.[1]

The *raison d'être* of the horse-shoe at the entrance of shops and other frequented buildings has been attributed to a belief that, among the many people continually passing through the doorway, some one might, unobserved, bring in ill-luck or work mischief. But these safeguards not only form a sufficient barrier against obnoxious hags and sorcerers, but are potent against ghosts and all manner of evil creatures. When the Oxford undergraduate " sports his oak " to prevent the untimely entrance of dunning tradespeople, he shuts out friendly visitors as well; but the faithful horse-shoe, by a process of natural selection, debars only objectionable spirits, and is a formidable obstacle to the demon of ill-luck.

---

[1] Robert Ford, *Thistledown*, p. 262.

XV. THE LUCKY HORSE-SHOE IN GENERAL

He laughs like a boor who has found a horse-shoe.
                                        Dutch proverb.

Throughout Germany the belief obtains that a horse-shoe found on the road, and nailed on the threshold of a house with the points directed outward, is a mighty protection not only against hags and fiends, but also against fire and lightning ; but, *reversed*, it brings misfortune. In eastern Pennsylvania, however, even in recent times, the horse-shoe is often placed with the prongs pointing inward, so that the luck may be spilled into the house. The horse-shoe retains its potency as a charm on the sea as well as on land, and it has long been a practice among sailors to nail this favorite amulet against the mast of a vessel, whether fishing-boat or large sea-going craft, as a protection against the Evil One. The shoe of a "wraith-horse," the mythical offspring of a water-stallion, is especially esteemed by Scotch mariners for this purpose.[1]

In Bohemia only exists the superstition exactly opposite to that elsewhere prevalent, namely, that whoever picks up a horse-shoe thereby *ipso facto* picks up ill-luck for himself, — a notable example in folk-lore of the exception which proves the rule. The Bohe-

[1] Gregor, *Scotch Folk-Lore.*

mians, however, believe a nailed-up horse-shoe to be a cure for lunacy.[1]

As a general rule, the degree of luck pertaining to a horse-shoe found by chance has been thought to depend on the number of nails remaining in it: the more nails the more luck.[2]

In Northumberland the holes free of nails are carefully counted, as these indicate, presumably in years, how soon the finder of the shoe may expect to be married.[3] The peasants of northern Portugal prefer mule-shoes having an uneven number of nail-holes, as counteractives of the evil influences of the dreaded, omnipresent witches known as the *Bruxas*.[4]

In Derbyshire it is customary to drive a horse-shoe, prongs upward, between two flagstones near the door of a dwelling.[5] This position is sometimes explained by saying that, so placed, the luck cannot spill out.

In a short poem called "The Lucky Horse-Shoe," by James T. Fields, an amusing account is given of a farmer who picked up an old horse-shoe from the road, and nailed it upon the door of his barn with the prongs downward. But, far from bringing him luck, Fortune

---

[1] A. Wuttke, *Der deutsche Volksaberglaube*. Berlin, 1869.
[2] Robert Thorne, M. A., *A Dictionary of Rare and Curious Information*.
[3] *The Denham Tracts*.
[4] *Fortnightly Review*.
[5] Sidney Oldall Addy, M. A., *Household Tales*. 1895.

thereafter frowned upon him; his hay crop failed, a drought blighted his vegetables, and his hens refused to lay.

The good farmer, discouraged and perplexed, confided his woes to the sympathetic ear of an aged wayfarer who chanced to pass by, relating how misfortunes had pursued him since he had fastened up the old horse-shoe.

> The stranger asked to see the shoe;
> The farmer brought it into view;
> But when the old man raised his head,
> He laughed outright and quickly said:
> " No wonder skies upon you frown,
> You 've nailed the horse-shoe upside down;
> Just turn it round, and soon you 'll see
> How you and Fortune will agree."

The farmer profited by the friendly suggestion and reversed his luck-token, whereupon the capricious goddess fairly beamed upon him. His barn was soon filled with hay, his storehouses were packed with the kindly fruits of the earth, while his wife presented him with twins.

Farmers may well take heed *how* they nail up horseshoes over the doors of their barns. To obtain the best results, it would seem advisable to place a pair of these useful articles on each farm building, one with the points upward, the other reversed; for in this way they may not only hope to win Fortune's smiles, but also to keep all witches and unfriendly spirits at a respectful distance.

In an interesting story for children in " St. Nicholas," April, 1897, by Rudolph F. Bunner, entitled " The Horse-Shoe of Luck," the writer introduces Luck in the character and garb of a wandering clown or jester, mounted upon a white horse. This jovial traveler seeks a night's lodging at a wayside farmhouse, and when he has almost reached its hospitable door, his steed casts a shoe, which the farmer hastens to pick up and carefully hangs on a hook above the door. Luck proved to be a most amusing fellow, and after supper he entertained the children of the household in a royal manner, showing them, among other things, how to drop china and glass without breaking them, and how to tumble down stairs without getting hurt. So the evening passed merrily enough, and all retired for the night in a happy frame of mind. Early in the morning the farmer was awakened by the splash of raindrops upon his face, and, hastily arising, he discovered that the roof had sprung a leak, and that his guest had unceremoniously departed. Nettled by such conduct, the farmer and his family hastened in pursuit of the fleeing stranger, guided by the hoof-prints of his white horse; and when they had overtaken him, the farmer reproached his late guest for having left his house so abruptly. Whereupon Luck replied: " I left you, not because you could not even nail my horse-shoe over your door, but hung it upside down, so the luck ran out at the ends, but because of your own mistake. You trusted to me; you trusted to Luck. Ah ha!"

In the northernmost districts of Scotland exists a belief that if the first shoe put on the foot of a stallion be hung on the byre door, no harm will come near the cows; and in the same region, if a horse-shoe be placed between the houses of quarrelsome neighbors, neither incurs any risk of evil as a result of the other's ill-wishes.[1]

As a means of warding off impending sickness from cattle, and in order that they may thrive during the summer, the Transylvanian peasants place broken horse-shoes in the animals' drinking-troughs on St. John's Day, June 24.

In Lincolnshire, not many years ago, there prevailed a custom of "charming" ash-trees by burying horse-shoes under them. Twigs from a tree thus magically endowed were believed to be efficacious in curing cattle over which a shrewmouse had run, or which had been exposed to the glance of an evil eye. To effect a cure in such cases, it was only necessary to gently stroke the affected animal with one of these twigs.[2]

Some years ago, a Golspie fisherman who owned a

[1] Edward W. B. Nicholson, M. A., *Golspie*. Edinburgh, 1897.
[2] *Notes and Queries*, 5th series, vol. ix. p. 65. January, 1878.

small boat was favored with an extraordinary run of luck in his fishing, and as a result of his good fortune was enabled to buy a larger vessel, selling the old one to a neighbor. From that time, however, his lucky star seemed to wane, and good " catches " were infrequent. Casting about in his mind for the reason of this, he bethought him of a stallion's shoe which was fastened inside his former boat, and which had been given him by a " wise person." But both boat and horse-shoe were now in the hands of his neighbor, who maintained with reason that the lucky token was now *his* property, as he had purchased " the boat and its gear." And ever thereafter the disconsolate fisherman attributed his lack of success in that season to his own folly in having parted with the stallion's shoe.[1]

The horse-shoe figures often in traditions of the sea as a protection to sailors. When the ghostly ship of the Flying Dutchman meets another vessel, some of its uncanny crew approach the latter in a boat and beg them to take charge of a packet of letters.

These letters must be nailed to the mast, else some misfortune will overtake the ship; especially if there be no Bible on board, nor any horse-shoe fastened to the foremast.

In the month of September, 1825, lightning struck a brigantine which lay at anchor in the Bay of Armiso,

[1] Rev. James Macdonald, *Religion and Myth*, p. 92.

in the Adriatic. A sailor was killed by the bolt, and tradition says that on one of his hips was seen the perfect representation of a horse-shoe, a counterpart of one nailed to the vessel's foremast in accordance with the custom in vogue on the Mediterranean.[1]

The same custom is common in German inland waters, as, for example, on the river craft which ply on the Elbe below Hamburg, and on those which navigate the Trave, at Lubec. On the latter vessels horse-shoes are usually fastened to the stern-post, instead of to the mast.

In a German work, entitled "Seespuk," by P. G. Heims, page 138, the writer remarks that, among seafaring people, the old pagan emblem, the horse-shoe, whose talismanic origin is so closely associated with horse-sacrifice and the use of horse-flesh as food among the heathen nations of the North, is even now the most powerful safeguard aboard ship against lightning and the powers of evil.

There are comparatively few small vessels laden with wood, fruit, vegetables, or other merchandise, sailing between Baltic Sea ports, upon whose foremast, or elsewhere upon deck, horse-shoes are not nailed.

Indeed, continues the same writer, this symbol has a notable significance in German art as well, a fact attributable less to its graceful curving shape than to the

[1] *Novellenzeitung*, sechster Jahrgang, No. 51, p. 812.

deeply rooted superstitions, relics of barbaric times, which yet cling to it.

Whether we regard the horse-shoe as a symbol of Wodan, the chief deity of the northern nations, as deriving magical power from its half-moon shape, as a product of supernatural skill in dealing with iron and fire, or as appertaining to the favorite sacrificial animal of antiquity, the pagan source of its superstitious use is equally evident.

The horse-shoe, whether as an amulet or as a sign of good luck, has nothing to do with the Christian religion. In either case it is a wholly superstitious symbol, and savors of paganism; it is in fact an inheritance from our heathen ancestors, a barbaric token, unworthy even to be named in connection with the Sacred Cross. Yet throughout many centuries it has captivated the popular fancy, and its emblematic use appears to be as firmly established to-day as ever in many parts of the world.

It is popularly believed that the chance finding of a horse-shoe greatly enhances its magical power; and it is claimed, moreover, by some writers, to be an axiom in folk-lore that talismanic objects thrust upon one's notice, as it were, are direct gifts from the goddess Fortune, and hence possessed of a special value for the finder. Such a notion is as clearly of pagan origin as the custom of bowing to the new moon, or of fixing representations of horses' heads upon the gables of houses in order to terrify wandering spirits of evil.

In "Curiosities of Popular Customs," by William S. Walsh (p. 665, 1898), it is stated that the Northern peoples were wont to offer sacrifices to Wodan after the harvest, and that the little cakes still baked on St. Martin's Day, November 11, throughout Germany, are shaped like a horn or horse-shoe, which was a token of the pagan god. Although not susceptible of proof, it seems highly probable that we have here another relic of idolatry. It is a point worthy of note, moreover, that Wodan was not only an all-powerful deity, corresponding to the Greek Zeus and Roman Jupiter, but that he was also a great magician, and hence quite naturally the horse-shoe, as one of his symbols, inherits magical attributes.

In Tuscany a horse-shoe when found is placed in a small red bag with some hay, which the Tuscans consider also a luck-bringing article, and the twofold charm is kept in its owner's bed.[1]

Dr. Robert James, an English physician of the eighteenth century, and the inventor of a well-known fever-powder, ascribed his success in acquiring a fortune to his good luck in having once found a horse-shoe on Westminster Bridge. The sincerity of his faith was attested by the adoption of the horse-shoe as his family crest.

[1] C. G. Leland, *Etruscan Roman Remains*.

Brand quotes from John Bell's MS. " Discourse on Witchcraft " (1705) as follows : —

Guard against devilish charms for Men or Beasts. There are many sorceries practiced in our day, against which I would on this occasion bear my testimony, and do therefore seriously ask you, what is it you mean by your observation of Times and Seasons as lucky or unlucky? What mean you by your many Spells, Verses, Words, so often repeated, said fasting or going backward? How mean you to have success by carrying about with you certain Herbs, Plants, and branches of Trees? Why is it that, fearing certain events, you do use such superstitious means to prevent them, by laying bits of Timber at Doors, carrying a Bible merely for a Charm, without any farther use of it? What intend ye by opposing Witchcraft to Witchcraft, in such sort that, when ye suppose one to be bewitched, ye endeavour his Relief by Burnings, Bottles, Horse-shoes, and such like magical ceremonies?

In some Roman Catholic countries the priests are wont to brand cows and pigs on the forehead with the mark of a horse-shoe, to insure them against disease.[1] It was, moreover, an old Scotch superstition, or *freet*, to pass a horse-shoe thrice beneath the belly and over the back of a cow that was considered elf-shot.[2]

Among the Wendish inhabitants of the *Spreewald*, in North Germany, the lucky finder of a horse-shoe is careful not to tell any neighbor of his good fortune, but proceeds at once to fasten the shoe over the door

[1] Thomas A. Wise, M. D., *History of Paganism in Caledonia.*
[2] *The Scottish Gallovidian Encyclopædia.* London, 1824.

of his house, or on the threshold, with three nails, and by three blows of a hammer, so that evil spirits may not enter.

We have seen that a horse-shoe picked up on the road is often prized as no mean acquisition by the finder thereof. It may not be out of place to give here a literal translation of a spell for the protection of a horse's hoof when a shoe has been lost. The original appeared in Mone's "Anzeiger" in 1834, and is written in the dialect known as "Middle High German," which was in vogue from the twelfth to the sixteenth centuries:—

When a horse has lost one of its iron shoes, take a bread-knife and incise the hoof at the edge from one heel to the other, and lay the knife crosswise on the sole and say: "I command thee, hoof and horn, that thou breakest as little as God the Lord broke his Word, when he created heaven and earth." And thou shalt say these words three hours in succession, and five *Paternosters* and five *Ave Marias* to the praise of the Virgin. Then the horse will not walk lame until thou happenest to reach a smithy.

The Germans have a saying in regard to a young girl who has been led astray, — "She has lost a horse-shoe." This saying has been associated with the shoe as a symbol of marriage, an idea found both in the northern and Indian mythologies. But the phrase has been also thought to refer to the horse-shoe shaped *gloria* which crowns the head of the Virgin, the horse-shoe thus becoming the symbol of maidenly chastity.[1] Again, it has been suggested, in reference to the same phrase, that the horse-shoe is a symbol of the V (or first letter of the word *Virgo*), which is used in church records to designate the unmarried state, just as the word "spinster" is used in legal documents.

The ancient Irish were wont to hang up in their houses the feet and legs of their deceased steeds, setting an especial value upon the hoofs;[2] and with the Chinese of to-day a horse's hoof hung up indoors is supposed to have the same protective influence over a dwelling that a horse-shoe has elsewhere. In south-western Germany it is still a common practice to nail a hoof over the stable-door; and in the Netherlands a horse's foot placed in a stable is thought to keep the horses from being bewitched.[3]

Burton, in his "Anatomy of Melancholy," admits a belief in the virtues of a ring made from the hoof of the right foot of an ass, when carried about as an amulet.

Occasionally, though rarely, the horse-shoe is thought to have been employed by the witches themselves in furtherance of their mischievous designs.

In the "Revue des traditions populaires," vol. ii. 1887, an anecdote is related of a veteran Polish cavalry-

[1] Petersen, *Hufeisen*, p. 8.
[2] Camden's *Britannia*.
[3] Thorpe's *Northern Mythology*.

man who had served under Napoleon I. While bivouacking with a detachment of lancers in a village of eastern Prussia, he and several others lodged in the house of an old peasant woman, and their horses were accommodated in her barn. It was shortly noticed that the animals appeared depressed and refused the hay and grain provided for them, whereupon the soldiers concluded that they were under some spell and began a search for the cause. They soon found an old horse-shoe with three nails remaining in it, and one of these was quickly driven out with a hammer. Instantly the horses began to snort and exhibited signs of restlessness. On the removal of the second nail they held up their heads proudly, and when the third nail was hammered out they fell upon their provender and devoured it voraciously. The cavalrymen were now convinced that their horses had been the victims of some deviltry at the hands of their hostess, whom they believed to be a sorceress. Before their departure, therefore, they gave her a good beating with their sabre scabbards to teach her not to practice her nefarious arts upon the horses of honest people.

XVI. THE HORSE-SHOE AS A PHALLIC SYMBOL

It will suffice merely to allude to the theory of the phallic origin of the superstitious use of the horse-shoe, a branch of our subject capable of much elaboration.

The horse-shoe is still the conventional figure for the *yoni* (a phallic emblem) in modern Hindu temples. This theory is discussed in "Ancient Faiths embodied in Ancient Names," by Thomas Inman, M. D., London, 1873; and in "A Discourse on the Worship of Priapus," by Richard Payne Knight, Esq., London, 1865.

Phallic ornaments are of great antiquity, and amulets of this character have been found in the earliest Etruscan tombs. Specimens are also to be seen in the various Italian museums.

The *yoni* symbol guards the entrances of ancient temples in Mexico and Peru, as well as in India.

Ornate Mexican sacred stones of the horse-shoe form, relics of the ancient Maya tribes, are classed in the National Museum at Washington, D. C., as representative of fecundity and nature-worship; and horse-shoe symbols are found in Aztec manuscripts relating to agriculture as signs of abundance.[1]

Phallic charms are seen above the entrances of houses and over tent-doors in north Africa to avert the evil eye, and to bring health and good fortune. Much information on this subject may be found in a chapter on serpent and phallic worship in "Rivers of Life," by Major-General J. G. R. Forlong, London, 1883; and in an essay on "Phallism in Ancient Religions," by C. Staniford Wake, 1888.

[1] Francis Parry, F. R. G. S., *The Sacred Symbols and Numbers of Aboriginal America in Ancient and Modern Times.*

On a curious tablet found near a prehistoric mound in the vicinity of the village of Cahokia, Saint Clair County, Illinois, are portrayed human faces with bird-like profiles, diamond-shaped eyes, and low foreheads surmounted by ornamental crowns or head-dresses. The mouths are wide open, and in front of them are represented symbols having a well-defined horse-shoe form. These symbols, although probably of phallic origin, are thought to signify the principle of life residing in the breath, just as in India the horse-shoe is an emblem of the soul.[1]

XVII. THE HORSE-SHOE AS A SYMBOL ON TAVERN SIGN-BOARDS

The horse-shoe, associated usually with some other symbol, is not infrequently seen displayed on the signs of British taverns. There is a well-known hostelry bearing this sign and name on Tottenham Court Road in London. To quote from "The History of Sign-boards," by Jacob Larwood and John Camden Hotten : —

The Three Horse-shoes are not uncommon, and the single shoe may be met with in many combinations, arising from the old belief in its lucky influences. Thus the *Horse and Horse-Shoe* was the sign of William Warden at Dover, as appears from his token. The *Sun and Horse-Shoe* is still a public-

[1] *The American Antiquarian,* vol. xii. p. 356 ; vol. xiii. p. 58.

house sign in Great Tichfield Street, and the *Magpie and Horse-Shoe* may be seen carved in Fetter Lane ; the magpie is perched within the horse-shoe, a bunch of grapes being suspended from it.   The *Horns and Horse-shoe* is represented on the token of William Grainge, in Gutter Lane, 1666, a horse-shoe within a pair of antlers.   The *Hoop and Horse-shoe* on Tower Hill was formerly called the *Horse-shoe.*

Miller Christy, in his book "The Trade Signs of Essex," says that horse-shoe signs probably owe their origin partly to the fact that this symbol appears on the arms of the Farriers' Company, and partly to the old practice of fastening a horse-shoe upon the stable-door or elsewhere as a witch-scarer.   In the county of Essex the horse-shoe may be seen upon the signs of beer-houses at Great Parndon, Braintree, Waltham Abbey, and High Ongar.

There was formerly more than one noted inn in London known as the Half-Moon, and a street of that name, leading from Piccadilly, is well known.   The name and symbol of the *full* moon, however, seldom appear on sign-boards.   Butler asks in "Hudibras:" —

> Tell me, but what's the nat'ral cause,
> Why on a sign no painter draws
> The full moon, but the half ?

The reason is doubtless because of the favorable auspices associated from time immemorial with the crescent moon.

One need hardly accept as plausible the explanation

sometimes offered, namely, that the half-moon tavern symbol is a silent invitation to eat and drink to one's full capacity; a hint, as it were, to follow the crescent moon's example and " get full."

XVIII. HORSE-SHOES ON CHURCH-DOORS

The origin of the horse-shoe as a charm has been ascribed to its resemblance to the metallic aureole or *meniscus* formerly placed over the heads of images of patron saints in churches, and which is also represented in ancient pictures of the Virgin.

This aureole, or more properly *nimbus*, was probably of pagan origin, for in early times circles of stars frequently ornamented the heads of statues of the gods, as emblematic of divinity. In speaking of certain ancient relics found in Ireland, Mr. W. G. Wood-Martin (" Pagan Ireland," p. 492) says : —

Thin crescentic plates, with the extremities terminating in flat circular disks, are the ornaments most frequently discovered. In form they are identical with the half-moon-shaped ornaments in use among the Greeks and Romans, and with the *nimbi* on carvings of the Byzantine school; and they differ but little from the ring which now is conventionally placed around the head of a saint. Thus this glory can be traced back to pagandom. The crescentic plate appears to have been primarily the badge of some distinguished person, a chief or king; then it became the emblem of one considered to be a very holy person, for in Ireland, in the early days of

Christianity, the saints were derived principally from the aristocracy.

In the collection of the Royal Irish Academy is a golden tiara or diadem, said to have been found in County Clare. This relic, which measures about a foot in height and the same in breadth, is thought to have been a head-dress of some pagan or early Christian chieftain.

In the earlier years of the church these crescent symbols were avoided as savoring of heathenism; but without any thought of its significance, it became customary in the Middle Ages to place a circular brass plate upon the heads of statues as a protection from snow or rain. Hence arose the practice of similarly adorning images and paintings in churches.[1]

In later times these crescent-shaped pieces of metal were sometimes nailed up at the entrance of churches, and so came to be regarded as protective emblems.[2] The horse-shoe was an easily available substitute for the halo or glory, and so was often placed upon the doors of churches, especially in the southwest of England, as it was generally believed in olden times that evil spirits could enter even consecrated edifices. Aubrey, in his "Miscellanies," mentions having seen under the porch of Staninfield Church, in Suffolk, an inscription with the

---

[1] Leopold Wagner, *Manners, Customs, and Observances.*
[2] S. H. Killikelly, *Curious Questions.*

device of a horse-shoe, intended to exclude witches, and
he naïvely remarks that one would imagine holy water
amply sufficient for the purpose.

On the south door of the parish church of Ashby-
Foville, in Leicestershire, were formerly two ancient
horse-shoes of great size, one of them measuring 16 by
11½ inches, or more than twice as large as an average
modern shoe.

As it does not seem likely that such shoes were made
to fit horses' feet, in the absence of traditional information regarding them, it appears probable that they
were intended solely to bar the ingress of witches.[1]

In St. Martin's Church, Canterbury, the oldest in
England, the sacristan shows visitors the site of an early
English door on the south side, and a Norman doorway
in the middle of the northern wall, both long since
blocked up. Infants to be baptized were formerly
brought into the church by the south entrance, and
after the ceremony the north door was thrown open to
permit the egress of evil spirits expelled by baptism.
For in early times demons were believed to come from
the north, where the habitations of the Norse gods
were also thought to be. The pagans, when worship-
ing their deities, looked towards the north; but
Christians engaged in prayer turned their faces east-
ward and lifted up their hands; they regarded the

---

[1] *Leicestershire and Rutland Notes and Queries,* vol. ii. 1891–93.

north as "the unblessed heathen quarter." The unexplored Arctic regions, where night[1] reigned much of the time, were thought to belong especially to the Devil, or spirit of darkness;[2] and the same idea is conveyed in several passages of Holy Scripture, as, for example, in Jeremiah iv. 6: "I will bring evil from the north, and a great destruction."

In the Middle Ages the rose-windows in the north and south transepts of Lincoln Minster were called the two eyes of the cathedral, the former being known as the *Dean's Eye*, ever on the watch against the attacks of Lucifer, who had his abode "in the sides of the north" (Isaiah xiv. 13); while the window in the south transept was called the *Bishop's Eye*, "courting the influence of the Holy Spirit, of which the south wind was a type." Apropos of evil spirits entering consecrated places, there is a quaint legend about a little stone figure yclept the *Lincoln Imp*, which is to be seen perched upon a corbel of a column on the north side of the Angel Choir of the same cathedral. According to one version of the legend, when Bishop Remigius came to Lincoln, in the year after the Norman Conquest, the Devil was sorely tried; for until that time he had had undisturbed control of affairs in the town and neighborhood. In vain the Evil One

---

[1] Grimm, p. 34.

[2] J. Scheible, *Das Kloster*, vol. ix. p. 422.

sought to hinder the completion of the church, and finally he waylaid the bishop outside the building and attempted to kill him. But the good bishop at this critical time called upon the Blessed Virgin Mary for assistance, and she sent a tempest of wind which so buffeted and distracted the Devil that he sought refuge inside the church, not daring to venture out because of the fierce wind, which prevails a good part of the time even nowadays, and which is still awaiting the Devil's reappearance!

> The Bishop, we know, died long ago;
> The wind still waits, nor will he go
> Till he has a chance of beating his foe;
> But the Devil hopp'd up without a limp,
> And at once took shape as the Lincoln Imp.
> And there he sits atop the column,
> And grins at the people who gaze so solemn.
> Moreover, he mocks at the wind below,
> And says, "You may wait till doomsday, O!"[1]

In southern Germany, Bavaria, and Tyrol, the horse-shoe symbol is to be seen on church-doors, as an emblem of St. Leonard, the guardian and protector of horses and travelers; and it is usually associated with some romantic legend, having oftentimes an historic basis. Traditions relating to horse-shoes on church-doors are, indeed, plentiful in the popular literature of Germany, and a few examples are given later. St.

[1] Arnold Frost, *The Ballad of the Wind, the Devil, and Lincoln Minster.* Lincoln. 1897.

Leonard's Day, November 6, had its special observances. The peasants were wont to bring their horses to some church dedicated to that worthy, and ride them thrice around the sacred building, a procedure which was believed to be highly auspicious.[1] It was, moreover, customary for noblemen, before starting on an equestrian journey, to fasten a horse-shoe on the church-door as a votive offering to St. Leonard.[2]

Especial honor is accorded to this saint on the day of his festival, at Fischhausen, a seaport village in northeastern Prussia. On that occasion the parish church is surrounded by farm wagons and other vehicles drawn by gayly decorated horses, for here the country people have a grand rendezvous; young women in holiday attire drive hither the cows, which have been brought from their summer quarters in the upland pastures, that they, too, may participate in the festivities. A religious service, largely attended by the peasants, is first held in the church, and then follow the outdoor exercises, of which a chief feature consists in driving the horses three times around the building at a rapid pace.[3]

During the prevalence of a severe epizoötic in Wür-

---

[1] J. W. Wolf, *Beiträge zur deutschen Mythologie*, p. 91.

[2] Ignaz V. Zingerle, *Sitten, Bräuche und Meinungen des Tiroler Volkes.* Innsbruck, 1857.

[3] Herman Schmid and Karl Stieler, *The Bavarian Highlands and the Salzkammergut.*

temberg many years ago, the people removed the shoes
from their horses' feet, and hung them on the walls of
churches as propitiatory offerings. Various other iron
implements, such as chain traces, were thus similarly
displayed.

An ancient St. Leonard's Chapel, in the town of
Laupheim, is encircled by an iron chain, which is said
to have been forged from horse-shoes thus piously con-
tributed.[1] The largest church dedicated to this saint is
at Tölz, in upper Bavaria, and its altar is likewise surrounded by an iron chain.

Pictures of St. Leonard are sometimes placed upon
stable-doors to bring luck; he is usually represented as
holding a pastoral staff, while on one side is seen a colt
or filly, on the other a sick ox, and at his feet is a ewe
lamb.

In northern Germany, St. George, as a successor
of Wodan, is one of the special guardians and protec-
tors of horses. On the festal day of this saint, April
23, the peasants gather in large numbers around some
church dedicated to him, and their horses and vehicles,
numbering sometimes many hundreds, are drawn up in
a circle around the sanctuary. After the parish priest
has delivered a sermon in the church, he comes to the
door and blesses each horse separately as the animal is
led past, meanwhile sprinkling him with holy water.

[1] Anton Birlinger, *Sagen, Legenden und Volksaberglauben*, vol. i. p. 49.

Then the young men mount their best horses and ride them three times at full speed around the church, shouting lustily meanwhile.

Jähns remarks that this ceremony is doubtless a relic of some pagan rite, and that in many places a venerable tree, instead of a Christian church, is chosen as the place of rendezvous on St. George's Day. During the ride around the tree, an aged peasant standing in its shade throws upon each horse, as it passes, a little moist earth taken from about the roots of the sacred tree, and this insures the animal against sickness until the following spring, especially if some of the earth be placed in a bag and hung up in the stable.

As the hammer was Thor's emblem, so the horse-shoe has been thought to possess a certain mystic significance as a symbol of the heathen god Wodan; and it has been assumed that the ancient churches, upon whose doors horse-shoes are still to be seen, were built upon the sites of pagan temples dedicated to that deity. It has been argued, moreover, that the modern use of a horse-shoe as a talisman, and the placing of horses' heads on peasants' houses, are relics of heathendom, and have a mysterious affinity with the hoof-print legends of Teutonic mythology. Such a theory appears plausible enough in view of the fact that many of the superstitious customs and beliefs of modern times are known to have existed before the Christian era.

XIX. HORSE-SHOE LEGENDARY LORE

1. Within recent years two horse-shoes were to be seen on the door of the parish church of Haccombe in Derbyshire. A romantic legend associated with these horse-shoes is the theme of a ballad supposed to have been written by a master of Exeter Grammar School in the early part of the nineteenth century. The ballad graphically describes a race for a wager between a certain Earl of Totnes, mounted on a Derbyshire roan, and one Sir Arthur Champernowne, on a fleet Barbary courser. The race was won by the earl, who thereupon rode straight to the door of Haccombe Church,

> And there he fell on his knees and prayed,
> And many an *Ave Maria* said;
> Bread and money he gave to the poor,
> And he nailed the roan's shoes to the chapel door.[1]

2. In the traditionary lore of the Harz Mountains there is a weird tale of four horse-shoes, which for ages were to be seen on the door of a church in the suburbs of Klettenburg.

Once upon a time, so runs the story, a great drinking-match was held on a Sunday morning at Elrich. The prize was a golden chain, and many knights assembled from near and far. The carousal lasted for some hours, until Count Ernest of Klettenburg, the only one who

[1] *Belgravia*, vol. iv. 1887.

could still keep on his feet, exultantly claimed the golden chain, which he hung about his neck. Then, mounting his horse, he rode homeward, and while nearing Klettenburg he heard the strains of even-song in a church dedicated to St. Nicholas. Urging on his steed, he rode madly through the open door straight to the altar. Then, so runs the legend, the horse's four shoes fell off, and horse and rider sank down together out of sight. In memory of this wonderful event, the four horse-shoes were placed on the door of the church, and for many years were regarded with awe by the simple countryfolk.[1]

3. In the construction of the Church of St. Stephen, at Tangermünde, in Prussian Saxony, a brick edifice of the fourteenth century, the members of two guilds, those of the blacksmiths and shoemakers, were of especial assistance; and in remembrance of this, a horse-shoe and an iron shoe-sole were built into the outer wall of the church. The former indicates that up to its level the blacksmiths had built the walls, and the latter shows that all the work above the horse-shoe was done by the shoemakers; such, at least, is the popular explanation, which may well be received *cum grano salis*.

4. In the parish church of Schwarzenstein, in east Prussia, hang two horse-shoes as reminders of the fol-

---

[1] *Yule-Tide Stories*, edited by Benjamin Thorpe. London, 1853.

lowing tradition: In the village of Eichmedien, one mile from Rastenburg, lived formerly as tavern-keeper a woman, who had earned an unenviable notoriety by her practice of charging double the proper fees for board and lodging. Late one night, when several of her guests accused her of being a cheat, she asseverated her honesty by holding up her hand, and saying in the form. of an oath: "If my score is not correct, may the Devil now jump on my back." The Evil One took the woman promptly at her word, transformed her into a mare, and rode her out of the village, laughing scornfully. At headlong speed he rode to a blacksmith's shop in Schwarzenstein, and demanded that his mare be shod at once. The blacksmith, routed out of his sleep, excused himself, pleading the lateness of the hour and the fact that there was no fire in his forge. The Devil insisted, however, and promised liberal payment if the work were done quickly. The blacksmith yielded at length, but had not proceeded far in shaping the shoes when the mare began to speak. "My cousin, don't you know me?" she said; "I am the tavern-keeper." Upon this the blacksmith was so horrified that neither threats nor entreaties could prevail to make him proceed with the shoeing, and before he had finished the third shoe a cock crowed, and immediately the spell was broken and the woman reassumed her own form. And to point the moral of this legend, and as a warning to cheats, the two horse-shoes which the smith had completed were nailed up in the village church at Schwarzenstein.

5. According to an old tradition, the Lapp king, Olaf Skötkonung (995–1030), wishing to become a Christian, asked his royal contemporary, Ethelred II. of England, to send him a teacher.   In response to this request Bishop Siegfried and three missionaries came to Sweden, and, landing on the southwestern coast, encamped the first night at Wexio, on Lake Sodre. Here the bishop saw in a vision a great company of angels, and thereupon determined to build a church at that place.   The pagan inhabitants, however, were hostile to the undertaking, and seized the three missionaries, Winaman, Unaman, and Sunaman, whom they beheaded, and caused their heads to be thrown into the water.

One night soon after this sad event Siegfried was walking along the shore of the lake, sighing and praying, when he espied three luminous objects approaching on the water, borne onward by the waves, and soon he recognized them as the heads of his friends.   And, behold, the first head said, " The dead shall be avenged." And a voice from the second head exclaimed, " When?" Then replied the third head in solemn tones, " On their children and children's children."   This prophecy was not, however, fulfilled to the letter, for through Siegfried's intercession Olaf consented to spare the lives of the murderers, on condition that they should build a Christian church in Wexio; and this church, which still exists, has on its coat-of-arms, or seal, the representation of three severed heads, in memory of the occurrence and its legend. In this church hung formerly a shoe of Wodan's famous steed Sleipnir, as a souvenir of the following tradition: When the church bells rang for the first time to summon the people to mass, Wodan came riding over the mountains, and, when nearing Wexio, Sleipnir, in a sudden fright, struck a rock with one of his feet, and the impress of the powerful blow remains in the rock to this day. But the shoe fell off and was placed in the church.[1]

6. Many years ago, so runs an old legend, a man obtained employment at a farm in Norway, where, unknown to him, the mistress was a witch. Although the man had plenty of good wholesome food, he did not thrive upon it, but became thinner each day. Being troubled at this, he sought the counsel of a wise man, from whom he learned the true character of his mistress. He learned, moreover, that she had been in the habit of transforming him into a horse at night while he slept, and riding him to Troms Church, a fact which fully accounted for his leanness.

The wise man also gave him a magical ointment, with

[1] J. Scheible. *Das Kloster*.

which to rub his head at bedtime, and by virtue of which, on awaking the next morning, he found himself standing by Troms Church with a bridle in his hand, while behind him were a number of horses bound together by their tails. Soon he perceived his mistress coming out of the church, and when she was near enough to him he threw the bridle over her head, and instantly she was transformed into a handsome mare, which he mounted and rode homeward. On his way, however, he stopped at a farrier's and had the animal shod with four new shoes, and on reaching home he told his master that he had bought a fine mare, that would be an excellent mate for one which he already had. His master bought the mare at a good price, but when he took the bridle off she disappeared, and in her place stood the mistress witch with new horse-shoes on her hands and feet. Thereupon the man related the wonderful tale of his experiences, and in consequence thereof the wife was turned out of doors, and never got rid of the horse-shoes.[1]

7. Once upon a time a gentleman of rank was driving with four horses along the highway which runs between the towns of Tübingen and Hirschau, in Würtemberg, and when opposite a roadside chapel he scoffed at a picture of the Madonna which adorned it. Immediately his horses came to a standstill, nor could he

[1] Thorpe's *Northern Mythology*, vol. ii. p. 190.

make them proceed, in spite of vigorous urging. At
length, in this dilemma, a priest was called, who imposed as a penance the removal of a shoe from the right
fore-foot of each horse, and after this had been done
the gentleman was enabled to continue his journey.
And in commemoration of this miracle one of the horse-
shoes was nailed upon the chapel-door, where it was
still to be seen in recent years.[1]

8. One Sunday morning a swarthy rider on a black
horse rode at full speed through the village of Nab-
burg, in Bavaria, directly to the blacksmith's shop, to
have his horse shod. "Will you not rest on a Sunday?" demanded the smith. "My steed and I journey to and fro, and care nothing for the Christian
Sunday," replied the horseman; "therefore shoe my
horse in the Devil's name, and I counsel thee speak no
pious word meanwhile, for no devout person has yet
obtained the mastery over this spirited animal." With
these words he sprang to the ground and stroked his
horse's flowing mane. The smith, though ill at ease,
began the work, and the horse was as quiet as if under
a spell, much to the astonishment of his master, who
could scarce believe his eyes. Three shoes were quickly
set, and the smith called to his assistant, "Now, then,
in God's name, hand me the last shoe!" Instantly the

[1] Ernst Meier, *Deutsche Sagen, Sitten und Gebräuche aus Schwaben.*
Stuttgart, 1852.

fiery steed reared and struck out wildly, casting a shoe
with such force against the wall that it remains to this
day embedded there. But the horse and his rider were
seen no more.[1]

9. In a wall on an estate called Ludwigstein, in
Schleswig-Holstein, is to be seen a large stone bearing
the imprint of a horse-shoe, wherewith is associated the
following tale: One morning many years ago a horseman was riding along the road when the church prayer-
bell rang, whereupon he swore an oath and said, "May
the Devil take me if I am not again on this very spot
this evening when the bell again sounds." And indeed
he kept his word, but at the stroke of the evening bell
his horse slipped upon the stone and broke a leg, and
the mark of a shoe is still to be seen there.

10. The Horse-Shoe imprint in the cemetery of the
Church of Our Lady at Münster. During the building of this beautiful Gothic church in the fourteenth
century, the Devil observed its shapely proportions
with increasing displeasure, and bethought himself of
various schemes to hinder the work's progress. Finally
he decided on trying to bewitch the architect's senses.
Accordingly he braided his hair, arrayed himself in
gay female attire, bedecked with costly jewels, and
appeared before the architect, whom he sought to
ensnare with soft words and gifts. But the latter

[1] Friedrich Panzer, *Bayerische Sagen und Bräuche*, vol. i. p. 127.

was not thus to be deceived. Leaning upon his measuring-rod, he listened unmoved to the beguiling conversation of the pretended belle, and rejected with scorn the gold and precious stones which she brought him. Thereupon the Devil became enraged, stamped upon the ground with vehemence, and disappeared, leaving behind him an evil smell; and the mark of one of the iron horse-shoes, wherewith he was shod, was deeply imprinted on a stone in the cemetery, and, according to popular report, is still to be found there.

The impressions on stone of figures of horse-shoes, of which there are numerous examples in northern Europe, are regarded by some archæologists as sacred symbols of the pagans or relics of the cult of Wodan, and as showing the sites of ancient altars and burial places; while others maintain that these figures were originally intended as boundary marks. Numerous traditions associate them with battles fought in these localities, and in the popular fancy they are imagined to indicate the favorite haunts of witches, the meeting-places where they held their revels, the horse-shoe mark being an imprint of the Devil's foot. These weird rendezvous were usually on the tops of mountains or hills, and are still known as Witches' Dance-Places in different parts of Europe, especially in Germany.

XX. RECAPITULATION OF THEORIES OF THE ORIGIN OF THE HORSE-SHOE SUPERSTITION

In the preceding pages an attempt has been made to furnish plausible reasons for the horse-shoe's universal popularity both as an amulet and as a token of good luck.   It is evident, however, that this superstition cannot be referred to any one particular starting-point. Just as the sources of a river may be manifold, consisting of numerous springs and tributaries, so, too, the belief in the horse-shoe's magical virtues is of complex origin, and can be traced to diverse beginnings.

It may be profitable, therefore, briefly to enumerate the different theories which have been advanced : —

1. At the *rite of the Passover*, the blood sprinkled upon the lintel and door-posts formed the chief points of an arch.   Hence the value of arch-shaped talismans.

2. The magical virtue of the horse-shoe against witches and fiends has been attributed to its *bifurcated form*, and to its resemblance to the *lunar crescent*. Charms of similar shape are known to have been in use among the ancient Chaldeans and Egyptians.

3. *Iron* and *steel*, metals having traditional power against evil-disposed fairies and goblins.

4. The *serpentine shape*.   Serpent-worship was nearly universal among primitive peoples, and amuletic

symbols of this form were in use in the days of ancient Rome.

5. The so-called *horse-shoe arch* as typifying a beneficent, protecting power.

6. The ancient conception of the earth as having the shape of a *round boat turned upside down* and corresponding to the Egyptian *Put-sign*.

7. *The Horse*. This animal was worshiped among the early Germanic tribes, and an English myth accredits to it luck-bringing qualities.

8. The Scandinavian superstition of the *Demon-Mare*.

9. The old astrological principle that *Mars*, the God of War and the War Horse, was hostile to *Saturn*, the liege-lord of witches.

10. The legend of *Saint Dunstan and the Devil*.

11. *Phallic Symbolism*.

12. The *Aureole* or *Nimbus*.

13. Supernatural faculties ascribed to *blacksmiths*.

14. The Egyptian hieroglyphic symbol ∩, signifying the *mystical door of life*.

15. *Horses' hoof-prints* in mythology and tradition.

16. The horse-shoe a symbol of the heathen god *Wodan*.

XXI. CONCLUSION

Whatever may be the origin of the superstitious employment of the horse-shoe, its adoption as a token of good luck appears to be comparatively modern, its earliest use having been for the exclusion of witches, evil spirits, and all such uncanny beings.

Before leaving the subject an extract may be given from an article in the " London World," August 23, 1753, against the repeal of the so-called Witch Act, wherein the writer offers the following satirical advice to whomever it might concern : —

To secure yourself against the enchantments of witches, especially if you are a person of fashion and have never been taught the Lord's Prayer, the only method I know of is to nail a horse-shoe upon the threshold. This I can affirm to be of the greatest efficacy, insomuch that I have taken notice of many a little cottage in the country with a horse-shoe at its door where gaming, extravagance, Jacobitism, and all the catalogue of witchcrafts have been totally unknown.

The world moves and civilization progresses, but the old superstitions remain the same. The rusty horse-shoe found on the road is still prized as a lucky token, and will doubtless continue to be so prized; for human nature does not change, and superstition is a part of human nature.

FORTUNE AND LUCK

If Fortune favor you, be not elated;
If she frown, do not despond.

AUSONIUS.

When Fortune means to men most good,
She looks upon them with a threatening eye.

King John, III. 4, 119.

When smiling Fortune spreads her golden ray,
All crowd around to flatter and obey;
But when she thunders from the angry sky,
Our friends, our flatterers, our lovers fly.

OVID.

Since Fortune is not in our power,
Let us be as little as possible in hers.

STEELE.

I. TYCHE, THE GRECIAN GODDESS OF GOOD LUCK

AMONG the more popular divinities of the early Grecians was Tyche, the goddess of good luck, whose worship, according to Plutarch, complemented that of Destiny. She ruled over accidental events, and was the dispenser alike of blessings and misfortunes; but when too lavish in the distribution of her favors she was liable to incur the jealousy of Nemesis, the goddess of retribution.

Tyche, the Goddess of Fortune, is not mentioned in the works of the earliest Grecian poets, but Homer and Hesiod both allude to an ocean nymph of this name who was gathering flowers with Proserpina when the latter was carried off by Pluto.

The Theban lyric poet Pindar appears to have originated the worship of Tyche, whom he celebrated in verse, and invested with the title Pharopolis, or Protectress of Cities;[1] and in Greece, towards the close of the fifth century B. C., this goddess was generally believed to be the ruler of worldly affairs. While Zeus was, indeed, the most powerful of the gods, Tyche was regarded by some as having the character of Providence;[2] yet she was more generally thought to be identical with Chance or Luck. The famous Ionic philosopher Anaxagoras said that Fortune was a cause unknown to human reason; for some things come by Necessity, some by fatal Destiny, and others by deliberate Counsel.[3]

II. THE ROMAN GODDESS FORTUNA

The worship of the Goddess of Chance, *Fortuna*, was introduced among the Romans from Greece during the reign of Servius Tullius, and soon became very

---

[1] *Cyclopædia of Arts.* Philadelphia.
[2] F. Allègre, *Étude sur la déesse grecque Tyché.* Paris, 1889.
[3] Plutarch's *Opinions of Philosophers.*

popular. Indeed, at one period Fortuna was the chief Italian divinity, and the plebeians and slaves held an annual festival on the twenty-fourth day of June in honor of her who could bestow riches and liberty. Pliny wrote that the Chance or Fortune by means of which we acquire so much is a divine power; and Plutarch, in his work on the Fortune of the Romans, attempts to show that the great achievements of that people were to be attributed to good luck rather than to sagacity or prowess. As an example he cites their escape from invasion by the opportune death of Alexander the Great at Babylon, B. C. 323, at a time when he was preparing to overwhelm Italy with his armies.

The Roman biographer, Cornelius Nepos, in speaking of the Greek general, Emenes the Cardian (B. C. 361–317), said that, even if the favors shown him by Fortune had been commensurate with his great abilities, he would not for that reason have been more eminent; for great men should be measured by their qualities, and not by their good or bad fortune. The Dutch *savant*, Desiderius Erasmus, wrote that Diogenes was wont to rebuke with asperity those who blamed the goddess when their affairs did not prosper; and he also severely criticised the prevalent habit of craving at the hands of Mistress Fortune, not such things as were substantially good, but rather such as seemed to be so in the fancy of the petitioners. Philip of Macedon, on

the receipt of the news of great victories won by his
generals, thanked Fortune for her great goodness, mod-
estly beseeching of her only some "light and shrewd
turn again at another season." And Erastus, commenting on Philip's moderation and good sense in not
being unduly elated by prosperity, quaintly remarked
that this great king, having profound wisdom and experience, did not insolently leap and skip about on the
receipt of joyful tidings, but rather mistrusted the
pampering of Fortune, whom he knew to be a fickle
jade.

III. THE CHARACTER OF FORTUNE

Of all the pagan deities, Fortune was the most absolute and the most universally worshiped; for she kept
all men at her feet, the prosperous through fear and
the unfortunate through hope.[1] She was also an eccentric goddess, not only favoring the brave, according
to the familiar maxim of Terence, but likewise being
decidedly partial to fools, if we may believe another
classical saying, *Fortuna favet fatuis.* And again, as
an ancient poet wrote, *Legem veretur nocens, Fortu-
nam innocens.* The satirist Juvenal said that, if men
were discreet, Fortune had no power over them. When
she entered Rome she folded her wings as a sign that
she wished to remain there; and, as has been aptly

---

[1] Lyon, *Nouveau dictionnaire historique.* 1804.

remarked, she is there still, for the modern Roman is as firm a believer in luck, whether good or bad, as was the Roman citizen two thousand years ago.[1]   Among the ancients, a lucky event, something opportune occurring unexpectedly, was ascribed to a sudden caprice or whim on the part of the goddess, while success in an undertaking was thought to be due to her favor when in a sober mood.[2]

"Why was Fortune made a goddess?" asked St. Augustine, since she is so blind that she runs to anybody without distinction, and often passes by her admirers to cling to those who despise her.[3]   And Cicero remarked that Fortune was not only blind herself, but often deprived her votaries of sight.

Pliny, in discoursing about the religious beliefs current in his time, says: —

All over the world, in all places and at all times, Fortune is the only God whom every one invokes: she alone is spoken of; she alone is accused and is supposed to be guilty; she alone is in our thoughts, is praised and blamed, and is loaded with reproaches; wavering as she is, conceived by the generality of mankind to be blind, wandering, inconstant, uncertain, variable, and often favoring the unworthy.   To her are referred all our losses and all our gains, and, in casting up the accounts of mortals, she alone balances the two pages of our

[1] *History of Rome.*
[2] George Crabb, *English Synonymes.*
[3] Andrew Tooke. A. M.. *The Pantheon.*   Dublin. 1792.

sheet. We are so much in the power of chance, that chance itself is considered as a God.

The representations of Fortune, which are to be seen in ancient statues, bas-reliefs, medals, and coins, exhibit the many different attributes of her character. The earliest image of the goddess was probably at Smyrna, and was the work of the eminent sculptor Bupalus, who lived in the sixth century B. C. She was here shown as bearing on her head a hemisphere, and with the horn of Amalthæa in her left hand, thus typifying the distribution of all good things.[1]

Her lack of discernment has been symbolized by artists, who have portrayed her with a bandage before her eyes; with a rudder, as guiding worldly affairs; or with a wheel or ball, as types of instability. In a painting by Sulzer, Fortune is shown seated on a throne, which is borne aloft in the air by contrary winds. In her hand is a magic wand, and her countenance expresses inconstancy and fickleness, while in her train follow Riches, Poverty, Despotism, and Slavery. In the Villa d'Este, near the Italian town of Tivoli, is a painting by Zucchari showing Fortune astride of an ostrich, which has been supposed to be an allegorical intimation that the goddess has a preference for simpletons.[2] In her temple at Thebes, she

[1] Anthon's *Classical Dictionary*.
[2] F. Noel, *Dictionnaire de la fable*. Paris, 1803.

held Wealth in her arms. Sometimes she was accompanied by a winged youth named Favor, to denote how speedily her favors may fly away from us;[1] or by a winged Cupid, which has been thought to signify that, in Love, Beauty has a less permanent influence than Fortune.[2]

Her numerous titles were usually complimentary, as Golden or Royal Fortune, but she was disrespectfully spoken of by Horace, Ovid, and other writers, by whom she was characterized as unjust, fickle, and delighting in mischief. One reproachful epithet applied to her was *viscosa*, tenacious or sticky, because men are caught in her toils like birds in quicklime.[3]

The Abbé Banier, in his "Mythology and Fables of the Ancients," thus moralizes regarding Fortune, good and bad: —

As men have always highly valued earthly goods, 't is no wonder that they adored Fortune. Fools! who thus instead of acknowledging an intelligent Providence that distributes riches and earthly goods, from views always wise, though dark and placed beyond the reach of human discovery, addressed their vows to an imaginary Being, that acted without design and from the impulse of unavoidable necessity; for 't is beyond question that, in the Pagan system, Fortune was nothing else but Destiny. Accordingly she was confounded,

---

[1] P. Galtruchius, *History of the Heathen Gods.* 1671.
[2] Daniel Watson, A. M., *A History of the Gods and Goddesses.*
[3] Plutarch's *Roman Questions.*

as we shall see afterwards, with the *Parcœ*, who were themselves that fatal Necessity, which the poets have reasoned so much about.

We learn from the historian Suetonius that the early Roman emperors were wont to cherish small images of Fortune, which they venerated as special tutelary deities.

The goddess is said to have once appeared in a vision to the Emperor Galba, who reigned A. D. 68–69, and to have informed him that she was standing weary before his door, and that, if she were not quickly admitted, every one dear to him would become her prey. On awakening he found outside the entrance-hall of his palace a bronze figure of Fortune, which he concealed beneath his garments and carried to his summer residence at Tusculum. There he set apart a sanctuary for the image, and offered prayers to it each month, keeping, moreover, in its honor an all-night vigil every year. On one occasion Galba had intended to present his little guardian genius with a necklace of pearls and precious stones, but changed his mind and gave it to the Capitoline Venus. The following night Fortune, in angry mood, again appeared to the emperor in a dream, complaining that she had been cheated out of the intended gift, and threatening to take away the many benefits which she had bestowed upon him. Alarmed at this, Galba sent a messenger early in the

morning to prepare a sacrificial offering, and he himself
hastened to Tusculum, but found on the altar of the
sanctuary nothing but warm ashes; and near by stood
an old man clothed in black, holding in one hand a
glass plate containing incense, and in the other an
earthenware vessel full of sacrificial wine.[1]

Some verses containing uncomplimentary allusions to
the character of Fortune were formerly to be seen on
the wall of a chamber in Wressell Castle, Yorkshire,
a building of the latter part of the fourteenth century,
which was destroyed by fire in 1796 : —

The Proverbis in the syde of the utter chamber above of
the Hous in the Gardyng at Wresyll.

No thynge to fortune thou apply,
For her gyftis vanyshithe as doth fantasy,
The more thou receyvethe of her gyftis moste unsure,
The more to the aprochethe displeasure.

Then in blynde fortune put not thy truste.
For her brightness sone receyveth ruste.
Fortune is fykill, fortune is blynde.
Her rawardes be fekill and unkynde.

Forsake the glory of fortune('s) fyckillnes,
Of whom comythe worldly glory and yet much unkyndnes,
Put thy trust and in hym sett thy mynde,
Whiche when fortune faylithe will nevyr be unkynde.[2]

Among most civilized nations of the present day the
Goddess Fortune is not openly worshiped, although

[1] Roscher, *Lexicon der griechischen und römischen Mythologie*, p. 1523.
[2] *The Antiquarian Repertory*, vol. iv. p. 256.   London, 1784.

the Japanese have their seven Gods of Luck, which are comparatively modern deities, brought together from various sources, including their own primitive Shinto religion, Buddhism, and the Taouism of China.[1]

The Lamas of Tibet perform each year a peculiar scapegoat rite called the Chase of the Demon of Ill-luck. One of their number, in fantastic garb and with grotesquely painted face, sits in the market-place for a week previously, and on the day of the ceremony this worthy, who is known as a ghost-king, wanders about shaking a black yak's tail over the heads of the people, whereby their ill-luck is in some mystic way trans-ferred to him.[2]

IV. TEMPLES OF FORTUNE

Temples in honor of the Goddess Tyche were built at Elis, Corinth, and in other Grecian cities; and in the second century A. D. the eminent philanthropist, Herodes Atticus, erected for her a temple in Athens, the ruins of which are believed still to exist.[3]

The western suburb of Syracuse, in Sicily, was called Τύχη, after a temple of Tyche which adorned it.

Among the Italians the worship of Fortune became so popular that her temples outnumbered all others.

---

[1] Basil H. Chamberlin, *Things Japanese.*
[2] L. Austine Waddell, B. A., *The Buddhism of Tibet*, p. 512.
[3] *Mythology and Monuments of Ancient Athens.*

"We have built a thousand temples to Fortune and not one to Reason," remarked Fronto, the worthy tutor of the Emperor Marcus Aurelius. Of all these pagan edifices in Rome, but a single one now remains, the temple of Fortuna Virilis, now the church of Santa Maria Egiziaca.[1] It is a small Ionic tetrastyle building on the left bank of the Tiber, a little north of the so-called Temple of the Sun. But the most famous Italian temple of Fortune was at Preneste, an ancient Latin town, now called Palestrina. Here oracles were consulted and fugitives found a place of refuge.

In Great Britain there still exist a number of altars in honor of Fortune, which date from the Roman occupation. One of these, on the line of the wall of Antoninus in Scotland, was erected by soldiers of the second and sixth legions. Another altar, dedicated to the same goddess, was found at the headquarters of the sixth legion at Eboracum, the modern city of York, and is still to be seen at the museum there.[2] The inscription on this altar was copied by the writer during a recent visit to York, and reads as follows: —

DEÆ FORTUNÆ
SOSIA
IUNCINA
Q. ANTONI
ISAURICI
LEG. AUG.

[1] Rodolfo Lanciani, *Pagan and Christian Rome.*
[2] Thomas Wright, *The Celt, the Roman, and the Saxon.*

V. LUCK, ANCIENT AND MODERN

Our English word *luck*, according to some authorities, is of Scandinavian origin, while others consider it to be the past tense of an Anglo-Saxon verb meaning "to catch." Luck signifies, therefore, *a good catch*, and is analogous to the German *Glück*. It has been aptly remarked that very many so-called strong-minded persons, who would not for a moment admit that they are superstitious, are yet not insensible to the fascination of this little monosyllable. As Christian people, we profess to believe implicitly in Divine Providence; yet often because we cannot understand its workings, we so far relapse into paganism as to worship secretly the Goddess Fortune. The fact is, that superstition is an ineradicable element of human nature. The combined forces of religion, education, philosophy, and common sense are allied in a perpetual warfare against it. The thousand and one little credulities which form such an important part of modern folk-lore may be intrinsically the veriest whimsies and trifles, but they are evidence of the tenacity of traditional beliefs.

The modern sailor carries in his pocket a bit of sealskin, or an eagle's beak, to shield him from the lightning; and the Southern negro has his rabbit's foot, and a host of other outlandish fetiches, all for luck.

The millions of American negroes have, indeed, a

deeply-rooted love for the supernatural, and their character exhibits a peculiar blending of superstition and religion. Among the mixed colored races in Missouri, for example, we find a bewildering jumble of African Voodoo credulities, the traditions of the American Indian, and religious fanaticism. Thus, in "Voodoo Tales," by Mary A. Owen, we read of an old crone who kept her medicine-pipe and eagle-bone whistle alongside of her books of devotion, carried a rosary and rabbit's foot in the same pocket, and wore a saint's toe dangling on her bosom, and a luck-ball under her right arm.

It has been well said that only those whose minds are predisposed to entertain idle fancies are wont to regard misfortune as a natural sequence of the legion of alleged evil omens. Yet we know that in all ages and countries such notions have prevailed. The ancient Chaldeans made use of magic formulæ to ward off ill-luck, and Tacitus relates that the most trivial events were regarded as portentous by the Roman people. What a contrast to the credulity of a superstitious age is afforded by the often quoted remark of Cato the Censor, who refused to regard it as ominous when informed that his boots had been gnawed by rats! "If the boots had gnawed the rats," he said, "it might have portended evil."

There is a deal of philosophy in the Irish saying,

"Every man has bad luck awaiting him some time or other, but leave the bad luck to the last; perhaps it may never come."

In attributing the sundry and divers misfortunes of our lives to bad luck, we surely ignore the fact that these same unwelcome experiences are often the logical sequences of our own shortcomings, and that the fickle goddess cannot with fairness be made always to masquerade as our scapegoat.

THE FOLK-LORE OF COMMON SALT[1]

Jests, like salt, should be used sparingly.
Similitudes of Democritus.

I. ORIGIN AND HISTORY

THE origin of the use of common salt as a condiment is hidden in the mazes of antiquity. Although we have no evidence that this important article of diet was known to the antediluvians, there is still abundant proof that it was highly esteemed as a seasoner of food long before the Christian era. In a Greek translation of a curious fragment of the writings of the semi-fabulous Phœnician author, Sanchoniathon, who is said to have lived before the Trojan war, the discovery of the uses of salt is attributed to certain immediate descendants of Noah, one of whom was his son Shem.[2]

From the mythical lore of Finland we learn that Ukko, the mighty god of the sky, struck fire in the heavens, a spark from which descending was received by the waves and became salt. The Chinese worship

[1] Read at the Annual Meeting of the American Folk-Lore Society, New York, December 29, 1896.

[2] Banier's *Mythology.* London, 1739.

an idol called Phelo, in honor of a mythological personage of that name, whom they believe to have been the discoverer of salt and the originator of its use. His ungrateful countrymen, however, were tardy in their recognition of Phelo's merits, and that worthy thereupon left his native land and did not return. Then the Chinese declared him to be a deity, and in the month of June each year they hold a festival in his honor, during which he is everywhere eagerly sought, but in vain; he will not appear until he comes to announce the end of the world.

Among the Mexican Nahuas the women and girls employed in the preparation of salt were wont to dance at a yearly festival held in honor of the Goddess of salt, Huixtocihuatl, whose brothers the rain-gods are said, as the result of a quarrel, to have driven her into the sea, where she invented the art of making the precious substance.[1]

The earliest Biblical mention of salt appears to be in reference to the destruction of Sodom and Gomorrah. (Genesis xix. 24–26.) When King Abimelech destroyed the city of Shechem, an event which is believed to have occurred in the thirteenth century B. C., he is said to have " sowed salt on it," this phrase expressing the completeness of its ruin.[2] (Judges ix. 45.) It is cer-

---

[1] Bancroft, *Native Races*, vol. ii. p. 353.
[2] J. J. L. Ratton, M. D., M. C., *A Hand-Book of Common Salt.*

tain that the use of salt as a relish was known to the
Jewish people at a comparatively early period of their
history. For in the sixth chapter of the Book of Job
occurs this passage : " Can that which is unsavoury be
eaten without salt ? "

In Eastern countries it is a time-honored custom to
place salt before strangers as a token and pledge of
friendship and good-will. The phrase " to eat some
one's salt " formerly signified being in that person's
service, and in this sense it is used in the Book of Ezra,
iv. 14, where the expression, " we have maintenance
from the king's palace," means literally, " we are salted
with the salt of the palace," which implies being in the
service of the king. And from the idea of being in the
employment of a master, and eating his salt, the phrase
in question came to denote faithfulness and loyalty.[1]

As an instance of the superstitious reverence with
which salt is regarded in the East, it is related that
Yacoub ben Laith, who founded the dynasty of Persian
princes known as the Saffarides, was of very humble
origin, and in his youth gained a livelihood as a free-
booter. Yet so chivalrous was he that he never stripped
his victims of all their belongings, but always left them
something to begin life with anew.

On one occasion this gallant robber had forcibly and
by stealth entered the palace of a prince, and was about

---

[1] J. B. Friedrich, *Die Symbolik und Mythologie der Natur.*

departing with considerable spoil, when he stumbled over
an object which his sense of taste revealed to be a lump
of salt. Having thus involuntarily partaken of a pledge
of hospitality in another man's house, his honor over-
came his greed of gain and he departed without his
booty.[1]

Owing to its antiseptic and preservative qualities, salt
was emblematic of durability and permanence; hence
the expression " Covenant of Salt." It was also a symbol of wisdom, and in this sense was doubtless used by
St. Paul when he told the Colossians that their speech
should be seasoned with salt.

Homer called salt divine, and Plato described it as a
substance dear to the gods.

Perhaps the belief in its divine attributes may have
been a reason for the employment of salt as a sacrificial
offering by the Hebrews, Greeks, and Romans, all of
whom, moreover, regarded it as an indispensable relish.

Plutarch said that without salt nothing was savory or
toothsome, and that this substance even imparted an
additional flavor to wines, thus causing them " to go
down the throat merrily." And the same writer remarked that, as bread and salt were commonly eaten
together, therefore Ceres and Neptune were sometimes
worshiped together in the same temple.[2]

[1] Calmet's *Dictionary of the Holy Bible.*
[2] Philemon Holland, *The Morals or Miscellane Works of Plutarch.*

II. SALT UNCONGENIAL TO WITCHES AND DEVILS

Grimm remarks that salt is not found in witches' kitchens, nor at devils' feasts, because the Roman Catholic Church has taken upon herself the hallowing and dedication of this substance. Moreover, inasmuch as Christians recognize salt as a wholesome and essential article of diet, it seems plausible enough that they should regard it as unsuitable for the use of devils and witches, two classes of beings with whom they have no particular sympathy. Hence perhaps the familiar saying that " the Devil loveth no salt in his meat."

Once upon a time, according to tradition, there lived a German peasant whose wife was a witch, and the Devil invited them both to supper one fine evening. All the dishes lacked seasoning, and the peasant, in spite of his wife's remonstrances, kept asking for salt; and when after a while it was brought, he remarked with fervor, " Thank God, here is salt at last," whereupon the whole scene vanished.[1]

The abbot Richalmus, who lived in the old German duchy of Franconia in the twelfth century, claimed, by the exercise of a special and extraordinary faculty, to be able to baffle the machinations of certain evil spirits who took special delight in playing impish tricks upon churchmen. They appear, indeed, to have sorely tried

[1] Horst, *Dæmonomagie*. Frankfurt, 1818.

the patience of the good abbot in many ways, as, for
example, by distracting his thoughts during Mass and
interfering with his digestion, promoting discords in the
church music, and causing annoyance by inciting the
congregation to cough in sermon time.   Fortunately he
possessed three efficient weapons against these troublesome creatures, namely, the sign of the cross, holy
water, and salt.

"Evil spirits," wrote the abbot, "cannot bear salt."
When he was at dinner, and the Devil had maliciously
taken away his appetite, he simply tasted a little salt,
and at once became hungry.   Then, if soon afterwards
his appetite again failed him, he took some more salt,
and his relish for food speedily returned.[1]

In Hungarian folk-lore, contrary to the usual opinion, evil personages are fond of salt, for at those festive
gatherings described in old legends and fairy tales,
where witches and the Devil met, they were wont to
cook in large kettles a stew of horse-flesh seasoned with
salt, upon which they eagerly feasted.

Hence appears to have originated the popular notion
current among the Magyars that a woman who experiences a craving for salt in the early morning must be
a witch, and on no account should her taste be gratified.

Once upon a time, says tradition, a man crept into a

---

[1] Richalmus, *Liber Revelationum de Insidiis et Versutiis Dæmonum adver-*
sus Homines.

witch's tub in order to spy upon the proceedings at a meeting of the uncanny sisterhood.

Shortly thereafter the witch appeared, saddled the tub, and rode it to the place of rendezvous, and on arriving there the man contrived to empty a quantity of salt into the tub. After the revels he was conveyed homewards in the same manner, and showed the salt to his neighbors as proof positive that he had really been present at the meeting. Sometimes, however, salt is used in Hungary as a protection against witches. The threshold of a new house is sprinkled with it, and the door-hinges are smeared with garlic, so that no witch may enter.[1]

The peasants of Russian Esthonia are aware of the potency of salt against witches and their craft. They believe that on St. John's Eve witch-butter is maliciously smeared on the doors of their farm-buildings in order to spread sickness among the cattle. When, therefore, an Esthonian farmer finds this obnoxious butter on his barn-door or elsewhere, he loads his gun with salt and shoots the witch-germs away.[2]

The Hindus have a theory that malignant spirits, or *Bhúts*, are especially prone to molest women and children immediately after the latter have eaten confectionery and other sweet delicacies.

[1] Dr. Heinrich von Wlislocki, *Volksglaube und religiöser Brauch der Magyar*, p. 151.

[2] W. Mannhardt, *Germanische Mythen*. Berlin, 1858.

Indeed, so general is this belief that vendors of sweetmeats among school-children provide their youthful customers each with a pinch of salt to remove the sweet taste from their mouths, and thus afford a safeguard against the ever-watchful *Bhûts*.[1]

III. THE LATIN WORD "SAL"

Owing to the importance of salt as a relish, its Latin name *sal* came to be used metaphorically as signifying a savory mental morsel, and, in a general sense, wit or sarcasm.[2] It was formerly maintained by some etymologists that this word had a threefold meaning according to its gender. Thus, when masculine, it has the above signification, but when feminine it means *the sea*, and only when neuter does it stand for common salt. The characterization of Greece as "the salt of nations" is attributed to Livy, and this is probably the origin of the phrase "Attic salt," meaning delicate, refined wit. The phrase *cum grano salis* may signify the grain of common sense with which one should receive a seemingly exaggerated report. It may also mean moderation, even as salt is used sparingly as a seasoner of food.

Among the ancients, as with ourselves, *Sol* and *sal*, the Sun and salt, were known to be two things essential to the maintenance of life.

---

[1] W. Crooke, B. A., p. 147.
[2] Alexander Adam, LL. D., *Roman Antiquities*.

Soldiers, officials, and working people were paid either wholly or in part in salt,[1] which was in such general use for this purpose that any sum of money paid for labor or service of whatever kind was termed a *salarium*, or salary, that is, the wherewithal to obtain one's salt.[2]

Pliny remarked that salt was essential for the complete enjoyment of life, and in confirmation of this statement he commented on the fact that the word *sales* was employed to express the pleasures of the mind, or a keen appreciation of witty effusions, and, therefore, was associated with the idea of good fellowship and mirth.[3]

A certain mystic significance has been attributed to the three letters composing the word "sal." Thus, the letter S, standing alone, represents or suggests two circles united together, the sun and the moon. It typifies, moreover, the union of things divine and mundane, even as salt partakes of the attributes of each. A, alpha, signifies the beginning of all things; while L is emblematic of something celestial and glorious. S and L represent solar and lunar influences respectively, and the trio of letters stand for an essential substance provided by God for the benefit of his people. In a curious treatise on salt, originally published in 1770, the

---

[1] *Grosses Universal Lexicon.* Leipzig and Halle, 1742.
[2] John Borrow, F. R. S., *Travels in China.*
[3] *Natural History,* book xxxi. ch. 41.

writer launches forth in impassioned style the most extravagant encomiums upon this substance, which he avers to be the quintessence of the earth. Salt is here characterized as a Treasure of Nature, an Essence of Perfection, and the Paragon of Preservatives. Moreover, whoever possesses salt thereby secures a prime factor of human happiness among material things.[1]

The French people employ the word " salt " metaphorically in several common expressions. Thus, in speaking of the lack of piquancy or pointedness in a dull sermon or address, they say, " There was no salt in that discourse." And of the brilliant productions of a favorite author they remark, " He has sprinkled his writings with salt by handfuls." [2] In like manner they use the term *un epigramme salé* to denote a cutting sarcasm or raillery. Very apt also is the following definition by an old English writer : [3] " Salt, a pleasaunt and merrie word that maketh folks to laugh and sometime pricketh." The expression " to salt an invoice " signifies to increase the full market value of each article, and corresponds to one use of the French verb *saler*, to overcharge, and hence to " fleece " or " pluck." Thus the phrase *Il me l'a bien salé* means " He has charged me an excessive price." [4]

---

[1] Elias Artista Hermetica, *Das Geheimniss vom Salz.*
[2] *Il a répandu le sel à pleines mains dans ses écrits.*
[3] Baret, 1580.
[4] Brewer's *Dictionary of Phrase and Fable.*

IV. SALT EMPLOYED TO CONFIRM AN OATH

In the records of the Presbytery of Edinburgh, under date of September 20, 1586, is to be found the following description of an oath which Scotch merchants were required to take when on their way to the Baltic : —

Certan merchantis passing to Danskerne (Denmark) and cuming neir Elsinnure, chusing out and quhen they accompted for the payment of the toill of the goods, and that depositioun of ane othe in forme following, viz : Thei present and offer *breid* and *salt* to the deponer of the othe, whereon he layis his hand and deponis his conscience and sweiris.[1]

Gypsies likewise sometimes use bread and salt to confirm the solemnity of an oath. An example of this is recorded in the " Pesther Lloyd " of July 1, 1881. A member of a gypsy band in western Hungary had been robbed of a sum of money, and so informed his chief, who summoned the elders of the camp to a council. On an upright cross formed of two poles was placed a piece of bread sprinkled with salt, and upon this each gypsy was required to swear that he was not the thief. The real culprit, refusing to take so solemn an oath, was thus discovered.

Among the Jews the covenant of salt is the most sacred possible. Even at the present time, Arabian

[1] *Edinburgh Monthly Magazine*, June, 1817.

princes are wont to signify their ratification of an alliance by sprinkling salt upon bread, meanwhile exclaiming, "I am the friend of thy friends, and the enemy of thine enemies." So likewise there is a common form of request among the Arabs as follows: "For the sake of the bread and salt which are between us, do this or that." [1]

In the East, at the present day, compacts between tribes are still confirmed by salt, and the most solemn pledges are ratified by this substance. During the Indian mutiny of 1857 a chief motive of self-restraint among the Sepoys was the fact that they had sworn by their salt to be loyal to the English queen. [2]

The antiquity of the practice of using salt in confirmation of an oath is shown in the following passage from an ode of the Greek lyric poet Archilochus, who flourished during the early part of the seventh century B. C. : —

Thou hast broken the solemn oath, and hast disgraced the salt and the table.

In the year 1731 the Protestant miners and peasants inhabiting the "salt exchequer lands," prior to their banishment from the country by Leopold, Archbishop of Salzburg, held a meeting in the picturesque village of Schwarzach, and "solemnly ratified their league by

[1] Chevalier d'Arvieux, *Memoir*. Paris, 1735.
[2] J. J. Manley, M. A., *Salt and Other Condiments*, p. 90.

the ancient custom of dipping their fingers in salt."
The table at which this ceremony took place, and a
picture representing the event, are still shown at the
Wallner Inn, where the meeting was held.[1]

V. SALT-SPILLING AS AN OMEN

The widespread notion that the spilling of salt produces evil consequences is supposed to have originated
in the tradition that Judas overturned a salt-cellar at
the Paschal Supper, as portrayed in Leonardo da Vinci's
painting.   But it appears more probable that the belief
is due to the sacred character of salt in early times.
Any one having the misfortune to spill salt was formerly
supposed to incur the anger of all good spirits, and to
be rendered susceptible to the malevolent influences of
demons.[2]   When, in oriental lands, salt was offered to
guests as a token of hospitality, it was accounted a
misfortune if any particles were scattered while being
so presented, and in such cases a quarrel or dispute was
anticipated.[3]

Bishop Hall wrote, in 1627, that when salt fell
towards a superstitious guest at dinner, he was wont
to exhibit signs of mental agitation, and refused to be
comforted until one of the waiters had poured wine in

---

[1] Karl Baedeker, *The Eastern Alps*, p. 124.   1895.
[2] *Spectator*, vol. 66.   1891.
[3] *Gentleman's Magazine*, part i.   1833.

his lap.   And in Gayton's " Art of Longevity " we
find these lines : —

I have two friends of either sex, which do eat little salt or
none, yet are friends too; of both which persons I can truly
tell, they are of patience most invincible; whom out of temper no mischance at all can put; no, if towards them the salt
should fall.

The Germans have a saying, " Whoever spills salt
arouses enmity," and in some places the overthrow of a
salt-cellar is thought to be the direct act of the Devil,
the peace-disturber. The superstitious Parisian, who
may have been the unfortunate cause of such a mishap,
is quite ready to adopt this view, and tosses a little of
the spilled salt behind him, in order, if possible, to hit
the invisible Devil in the eye, which, temporarily at
least, prevents him from doing further mischief.[1] This
is probably a relic of an ancient idolatrous custom ; and
salt thus thrown was formerly a kind of sop to Cerberus, an offering to pacify some particular deity.   In
like manner the natives of Pegu, a province of British
Burmah, in the performance of one of their rites in
honor of the Devil, are wont to throw food over their
left shoulders to conciliate the chief spirit of evil.[2]

When salt was spilled at table the pious Roman was
wont to exclaim, " May the gods avert the omen ! " and

[1] Felix Liebrecht, *Die Symbolik und Mythologie der Natur.*
[2] Owen on *Serpents.*

the modern Sicilian, in such a case, invokes "the Mother of Light."

Among the Greeks it was customary to present salt to the gods as a thank-offering at the beginning of every meal. Louis Figuier, in " Les merveilles de l'industrie," places these three happenings in the category of ominous mishaps in a Grecian household : (1) the omission of a salt-cellar from among the furnishings of a dinner-table ; (2) the falling asleep of one of the guests at a banquet, before the removal of the salt-cellar to make place for the dessert ; (3) the overturning of this important vessel. It seems evident, therefore, that the origin of the belief in the ominous character of salt-spilling is of far greater antiquity than is popularly supposed ; and Leonardo da Vinci, in portraying Judas as upsetting a salt-cellar, probably had in mind the already well-known portentous significance of such an act. But some observers have failed to discover any trace of a salt-cellar in the original *Cenacolo* on the refectory wall of the Milanese convent. In the well-known engraving by Raphael Morghen, however, the overthrown salt-cellar is clearly delineated, and the spilled salt is seen issuing from it. An animated discussion on this moot-point enlivened the columns of " Notes and Queries " some years ago.

The following passage is to be found in a work entitled " Hieroglyphica, a Joanne Valeriano " (1586), being a treatise on ancient symbols : —

Alioqui sal amicitiæ symbolum fuit, durationis gratia. Corpora enim solidiora facit et diutissime conservat. Unde hospitibus ante alios cibos apponi solitum, quo amicitiæ firmitas ac perseverantia significetur. Quare plerique ominosum habent si sal in mensam profundi contigerit. Contra vero faustum si vinum atque id merum effusum sit.

Which has been rendered into English as follows: "Salt was formerly a symbol of friendship, because of its lasting quality. For it makes substances more compact and preserves them for a long time : hence it was usually presented to guests before other food, to signify the abiding strength of friendship. Wherefore many consider it ominous to spill salt on the table, and, on the other hand, propitious to spill wine, especially if unmixed with water." [1]

In Gaule's "Magastromancer" (1652), overturning the salt is mentioned in a list of "superstitious ominations." According to a popular Norwegian belief, one will shed as many tears as may suffice to dissolve the quantity of salt which he has spilled; [2] and in east Yorkshire, also, every grain of spilled salt represents a tear to be shed. Moreover, saltness has been thought to be an essential attribute of tears, and this intimate connection between the two may have given rise to

[1] The writer is indebted for this translation to John P. Hopkinson, Esq.

[2] Felix Liebrecht. *Zur Volkskunde.* 1877.

some of the many superstitions connected with salt.[1]
In Bucks County, Pennsylvania, in order to avert ill-
luck after salt has been spilled, one should not only toss
a pinch of the spilled salt over the left shoulder, but
should also crawl under a table and come out on the
opposite side.[2]

In the " British Apollo " (1708) are these lines : —

> We 'el tel you the reason
> Why spilling of Salt
> Is esteemed such a Fault,
> Because it doth ev'rything season.
>
> Th' antiques did opine
> 'T was of Friendship a sign,
> So served it to guests in decorum,
> And thought Love decayed,
> When the negligent Maid
> Let the salt-cellar tumble before them.

In New England the gravity of salt-spilling as an
omen, its deplorable severance of friendship's ties, and
the necessity for prompt remedial measures, are all fully
recognized.

And here the deft toss of the spilled particles over

---

[1] Shakespeare refers to this subject in several passages, and among
them the following : —

> How came her eyes so bright ?   Not with salt tears.
> > *Midsummer Night's Dream.*

> With tears as salt as sea.
> > *2 Henry VI.*

[2] *Current Superstitions*, edited by Fanny D. Bergen.

the left shoulder is not always adequate; for in order thoroughly to break the spell, these particles must be thrown on the stove.[1]

Gypsies have a saying, " The salt of strife has fallen."

From the idea of the desecration of a sacred substance, to which allusion has been made, doubtless arose the remarkable superstition that, as a penalty for spilling salt, one must wait outside the gate of Paradise for as many years as there are grains of salt spilled.[2]

In the Lansdowne MSS. 231 (British Museum) occurs this passage : —

The falling of salt is an authentic psağemt of ill-luck, nor can every temper contemn it; nor was the same a grall pgnostic among the ancients of future evil, but a pticular omination concerning the breach of friendship. For salt as incorruptible was ye symbole of friendship, and before ye other service was offered unto y^{eir} guests. But whether salt were not only a symbol of friendship w^h man, but also a fig. of amity and recociliation w^h God, and was therefore offered in sacrifices, is an higher speculation.

Herbert Spencer affirms [3] that the consciousness which harbors a notion that evil will result from spilling salt is manifestly allied to the consciousness of the savage,

[1] Clifton Johnson, *What they say in New England*, p. 92. 1896.
[2] M. J. Schleiden, *Das Salz*, p. 73.
[3] *The Study of Sociology*, p. 5.

and is prone to entertain other superstitious beliefs like those prevalent in barbarous lands. And although idolatry and fetich-worship do not flourish in civilized communities, yet many popular superstitions are akin in nature to the sentiments which prompt the savage to bow down before images of wood or stone.

VI. HELPING TO SALT AT TABLE

In the northern counties of England, and indeed quite generally in Anglican communities, it is reckoned unlucky to be helped to salt at table, and this idea has found expression in the popular couplet, " Help me to salt, help me to sorrow." In a small volume entitled " The Rules of Civility " (London, 1695), translated from the French, and quoted in " Brand's Popular Antiquities," is the following passage : —

Some are so exact they think it uncivil to help anybody that sits by them either with *salt* or *brains*. But in my judgment that is a ridiculous scruple, and if your neighbor desires you to furnish him (with salt), you must either take out some with your knife and lay it upon his plate, or if they be more than one, present them with the salt that they may furnish themselves.

In Russia there is a superstitious prejudice against helping one's neighbor to salt at table on account of the liability to quarrels thereby incurred. For in so doing one is thought to have the air of implying, " Well, you

have received your allowance of salt, now go away."
But if in proffering the salt one smiles amicably, all
danger of a quarrel is happily averted, and the act is
wholly relieved of its ominous character.[1]

The simple expedient of a second help is commonly
regarded as equally effective for this purpose, but it is
difficult to imagine whence was derived the alleged
potency of such an antidote, which is contrary to the
Pythagorean theory of the divine character of unity and
the diabolical attributes of the number two.

In many lands, however, it is only common courtesy
to help a friend to salt at table; but in Italy this delicate attention was formerly thought to be a mark of
undue familiarity, and, when salt was offered by one
gentleman to the wife of another, it was a sufficient
cause for jealousy and even quarrel.[2]

VII. SALT AS A PROTECTION TO YOUNG INFANTS

The mediæval Roman Catholic custom of using salt
to protect infants from evil prior to their baptism is
frequently alluded to in early romantic literature. In
an ancient ballad entitled " The King's Daughter," the
birth of a child occurs under circumstances which prevent the administration of the rite of baptism. The

---

[1] *Revue des traditions populaires*, tome i. 1886.
[2] *A Theological and Philosophical Treatise of the Nature and Goodnesse
of Salt*. Imprinted by Felix Kyngston for Richard Boyle at London, 1612.

mother, therefore, exposes the baby in a casket, and is careful to place by its side salt and candles.   The words of the ballad are : —

> The bairnie she swyl'd in linen so fine,
> In a gilded casket she laid it syne,
> Mickle saut and light she laid therein,
> Cause yet in God's house it had'na been.[1]

Mr. William G. Black, in his work on Folk-Medicine, says that in some districts of Scotland it was formerly a custom, previous to baptism, to carry some salt around the child " withershins," or backwards, — a procedure which was believed to protect the child from evil during its oftentimes long journey from the house to the church where the ceremony was to be performed. In Marsala the relatives of a new-born child do not sleep the first night, for fear of the appearance of witches.   Indeed, a watch is often kept for many nights, or until the child's baptism.   A light burns in the room constantly, and an image of some saint is fastened upon the house-door.   A rosary and a raveled napkin are attached to the image, and behind the door are placed a jug of salt and a broom.   When a witch comes and sees the saint's image and the rosary, she usually goes away at once; but even if these talismans are wanting, the salt, napkin, and broom afford adequate protection. For any witch before entering must count the grains of

---

[1] James Napier, *Folk-Lore*, p. 33.

salt, the threads of the napkin's fringe, and the twigs of which the broom is made. And she never has time enough for these tasks, because she cannot appear before midnight, and must hide herself before the dawn.[1]

This popular belief in the magical power of salt to protect infants from evil, especially in the period between birth and baptism, is exemplified in the following allusion to a foundling in a metrical " History of the Family of Stanley," which dates from the early part of the sixteenth century (Harleian MSS. 541, British Museum) : " It was uncrisned, seeming out of doubt, for salt was bound at its neck in a linen clout." [2]

In Sicily, too, it is sometimes customary for the priest to place a little salt in the child's mouth at baptism, thereby imparting wisdom. Hence the popular local saying in regard to a person who is dull of understanding, that the priest put but little salt in his mouth.[3] A similar usage is in vogue in the district of Campine in Belgium. The use of salt at baptism in the Christian Church dates from the fourth century. It was an early practice to place salt, which had been previously blessed, in the infant's mouth, to symbolize the counteraction of the sinfulness of its nature.[4]

[1] Pitré, vol. iv. p. 102.
[2] R. T. Hampson, *Medii Ævi Kalendarium.* London, 1841.
[3] Pitré, vol. ii. p. 161.
[4] Dr. Heino Pfannenschmid, *Das Weihwasser im heidnischen und christlichen Cultus.*

So, too, in the baptismal ceremonies of the Church of England in mediæval times, salt, over which an exorcism had been said, was placed in the child's mouth, and its ears and nostrils were touched with saliva, — practices which became obsolete at about the time of the reign of Henry VIII.

An octagonal font of the fifteenth century, in St. Margaret's Church, Ipswich, Suffolk, has upon one of its sides the figure of an angel bearing a scroll, on which appears a partially illegible inscription containing the words *Sal et Saliva*.[1]

Thomas Ady, in "A Perfect Discovery of Witches" (London, 1661), says that holy water, properly conjured, was used to keep the Devil in awe, and to prevent his entering churches or dwellings.

With such holy water Satanic influences were kept away from meat and drink, and from "the very salt upon the table."

In the Highlands of Scotland, instead of using salt as an amulet for the protection of young babies, it was customary for watchers to remain constantly by the cradle until the christening. For it was believed that spiteful fairies were wont to carry off healthy infants, leaving in their stead puny specimens of their own elfish offspring; and infants thus kidnapped were sometimes kept in fairyland for seven years. This well-known

[1] *Notes and Queries*, 6th series, vol. ix. p. 428. May, 1884.

popular belief gave rise to the word "changeling,"
which signifies a "strange, stupid, ugly child left by
the fairies in place of a beautiful or charming child
that they have stolen away." [1] And inasmuch as baby
elves were invariably stunted and of feeble intellect,
all idiotic and dwarfish children were thought to be
changelings. [2]

> From thence a faery the unweeting reft,
> There as thou slepst in tender swadling band,
> And her base elfin brood there for the left :
> Such men do *chaungelinges* call, so chaunged by fairies' theft. [3]

VIII. SALT AS A MAGICAL SUBSTANCE

The natives of Morocco regard salt as a talisman
against evil, and a common amulet among the Neapolitan poor is a bit of rock-salt suspended from the neck. [4]
The peasants of the Hartz Mountain region in Germany
believe that three grains of salt in a milk-pot will keep
witches away from the milk; [5] and to preserve butter
from their uncanny influences, it was a custom in the
county of Aberdeen, Scotland, some years ago, to put
salt on the lid of a churn. [6] In Normandy, also, the
peasants are wont to throw a little salt into a vessel

---

[1] *Century Dictionary.*
[2] Francis Grose, *Popular Superstitions.*
[3] Spenser's *Faerie Queene.*
[4] Clara Erskine Clement, *Naples.*
[5] Grimm's *Teutonic Mythology.*
[6] *The Folk-Lore Journal*, vol. vii. 1889.

containing milk, in order to protect the cow who gave the milk from the influences of witchcraft.

Peculiar notions about the magical properties of salt are common among American negroes. Thus in some regions a new tenant will not move into a furnished house until all objects therein have been thoroughly salted, with a view to the destruction of witch-germs.[1] Another example of the supernatural attributes ascribed to salt is the opinion current among uneducated people in some communities of its potency in casting a spell over obnoxious individuals. For this purpose it is sufficient either to sprinkle salt over the sleeping form of an enemy, or on the grave of one of his ancestors.[2] Another kind of salt-spell in vogue in the south of England consists in throwing a little salt into the fire on three successive Friday nights, while saying these words:—

> It is not this salt I wish to burn,
> It is my lover's heart to turn;
> That he may neither rest nor happy be,
> Until he comes and speaks to me.

On the third Friday night the disconsolate damsel expects her lover to appear.[3] Every one is familiar with the old saying, "You can catch a bird with your

[1] *Journal of American Folk-Lore*, No. xviii. 1892.
[2] *The Washington Post*, November 27, 1894.
[3] William Henderson, *Notes on the Folk-Lore of the Northern Countries of England*.

hand, if you first put some salt on its tail." This quaint
expression has been thought to imply that, if one can
get near enough to a bird to place salt on its tail, its
capture is an easy matter. The phrase, however, may
be more properly attributed to a belief in the magical
properties of salt in casting a spell over the bird.
Otherwise any substance might be equally effective for
the purpose of catching it. The writer remembers having read somewhere an old legend about a young man
who playfully threw some salt on the back of a witch
sitting next to him at table, and the witch thereupon
acquired such an increase of avoirdupois that she was
unable to move until the young man obligingly brushed
away the salt.

The ancient Teutons believed that the swift flight of
birds was caused by certain powerful spirits of the air.
Now salt is a foe to ghostly might, imparts weight to
bodies, and impedes their motion; therefore the rationale of its operation when placed upon a bird's tail is
easily intelligible.

In the Province of Quebec French Canadians sometimes scatter salt about the doors of their stables to prevent those mischievous little imps called *lutins* from
entering and teasing the horses by sticking burrs in
their manes and tails.[1] The *lutin* or *gobelin* is akin to
the Scandinavian household spirit, who is fond of chil-

[1] *Journal of American Folk-Lore*, No. 19. 1892.

dren and horses, and who whips and pinches the former
when they are naughty, but caresses them when good.[1]
In Marsala, west Sicily, a horse, mule, or donkey, on
entering a new stall, is thought to be liable to molesta-
tion by fairies.   As a precautionary measure, therefore,
a little salt is placed on the animal's back, and this is
believed to insure freedom from lameness, or other evil
resulting from fairy spite.[2]   Common salt has long
enjoyed a reputation as a means of procuring disen-
chantment.   It was an ingredient of a salve "against
nocturnal goblin visitors" used by the Saxons in England, and described in one of their ancient leech-books;[3]
while in the annals of folk-medicine are to be found
numerous references to its reputed virtues as a magical
therapeutic agent.   In Scotland, when a person is ailing
of some affection whose nature is not apparent, as much
salt as can be placed on a sixpence is dissolved in
water, and the solution is then applied three times to the
soles of the patient's feet, to the palms of his hands,
and to his forehead.   He is then expected to taste the
mixture, a portion of which is thrown over the fire while
saying, "Lord, preserve us frae a' skaith."[4]

[1] Keightley's *Fairy Mythology.*
[2] Giuseppe Pitré, *Usi e costumi, credenze e pregiudizi del popolo Siciliano,*
vol. iii. p. 426.   Palermo, 1889.
[3] *Leechdoms, Wortcunning, and Starcraft,* edited by Rev. Oswald Cockayne.   London, 1865.
[4] Rev. Charles Rogers, LL. D., *Scotland, Social and Domestic.*

The Germans of Buffalo valley in central Pennsylvania believe that a boy may be cured of homesickness by placing salt in the hems of his trousers and making him look up the chimney.[1]

In India the natives rub salt and wine on the affected part of the body as a cure for scorpion bites, believing that the success of this treatment is due to the supernatural virtue of the salt in scaring away the fiends who caused the pain.[2] An ancient Irish charm of great repute in cases of suspected "fairy-stroke" consisted in placing on a table three equal portions of salt in three parallel rows. The would-be magician then encircles the salt with his arm and repeats the Lord's Prayer thrice over each row. Then, taking the hand of the fairy-struck person, he says over it, "By the power of the Father and of the Son and of the Holy Spirit, let this disease depart and the spell of evil spirits be broken." Then follows a solemn adjuration and command addressed to the supposed demon, and the charm is complete.[3]

In Bavaria and the Ukraine, in order to ascertain whether a child has been the victim of bewitchment, the mother licks its forehead; and if her sense of taste reveals thereby a marked saline flavor, she is convinced

[1] *Journal of American Folk-Lore*, No. 13. 1891.

[2] James M. Campbell, *Notes on the Spirit-Basis of Belief and Custom.*

[3] Lady Wilde, *Ancient Legends, Mystic Charms, and Superstitions of Ireland.*

that her child has been under the influence of an evil eye.[1]

In the Swiss canton of Bern a person is believed to be amply fortified against all kinds of spiritual enemies by the simple expedient of carrying a piece of fresh bread and a psalm-book in the right and left coat pockets respectively, provided one is careful to have some rock-salt either in each vest pocket, or inside a briar-wood cane upon which three crosses have been cut.[2] In Bohemia a mother seeks to protect her daughter from evil glances by placing a little bread and salt in her pocket; and when a young girl goes out for a walk the mother sprinkles salt on the ground behind her, so that she may not lose her way.[3]

Holy water has been employed in the religious ceremonies of many peoples as a means of purifying both persons and things, and also to keep away demons. Sprinkling and washing with it were important features of the Greek ritual.

The holy water of the Roman Catholic Church is prepared by exorcising and blessing salt and water separately, after which the salt is dissolved in the water and a benediction pronounced upon the mixture. In the Hawaiian ritual, sea-water was sometimes preferred.[4]

---

[1] *Revue des traditions populaires*, tome vi. p. 43.   1891.

[2] *Zeitschrift für deutsche Mythologie und Sittenkunde*, Band iv.

[3] *Sitzungberichte der kaiserlichen Akademie der Wissenschaften.*

[4] Abraham Fornander, *An Account of the Polynesian Race*, vol. i.

A Magyar house-mistress will not give any salt to a woman who may come to the door and ask for it in the early morning, believing that any such would-be borrower is surely a witch; but in order to keep away all witches and hags, she strews salt on the threshold. On St. Lucien's Day neither salt nor fire must be taken out of the house.[1]

Among the Japanese, the mysterious preservative qualities of salt are the source of various superstitions. The mistress of a household will not buy it at night, and when purchased in the daytime a small quantity is thrown into the fire in order to prevent discord in the family, and to avert misfortune generally.[2]

In Scotland salt was formerly in high repute as a charm, and the salt-box was the first chattel to be removed to a new dwelling. When Robert Burns, in the year 1789, was about to occupy a new house at Ellisland, he was escorted on his route thither along the banks of the river Nith by a procession of relatives, and in their midst was borne a bowl of salt resting on the family Bible.[3]

In some places in the north of England the giving away of salt is a dangerous procedure; for if the salt thus given comes into the possession of an evil-wisher,

---

[1] *Aus dem Volksleben der Magyaren*, p. 111.
[2] William Elliot Griffis, A. M., *The Mikado's Empire*.
[3] Rogers, vol. iii. p. 288.

it places the donor entirely in the power of such a person.[1]

In upper Egypt, previous to the setting out of a caravan, it is customary for the native women to throw salt on burning coals, which are carried in earthen vessels and set down before the different loads. While so doing they exclaim, " May you be blessed in going and coming," and such incantations they believe render inert all the machinations of evil spirits.[2]

IX. MISCELLANEOUS REMARKS ON SALT

Among the peasants of the Spanish province of Andalusia the word "salt" is synonymous with gracefulness and charm of manner, and no more endearing or flattering language can be used in addressing a woman, whether wife or sweetheart, than to call her " the salt-box of my love." The phrase "May you be well salted" is also current as an expression of affectionate regard.[3]

Scotch fishermen have a traditional custom of salting their nets " for luck," and they also sometimes throw a little salt into the sea " to blind the fairies."

In the Isle of Man the interchange of salt is regarded as indispensable to every business transaction, while Manx beggars have even been known to refuse an alms if proffered without it.[4]

---

[1] Henderson, p. 217.   [2] Burkhardt's *Nubia*.
[3] M. J. Schleiden, *Das Salz*.   [4] Waldron's *History*.

In Syracuse, Sicily, salt has won distinction as a symbol of wisdom through a curious misinterpretation of the words *sedes sapientiæ* of the so-called Lauretane litany; these words becoming in the mouths of the people *sale e sapienza*,[1] salt and wisdom.

Salt and bread, representing the necessaries of life, are the first articles taken into the dwelling of a newly married pair in Russia. And in Pomerania, at the close of a wedding breakfast, a servant carries about a plate containing salt, upon which the guests place presents of money.[2]

In olden times bread and salt were reckoned the simplest and most indispensable articles of diet, and were offered to guests as a guarantee of hospitality and friendliness. The universal reputation of salt as a symbol of good-will is shown in the proverbs and current sayings of many nations. Cicero, in his treatise on Friendship, wrote that age increased the value of friendships, even as it improved the quality of certain wines; and he added further that there was truth in the proverb, "Many pecks of salt must be eaten together to bring friendship to perfection."

Inasmuch as salt is a necessary and wholesome article of diet, a generous use of it is reckoned beneficial. Evan Marlett Boddy, F. R. C. S., in his "History of

[1] Pitré.
[2] M. J. Schleiden, *Das Salz*, p. 71.

Salt," p. 78, comments with some asperity on the custom, prevalent at the tables of English gentlefolk, of placing salt in the tiniest receptacles, as if it were a most expensive substance. He regards it as anything but edifying "to see the host and his guests, in the most finical, grotesque manner, help themselves to the almost infinitesimal quantities of salt, as if it were a mark of good breeding and delicacy." On the contrary, he continues, such stupid customs of "good society" are truly indicative of mental weakness and profound ignorance.

In a treatise on the "Dignity and Utility of Salt," by Jean de Marcounille Percheron, Paris, 1584, this mineral is likened in value to the four elements recognized by the ancients, — earth, air, fire, and water; and indeed, on account of its importance for the maintenance of health in the animal economy, salt has been termed a "fifth element." So highly did the Thracians of old prize this commodity that they bartered slaves in exchange for it, whence originated the phrase *Sale emptum mancipium*.

The Egyptian geographer, Cosmas, stated that a salt currency was in use in Africa in the sixth century;[1] and Marco Polo wrote that salt was a common medium of exchange among certain Asiatic peoples in the thirteenth century. In Tibet, for example, pieces of salt

[1] *The Leisure Hour*, vol. xliii. p. 805. 1894.

shaped in a mould, and weighing about half a pound each, served as small change; eighty such pieces were equal in value to a *saggio* of fine gold, corresponding to the Roman *solidus*, worth about three dollars. Salt was, moreover, used as money at this time in Yun-Nan and other provinces of southwestern China.[1]

Felix Dubois, in his "Timbuctoo the Mysterious," p. 123, comments on the rarity of salt in the interior of the Soudan, and says that it is the most valuable commodity of that region, the *true gold* of the Soudanese. The bulk of the salt supply of Timbuctoo comes from the salt mines of Taudeny, which are situated in the great Sahara desert, some three hundred miles away to the north. Here the salt is found in abundance beneath a scanty layer of sand, and is dug up in lumps and fashioned into blocks. Small pieces of this rock-salt are useful to the traveler as money, and are readily accepted as such by the Soudanese merchants.

The camels of southern Mongolia require a certain amount of salt in order to remain in good condition. Instinctively, therefore, they browse upon the saline efflorescence which is found on the grassy plains or steppes of Asia. Baron Humboldt, in his "Aspects of Nature" (Berlin, 1808), wrote that these plains were covered with juicy, evergreen soda plants; and that many of them glistened from afar with flakes of exuded salt,

[1] *The Book of Ser Marco Polo.* London, 1874.

which much resembled newly fallen snow. When camels do not find this efflorescence, they sometimes show their craving for its saline flavor by taking white stones in their mouths, supposing them to be lumps of salt.[1]

Owing to the universality of its use, salt has been termed the " cosmopolitan condiment." The craving for this substance is not confined to man, but is shared by the lower animals, and its hygienic value for horses and cows is well known. Wild animals travel long distances over deserts and prairies, or through swamps and jungles, to reach " salt-licks."

It may be that this natural craving for salt, which is common to man and beast, may have suggested a custom of etiquette in Abyssinia. For when a native of that country desires to pay an especially delicate attention to a friend or guest, he produces a piece of rock-salt, and graciously permits the latter to lick it with his tongue ; a custom not a whit more ridiculous than the ceremonious offering of snuff and the social sneeze of modern civilization.

In certain portions of the Dark Continent salt is esteemed a great luxury, and is relished by native children quite as keenly as candy in more favored lands.

In the region of Accra, on the coast of Guinea, salt is said to rank next to gold in value; and according to

[1] Lieutenant-Colonel N. Prejevalsky, *Mongolia*, vol. i. p. 122.

Mungo Park, among the Mandingos and Bambarras, west African tribes, whose members are unusually intelligent, the phrase, "flavoring one's food with salt," implies the possession of wealth.[1]

The Namaquas, inhabitants of the Hottentot country, share so little the sentiments of their neighbors regarding salt that they consider it a superfluous article having no value whatever.

About the year 1830 there appeared in England a volume by a certain Doctor Howard, with the following curious title : "Salt, the forbidden fruit or food; and the chief cause of diseases of the body and mind of man and of animals, as taught by the ancient Egyptian priests and wise men and by scripture, in accordance with the author's experience of many years." [2]

As may well be imagined from its title, this book treats of salt as a most obnoxious substance, abstinence from which as an article of diet is essential to the maintenance of health.

The use of salt as an article of food was, moreover, thought to render one irascible and melancholic, and in illustration of this view may be quoted the following passage from "Euphues and his England," by John Lyly, Maister of Arte (1580) : —

In sooth, gentlemen, I seldome eate salte for feare of anger,

---

[1] J. J. Manley, M. A., *Salt and Other Condiments*.
[2] J. J. Manley, p. 13.

and if you give me in token that I want wit, then will you make cholericke before I eate it; for women, be they never so foolish, would ever be thought wise.

I staied not long for mine answer, but as well quickened by her former talke as desirous to cry quittance for her present tongue, said thus: "If to eat store of *salt*, cause one to fret; and to have no *salt*, signifies lack of wit, then do you cause me to marvel, that eating no *salt*, you are so captious; and loving no *salt*, you are so wise, when indeed so much wit is sufficient for a woman, as when she is in the raine can warne her to come out of it." [1]

In a recent article in the "Journal of Hygiene," the writer affirms that the general belief in the necessity of the use of salt for the maintenance of health is mischievous; for many people, in their zeal to make the most of a good thing, are wont to eat salt as a seasoner of all kinds of food. Thus an abnormal craving for the saline flavor is acquired and the condiment is used in excess, thereby unduly taxing the secretory organs, whereas in reality but a small quantity of salt is requisite. Persons addicted to the so-called "salt habit" have a perverted taste, and are naturally total failures as epicures; for how can any one assume to be a dainty feeder who disguises the true flavor of every dish, and whose palate refuses to be tickled by the choicest morsels, unless these smack strongly of salt?

But even in our times the use of salt as a relish is

---

[1] *Nares' Glossary*, vol. ii. p. 763.

sometimes deprecated as unnecessary, if not positively harmful. Thus it is argued that this substance arrests or retards the physiological processes of disintegration and renewal of the cells which compose the tissues of the living body, processes essential to the maintenance of life and health.

A recent advocate of this theory maintains that the fondness for salt shown by some domesticated animals is due to an acquired taste rather than to an instinctive craving; for dogs and cats easily grow to like such artificial products as ice-cream and beer. As to the occasional visits of wild animals to salt-licks, the fact that such visits are comparatively infrequent has been thought to prove that these animals periodically require the medicinal effects of saline waters, on the same principle which leads people of wealth and fashion to visit certain spas of Europe or America. The writer above mentioned suggests that, whereas each article of food has its own individual flavor, the addition of salt makes them all taste alike. And if an inveterate user of salt will forego this favorite condiment for a month, he will then for the first time be enabled properly to appreciate the true flavors of meats and vegetables.[1]

In the "Revelations of Egyptian Mysteries," by Robert Howard, the use of salt as a relish is character-

[1] *Cosmopolitan*, vol. xx. p. 94. 1894.

ized as an infringement of that law of nature which forbids animals to partake of mineral substances as food. History may, indeed, vouch for the antiquity of the custom, but can furnish no proof of its propriety. Indeed, the writer alleges in the above work that salt is a most pernicious substance, and the direct cause of many ills.

The idea conveyed by the phrase, "Enough is as good as a feast," applies in full force to the use of salt as a condiment, for an excess of this substance in one's food certainly spoils its flavor. According to one version of a Roumanian forest-myth, a prince, while following the chase, came upon a beautiful laurel-tree, whose branches were of a golden hue. This tree so pleased his fancy that he determined to have his dinner beneath its shade, and gave orders to that effect. Preparations were made accordingly; but during the temporary absence of the cook, a fair maiden emerged from the tree and strewed a quantity of salt upon the viands, after which she re-entered the tree, which closed over her. When the prince returned and began eating his dinner, he scolded the cook for using too much salt, and the cook quite naturally protested his innocence.

On the following day the same thing occurred, and the prince thereupon determined to keep watch, in order if possible to detect the culprit. On the third day, when the maiden came forth from the tree on mischief bent, the prince caught her and carried her away, and she became his loyal wife.[1]

This section may be appropriately concluded with the following translation of a Roman legend illustrating the value of common salt as an article of food:[2]—

The Value of Salt.   A Roman Folk-tale.

There was once a king who had three daughters, and he was very anxious to know which of them loved him most; he tried them in various ways, and it always seemed as if the youngest daughter came out best by the test. Yet he was never satisfied, because he was prepossessed with the idea that the elder ones loved him most.

One day he thought he would settle the matter once for all, by asking each separately how much she loved him. So he called the eldest by herself, and asked her how much she loved him.

"As much as the bread we eat," was her reply; and he said within himself, "She must, as I thought, love me the most of all; for bread is the first necessary of our existence, without which we cannot live. She means, therefore, that she loves me so much she could not live without me."

Then he called the second daughter by herself, and said to her, "How much do you love me?"

And she answered, "As much as wine."

"That is a good answer too," said the king to himself. "It is true she does not seem to love me quite so much as the eldest; but still, scarcely can one live without wine, so that there is not much difference."

[1] *Contemporary Review*, vol. xxxi.
[2] R. H. Busk, *Roman Legends*.

Then he called the youngest by herself, and said to her, "And you, how much do you love me?"

And she answered, "As much as salt."

Then the king said, "What a contemptible comparison! She only loves me as much as the cheapest and commonest thing that comes to the table. This is as much as to say, she does n't love me at all. I always thought it was so. I will never see her again."

Then he ordered that a wing of the palace should be shut up from the rest, where she should be served with everything belonging to her condition in life, but where she should live by herself apart, and never come near him.

Here she lived, then, all alone. But though her father fancied she did not care for him, she pined so much at being kept away from him, that at last she was worn out, and could bear it no longer.

The room that had been given her had no windows on the street, that she might not have the amusement of seeing what was going on in the town, but they looked upon an inner court-yard. Here she sometimes saw the cook come out and wash vegetables at the fountain.

"Cook, cook!" she called one day, as she saw him pass thus under the window.

The cook looked up with a good-natured face, which gave her encouragement.

"Don't you think, cook, I must be very lonely and miserable up here all alone?"

"Yes, Signorina," he replied; "I often think I should like to help you to get out; but I dare not think of it, the king would be so angry."

"No, I don't want you to do anything to disobey the king," answered the princess; "but would you really do me a favor, which would make me very grateful indeed?"

"Oh, yes, Signorina, anything which I can do without disobeying the king," replied the faithful servant.

"Then this is it," said the princess. "Will you just oblige me so far as to cook papa's dinner to-day without any salt in anything? Not the least grain in anything at all. Let it be as good a dinner as you like, but no salt in anything. Will you do that?"

"I see," replied the cook, with a knowing nod. "Yes, depend on me, I will do it."

That day at dinner the king had no salt in the soup, no salt in the boiled meat, no salt in the roast, no salt in the fried.

"What is the meaning of this?" said the king, as he pushed dish after dish away from him. "There is not a single thing I can eat to-day. I don't know what they have done to everything, but there is not a single thing that has got the least taste. Let the cook be called."

So the cook came before him.

"What have you done to the victuals to-day?" said the king sternly. "You have sent up a lot of dishes, and no one alive can tell one from another. They are all of them exactly alike, and there is not one of them can be eaten. Speak!"

The cook answered: —

"Hearing your Majesty say that salt was the commonest thing that comes to table, and altogether so worthless and contemptible, I considered in my mind whether it was a thing that at all deserved to be served up to the table of the king; and, judging that it was not worthy, I abolished it from the king's kitchen, and dressed all the meats without it. Barring this, the dishes are the same that are sent every day to the table of the king."

Then the king understood the value of salt, and he compre-

hended how great was the love of his youngest child for him;
so he sent and had her apartment opened, and called her to
him, never to go away any more.

X. THE SALT-CELLAR

The rhetorician Arnobius, in his work "Disputationes
contra Gentes," wrote that the pagans were wont to
sanctify or hallow their tables by setting salt-cellars
thereon. For owing to the fact that salt was employed
at every sacrifice as an offering to the gods, and owing
moreover to its reputed divine attributes, receptacles
containing salt were also held sacred.

Indeed, the salt-cellar partook of the nature of a
holy vessel, associated with the temple in general, and
more particularly with the altar.[1]

Pythagoras said that salt was the emblem of justice;
for as it preserves all things and prevents corruption,
so justice preserves whatever it animates, and without
it all is corrupted. He therefore directed that a salt-
cellar should be placed upon the table at every meal, in
order to remind men of this emblematic virtue of salt.[2]

The Romans considered salt to be a sacred article of
food, and it was a matter of religious principle with
them to see that no other dish was placed upon the
table before the salt was in position.[3] A shell served

[1] Schleiden, p. 73.
[2] M. Dacier, *The Life of Pythagoras*, p. 60.   London, 1707.
[3] Feu M. Jean François Buddeus, *Traité de l'athéisme et de la superstition*.

as a receptacle for salt on the table of the Roman peasant, but at the repast of the wealthy citizen the silver salt-cellar, which was usually an heirloom, was placed in the middle of the table; and the same custom prevailed in England in mediæval times.

In a work entitled "Antiquitates Culinariæ," compiled by the Rev. Richard Warner, London, 1791, are to be found, reprinted from an old paper-roll, elaborate directions for the preparation of the banquet-table on the occasion of a great feast at the enthroning of George Neville as Chancellor of England and Archbishop of York in the sixth year of Edward the Fourth, A. D. 1466.

After the laying of the "chiefe napkin," the officials of the king's household charged with such duties were directed to bring salt, bread, and trenchers, and to "set the salt right under the middest of the cloth of estate."

Minute directions follow regarding the proper disposition of the trenchers, knives, spoons, and bread, and their exact relations to the salt, which was treated with special deference throughout the ceremony.

The Hon. Horace Walpole published an account of the formalities observed at the "setting" of Queen Elizabeth's dinner-table, as described by a German traveler who was present on such an occasion. After the table-cloth had been spread two gentlemen appeared, one bearing a rod and the other having a salt-cellar, a plate, and bread. After kneeling three times with the utmost reverence, they placed these three articles upon the table and withdrew. Later in the ceremony came an unmarried lady dressed in white silk, and a matron carrying a tasting-knife. The former, having thrice prostrated herself, approached the table in the most graceful manner, and rubbed with bread and salt the plates provided for the guests. After this the yeomen of the guard, clad in scarlet, and each with a golden rose upon his back, entered bare-headed, bringing a course of four-and-twenty dishes. In the households of the English nobility a similar custom prevailed. A rhythmical code of instructions to servants of the fifteenth century required that the salt should always be the first article placed on the festive board after the cloth was laid : [1] —

> Tu dois mettre premièrement en tous lieux et en tout hostel
>   La nappe, et après le sel ;
> Cousteaulx, pain, vin et puis viande,
> Puis apporter ce qu'on demande.

In the "Haven of Health" (Thomas Coghan, London, 1636) are these verses, quoted from an earlier author :—

> Sal primo poni debet, primoque reponi,
> Omnis mensa male ponitur absque sale.

[1] Thomas Wright, *A History of Domestic Manners in England during the Middle Ages.*

A curious little treatise, with the title "How to serve a Lord," specifies how the principal salt-cellar shall be placed :—

Thenne here-uppon the boteler or panter shall bring forthe his pryncipall salte . . . he shall sette the saler in the myddys of the tabull accordyng to the place where the principall soverain shall sette . . . thenne the seconde salte att the lower ende . . . then salte selers shall be sette uppon the syde tablys.

The custom of placing salt upon the table before all else is thought to have originated in the ancient conception of this substance as the symbol of friendship; and indeed no banquet, however elaborate, was complete without it. The salt was, moreover, the last article to be removed from the hospitable board.

It was as though our forefathers thereby intended that the guests, seeing salt on the table, might realize that they were "invited in love and were loved before they came;" and the fact that it was allowed to remain after the other dishes had been removed might serve to remind them that while feasts, like many other good things, come to an end, love and friendship may be perpetual.[1]

Macrobius wrote, in the fifth century A. D., that the ancients did not consider themselves as either welcome or safe at a banquet unless the salt and the shrines of

[1] Richard Boyle. 1612.

their gods were placed upon the table; the former indicating a cordial greeting, and the latter being a guarantee of protection.

The ancient "Boke of Keruynge" says: "Than set your salt on the ryght syde where your soverayne shall sytte, and on ye lefte syde the salte set your trenchours."

Mediæval salt-cellars were often elaborate pieces of silver. In Paul Lacroix's "Manners, Customs, and Dress during the Middle Ages" are illustrations of an enameled silver salt-cellar with six facings, representing the labors of Hercules, which was made at Limoges for the French king, Francis I., in the early part of the sixteenth century. At Corpus Christi College, Cambridge, England, is preserved an elegantly wrought silver and golden salt-cellar which belonged to Matthew Parker, who was appointed Archbishop of Canterbury in 1558.[1]

In the "Art Journal" (vol. xxxix. 1887) is a description of the state salt-cellar of Mostyn Hall, Flintshire, North Wales, which had been recently discovered in an ancient chest. This magnificent piece of plate, which bears the London date-mark 1586–87, is eighteen and one half inches in height and of cylindrical form, surmounted by a vase, and richly ornamented with groups of fruit, foliage, animals, and birds.

In mediæval England the chief salt-cellar was some-

[1] Chambers's *Book of Days*.

times in the form of a silver ship, thus suggesting both
the briny deep and the craft which sails thereon.

King Henry III. ordered twenty silver salts in the
year 1243.[1]

In the room containing the crown jewels, in the
Tower of London, are to be seen eleven magnificent
golden salt-cellars, the oldest dating from the reign of
Elizabeth. Of these the so-called state salt-cellar,
which is a model of the White Tower, was presented
by the city of Exeter to King Charles II., and was
used at coronation banquets.

Descriptions and illustrations of old English salt-
cellars of different epochs are to be found in a volume
entitled "Old English Plate," by Wilfred Joseph
Cripps, M. A., F. S. A., London, 1886; and in "Old
Plate," by J. H. Buck, New York, 1888. In the former work mention is made of a magnificent salt-cellar,
"in the form of an olifaunt," the property of John,
Earl of Warrenes, in 1347; and another, "in the shape
of a dog," belonging to Edmund Mortimer, Earl of
March, in 1380.

From an early period until the close of the seventeenth century, the rank of guests at a banquet in
wealthy households, as in the halls of country squires,
in England, was indicated by the situation of their
places at table with reference to the massive silver

[1] Emily S. Holt, *Ye Olden Time*, p. 130.

centre-pieces which contained the salt,[1] sometimes called the " salt-vat " or " salt-foot."

At the head of the table, which was called *the board's end*, and " above the salt," sat the host and his more distinguished guests; and during the reigns of Henry VII. and VIII. it was enjoined upon the ushers to see that no person occupied a higher place than he was entitled to. Probably no penalty was imposed upon guests who unwittingly selected a more honorable seat than their rank warranted, other than removal to a lower position. But in the less civilized era of the eleventh century, the laws of King Canute provided that any person sitting at a banquet above his position should be " pelted out of his place by bones, at the discretion of the company, without the privilege of taking offense." [2]

In a book called " Strange Foot-Post, with a Packet full of Strange Petitions," by Nixon (London, 1613), the author says in reference to a poor scholar : —

Now, as for his fare, it is lightly at the cheapest table, but he must sit under the salt, that is an axiome in such places; then having drawne his knife leisurably, unfolded his napkin mannerly after twice or thrice wiping his beard, if he have it, he may reach the bread on his knife's point.

The " Babees Book" (1475) says : " The salt also

---

[1] Fosbroke, *Encyclopædia of Antiquities*.

[2] *Leges Curiales Regis Canuti ; apud Bartholin*, p. 583 ; J. S. Forsyth, *The Antiquary's Portfolio*. London, 1825.

touch not in his salere with nokyns mete, but lay it honestly on the Trenchoure, for that is curtesy;" and the "Young Children's Book" (1500) contains this passage: "It was not graceful to take the salt except with the clene knyfe; far less to dip your meat into the salt-cellar."

Joseph Hall, in his "Satires" (1597), speaking of the conditions imposed by a gentle squire upon his son's tutor, says that the latter was required to sleep in a trundle-bed at the foot of his young master's couch, and that his seat at table was invariably "below the salt."

Again, in a volume of "Essayes," by Sir William Cornwallis (1632), occurs the following: —

There is another sort worse than these, that never utter anything of their owne, but get jests by heart, and rob bookes and men of prettie tales, and yet hope for this to have a roome *above the salt*.

Quite apropos to our subject are the words of an old English ballad: —

> Thou art a carle of mean degree,
> Ye salt doth stand twain me and thee.

The following passage from Smyth's "Lives of the Berkeleys" refers to Lord Henry Berkeley, who dwelt in Caludon Castle, near Coventry, in Warwickshire, in the latter part of the sixteenth century, and may serve to illustrate the importance of the central salt-cellar as a boundary: —

At Christmas and other festivals when his neighbors were

feasted in his hall, he would, in the midst of their dinner, rise from his own, and going to each of their tables, cheerfully bid them welcome; and when guests of honor and high rank filled his own table, he seated himself at the lower end; and when such guests filled but half his board and those of meaner degree the other half, he would take his own seat between them in the midst of his long table *near the salt*, which gracious considerate acts did much to gain the love that his people had for him.

And in commenting on this passage a recent writer remarks that his haughty wife, Lady Katherine, high-born and beautiful and clever though she was, could hardly be imagined as sitting "below the salt," out of consideration for the feelings of an inferior.[1]

In the houses of well-to-do farmers among the Scottish peasantry in the latter part of the eighteenth century, a linen cloth was sometimes spread over the upper portion of the dinner-table, where sat the farmer and the members of his family. Quite commonly, however, a chalk-line divided this end of the board from the lower portion where the hired laborers were seated; and in the more pretentious households the salt-dish served as a boundary.[2]

In "Nares' Glossary," vol. ii. p. 763, under the heading "Above or Below the Salt," the writer comments on the invidious distinctions formerly made between

[1] Elizabeth Hodges, *Some Ancient English Homes.*
[2] Rogers, vol. i. p. 233.

guests seated at the same table, and quotes as follows from Ben Jonson's "Cynthia's Revels" in reference to a conceited fop : —

His fashion is not to take knowledge of him that is beneath him in clothes ; he never drinks below the Salt.

The Innholders Company still adheres to the custom of indicating rank and social position at table by means of a handsome salt-cellar of the time of James I., to which is assigned the responsible function of dividing the Court from the Livery at the Livery dinners; the latter occupying the seats corresponding to those of the retainers in the old-time baron's hall.[1]

Among the Puritans in New England "the salt-cellar was the focus of the old-time board." Our ancestors brought with them from beyond the sea, not only the ideas regarding table etiquette prevalent in the old country, but also such tangible vanities as silver plate. Miss Alice Morse Earle, in her book on the "Customs and Fashions of Old New England," says that the "standing salt" was often the handsomest article of table furniture, and mentions among the belongings of Comfort Starr, of Boston, in 1659, a "greate silver-gilt double salt-cellar." Early in the eighteenth century these ponderous silver vessels were superseded by the little "trencher salts," of various patterns, which are still in use.

[1] P. H. Ditchfield, M. A., F. S. A., *Old English Customs.* 1896.

THE OMENS OF SNEEZING

He is a friend at sneezing time ; the most that can be got from him is a "God bless you ! " — *Italian proverb*.

I. IN ANCIENT TIMES

THE ancient Egyptians regarded the head as a citadel or fortress in which the reasoning faculty abode.[1] Hence they especially revered any function seemingly appertaining to so noble a portion of the body, and dignified even the insignificant act of sneezing by attributing to it auguries for good or evil, according to the position of the moon with reference to the signs of the zodiac.[2] The Greeks and Romans also, by whom the most trivial occurrences of every-day life were thought to be omens of good fortune or the reverse, considered the phenomena of sneezing as not the least important in this regard. Homer tells us in the Odyssey that the Princess Penelope, troubled by

[1] Martin Schoock, *De Sternutatione Tractatus Copiosus.* Amsterdam, 1664.

[2] Joh. Gerhardus Menschen, *Disquisitio Philologica de Ritu Salutandi Sternutantes.* Kiloni. 1704.

the importunities of her suitors, prayed to the gods for the speedy return of her husband Ulysses. Scarcely was her prayer ended when her son Telemachus sneezed, and this event was regarded by Penelope as an intimation that her petition would be granted.

Aristotle said that there was a god of sneezing, and that when in Greece any business enterprise was to be undertaken, two or four sneezes were thought to be favorable. If more than four, the auspices were indifferent, while one or three rendered it hazardous to proceed.[1] About this, however, there appears to have been no unvarying rule. Sneezing at a banquet was considered by the Romans to be especially ominous; and when it unfortunately occurred, some of the viands were brought back to the table and again tasted, as this was thought to counteract any evil effects. The Greeks considered that the brain controlled the function of sneezing. They were therefore as careful to avoid eating this portion of any animal as the Pythagoreans were to avoid beans as an article of diet.[2]

It is related that just before the battle of Salamis, B. C. 480, and while Themistocles, the Athenian commander, was offering a sacrifice to the gods on the deck of his galley, a sneeze was heard on the right hand, which was hailed as a fortunate omen by Euphrantides

[1] John Potter, D. D., *Antiquities of Greece*.
[2] Francis Rous, *Archæologiæ Atticæ*. London, 1685.

the Soothsayer. Again, it happened once that while Xenophon was addressing his soldiers, referring to the righteousness of their cause and the consequent divine favor which might be expected, some one chanced to sneeze. Pausing in his address, the great general remarked that Jupiter had been pleased to send them a happy omen, and it seemed therefore but right to make an offering to the gods. Then, after all the company had joined in a hymn of thanksgiving, the sacrifice was made, and Xenophon continued with his exhortation.

Among the ancients sneezing to the right was considered fortunate and to the left unlucky. In some erotic verses with the title " Acme and Septimius," by the Roman poet, Catullus (B. C. 87–47), are these lines, twice repeated : —

> Love stood listening with delight,
> And sneezed his auspice on the right.

The omens of sneezing were thought to be of especial significance in lovers' affairs, and indeed the classic poets were wont to say of beautiful women that Love had sneezed at their birth. The Italian poet, Propertius, while asserting his enduring affection for Cynthia, the daughter of the poet Hostius, thus apostrophizes the chief theme of his eulogies: " In thy new-born days, my life, did golden Love sneeze loud and clear a favoring omen."

The Egyptians, Greeks, and Romans regarded the act

of sneezing as a kind of divinity or oracle, which warned them on various occasions as to the course they should pursue, and also foretold future good or evil.[1]

Plutarch said that the familiar spirit or demon of Socrates was simply the sneezing either of the philosopher himself or of those about him. If any person in his company sneezed on his right hand, Socrates felt encouraged to proceed with the project or enterprise which he may have had in mind. But if the sneeze were on his left hand, he abandoned the undertaking. If he himself sneezed when he was doubtful whether or not to do anything, he regarded it as evidence in the affirmative; but if he happened to sneeze after any work was already entered upon, he immediately desisted therefrom.[2] The demon, we are told, always notified him by a slight sneeze whenever his wife Xantippe was about to have a scolding fit, so that he was thus enabled opportunely to absent himself. And in so doing Socrates appears to have given proof, were any needed, of his superior wisdom; for Xantippe had been known to upset the supper-table in her anger, and that, too, when a guest was present.

On a column in the garden of the House of the Faun, at Pompeii, there is a Latin inscription which may be freely translated as follows: —

[1] *Encyclopédie méthodique.* Paris, 1788.
[2] *U. S. Literary Gazette*, vol. iv. 1826.

Victoria, good luck to thee and wherever thou wilt, sneeze pleasantly.[1]

Clement of Alexandria, in a treatise on politeness, characterizes sneezing as effeminate and as a sign of intemperance.

Probably the only Biblical reference to the subject of sneezing is in 2 Kings iv. 35, where the son of the Shunamite sneezed seven times and then revived at the prayer of Elisha.

Hor-Apollo, in his treatise on Egyptian hieroglyphics, says that the inhabitants of ancient Egypt believed that the capacity for sneezing was in inverse ratio to the size of the spleen; and they portrayed the dog as the personification of sneezing and smelling, because they believed that that animal had a very small spleen. On the other hand, they held that animals with large spleens were unable to sneeze, smell, or laugh, that is, to be open, blithe, or frank-hearted.[2]

The function of the spleen in the animal economy is not fully understood to-day. If the above theory were correct, we should expect that the removal of a dog's spleen would incite excessive sternutation and render more acute the sense of smell, whereas the only marked result of the operation is a voracious appetite. The

---

[1] Eustace Neville Rolfe, B. A., *Pompeii, Popular and Practical.* London, 1888.

[2] Gerald Massey, *The Natural Genesis*, vol. i. pp. 83-85.

theory is certainly unique, as well as illogical and absurd.

St. Augustine wrote that, in his time, so prevalent was faith in the omens of sneezing that a man would return to bed if he happened to sneeze while putting on his shoes in the morning.

The learned English prelate, Alcuin (735–804), expressed the opinion that sneezings were devoid of value as auguries except to those who placed reliance in them. But he further remarked that "it was permitted to the evil spirit, for the deceiving of persons who observe these things, to cause that in some degree prognostics should often foretell the truth." [1]

In an ancient Anglo-Saxon sermon, a copy of which is in the library of Cambridge University, England, reference is made to certain superstitions existing among the Saxons before their conversion to Christianity. The writer says: "Every one who trusts in divinations, either by fowls or by sneezings, or by horses or dogs, he is no Christian, but a notorious apostate."

II. MEDIÆVAL BELIEFS ABOUT SNEEZING

From certain ancient Welsh poems, it appears that sneezing was considered unlucky in Wales in the twelfth century; [2] but in Europe generally, in mediæval

---

[1] Henderson, p. 128.
[2] *Mélusine*, vol. iv. 1888–89.

times, the sneeze of a cat on the eve of a wedding was reckoned auspicious.[1]   In the writings of the French poet, Pierre de Ronsard (1524–85), the opinion is expressed that not to sneeze while regarding the sun is a sign of ill-luck; and from Doctor Hartlieb's "Book of all Forbidden Arts, Unbelief, and Sorcery," 1455, we learn that in Germany there was a popular belief that three sneezes indicated the presence of four thieves around the house.

Jerome Cardan, the noted Italian philosopher and physician (1501–76), in speaking of genii or familiar spirits, remarked that, in his opinion, sneezing was a supernatural phenomenon, and, like the sound of ringing in the ears, was premonitory of some event of importance.[2]

Some idea of the credulous notions on the subject of sneezing which were prevalent in England during Queen Elizabeth's reign may be obtained from the following extracts from the "Burghley Papers," Lansdowne MSS. (No. 121) in the British Museum.[3]

1. If that any man talk with another about any matter and snese twise or iiij tymes, let him by and by arise, yf he sett, or yf he be stand, let him move hymself and go straightway without any stays about his business, for he shall prosper.

[1] William Jones, *Credulities.*

[2] John Beaumont, Gent., *A Treatise of Spirits.*   London, 1705.

[3] *Twelfth Annual Report of the Thirteen Club of New York,* January, 1894.   The writer has also consulted the original manuscript.

2. Yf he snese more than iiij tymes, let him staye, for it is doubtful how he shall spede.

3. Yf a man snese one or iij tymes, let him proceed no further in any matter, but let all alone, for it shall com to nought.

4. Yf two men do snese bothe at one instant, yt is a good syne, and let them go about their purpose, yf that it be either by water or land, and they shall prosper.

5. To snese twise is a good syne, but to snese once or iij times is an yll syne. If one come suddenly into an house and snese one tyme, yt is a good token.

6. One snese in the night season made by any of the household betokenyth good luck to the house, but yf he make two sneses, yt signifieth domage.

7. Trewe yt is that he who snesith takit pte (part) of the signification in this condition, that he pte some pte with other.

8. Yf that any man snese twyse iij nightes together, it is a tokyn that one of the house shall dye, or else some greatt goodness or badness shall happon in the house.

9. Yf a man go to dwell in an house and snese one tyme, lett him dwell there, but yf he snese twyse, lett him not tarry, neither let him dwell therein.

10. Yf a man lye awake in his bedd and snese one tyme, it is a syne of some great sickness or hyndraunce.

11. Yf a man sleape in his bedde and snese one tyme, it betokenyth greatt trouble, the death of some person or extreme hyndraunce in the loss of substaunce.

12. Yf a man lye in his bedde and make a snese one tyme, it is a good syne both of health and lucre, but if he sleape it is moche better.

13. Yf a man snese twyse three nights together, it is a good syne, whatsoever he go aboutt.

14. Yf a man travell by the ways and come into an Inne and snese twyse, let him departe out of the house and go to another or else he shall not prosper.

15. Yf a man go forthe to seke worke and laye hands of it and then snese one tyme, let hym departe, leaving his worke behind hym, and seke worke elsewhere, and so shall do well; but yf he snese twyse let hym take his worke and go no further.

16. If any man, after he haue made a bargayne with another for any thing and then snese one tyme, it signifieth that his bargayne will not continue.

17. Yf a man rise betymes on a Monday mornyng out of his bedd and snese one tyme, yt is a token that he shall prosper and gayne all that week, or haue some other joye and comoditie.

18. But yf he snese twyse, yt is cleane contrary.

19. Yf a man lose a horse or anything els, and is stopping (*sic*) out of his dore to seke it, do snese one tyme, yt is a token he shall haue it agayne, but yf he snese twyse he shall never haue it agayne.

20. Yf a man ryse betyme on a Sonday and snese ii tymes, yt is a good tokyn, but if he snese one tyme, it is an yll tokyn.

21. Yf a man at the very beginning of dinner or supper be minded to eat, and snese twyse, yt is a good tokyn, but yf he snese one time, yt is an yll syne.

22. Yf a man lye sicke in bed and mystrusts himselfe, and snese one tyme, yt is a tokyn of deathe, but if he snese twyse he shall escape.

23. A woman being very sicke, yf she snese one tyme, yt is a syne of health, but if she snese twyse, she shall-dye.

III. MODERN SUPERSTITIONS ABOUT SNEEZING

Sneezing at the commencement of an undertaking, whether it be an important enterprise or the most commonplace act, has usually been accounted unlucky. Thus, according to a modern Teutonic belief, if a man sneeze on getting up in the morning, he should lie down again for another three hours, else his wife will be his master for a week.[1] So likewise the pious Hindu, who may perchance sneeze while beginning his morning ablutions in the river Ganges, immediately recommences his prayers and toilet; and among the Alfoorans or aborigines of the island of Celebes in the Indian archipelago, if one happens to sneeze when about leaving a gathering of friends, he at once resumes his seat for a while before making another start.[2]

When a native of the Banks Islands, in Polynesia, sneezes, he imagines that some one is calling his name, either with good or evil intent, the motive being shown by the character of the sneeze. Thus a gentle sneeze implies kindly feeling on the part of the person speaking of him, while a violent paroxysm indicates a malediction.

In the latter case he resorts to a peculiar form of divination in order to ascertain who it is that curses

[1] Grimm's *Teutonic Mythology*.
[2] A. Featherman, *The Social History of the Races of Mankind*.

him.   This consists in raising the arms above the head
and revolving the closed fists one around the other.
The revolution of the fists is the question, "Is it such
an one?"   Then the arms are thrown out, and the
answer, presumably affirmative, is given by the cracking of the elbow-joints.[1]

In Scotland even educated people have been known
to maintain that idiots are incapable of sneezing,[2] and
hence, if this be true, the inference is clear that the
act of sternutation is *prima facie* evidence of the
possession of a certain degree of intelligence.

British nurses used to think that infants were under
a fairy spell until they sneezed.   "God sain the bairn,"
exclaimed an old Scotch nurse when her little charge
sneezed at length, "it's no a warlock."

The Irish people also entertain similar beliefs.   Thus
in Lady Wilde's " Ancient Cures, Charms, and Usages
of Ireland " (p. 41) is to be found the following description of a magical ceremony for the cure of a fairy-
stricken child.   A good fire is made, wherein is thrown
a quantity of certain herbs prescribed by the fairy
women; and after a thick smoke has risen, the child is
carried thrice around the fire while an incantation is
repeated and holy water is sprinkled about liberally.
Meantime all doors must be closed, lest some inquisitive

---

[1] R. H. Codrington, D. D., *The Melanesians.*
[2] *Notes and Queries,* 1st series, vol. xii.

fairy enter and spy upon the proceedings; and the magical rites must be continued *until the child sneezes three times*, for this looses the spell, and the little one is permanently redeemed from the power of witches.

Among uncivilized peoples the sneeze of a young child has a certain mystic significance, and is intimately associated with its prospective welfare or ill-luck. When, therefore, a Maori infant sneezes, its mother immediately recites a long charm of words. If the sneeze occurs during a meal, it is thought to be prognostic of a visit, or of some interesting piece of news; whereas in Tonga it is deemed an evil token.

So, too, among the New Zealanders, if a child sneeze on the occasion of receiving its name, the officiating priest at once holds to its ear the wooden image of an idol and sings some mystic words.

In a note appended to his "Mountain Bard," the Ettrick Shepherd says, regarding the superstitions of Selkirkshire: "When they sneeze in first stepping out of bed in the morning, they are thence certified that strangers will be there in the course of the day, in numbers corresponding to the times they sneeze." [1]

It was a Flemish belief that a sneeze during a conversation proved that what one said was the truth,[2] a

[1] Rev. Charles Rogers, LL. D., F. S. A., *Scotland, Social and Domestic.*
[2] Alexandre Desrousseaux, *Mœurs populaires de la Flandre française.*

doctrine which must have commended itself to snuff-takers.

In Shetlandic and Welsh folk-lore the sneeze of a cat indicates cold north winds in summer and snow in winter; [1] and the Bohemians have an alleged infallible test for recognizing the Devil, for they believe that he must perforce sneeze violently at sight of a cross. [2]

According to a Chinese superstition a sneeze on New Year's Eve is ominous for the coming year; and, to offset this, the sneezer must visit three families of different surnames, and beg from each a small tortoise-shaped cake, which must be eaten before midnight. [3]

In Turkistan, when a person to whom a remark is addressed sneezes, it is an asseveration that the opinion or statement is correct, just as if the person accosted were to exclaim, "That is true!" In the same country three sneezes are unlucky. When, also, any one hiccoughs, it is etiquette to say, "You stole something from me," and this phrase at such times is supposed to produce good luck. [4]

The Japanese attach significance to the number of times a man sneezes. Thus, one sneeze indicates that some one is praising him, while two betoken censure or disparagement; a triple sneeze is commonplace, and

[1] *Gentleman's Magazine*, vol. 252, p. 237. January, 1882.
[2] Wuttke, p. 243.
[3] *Philadelphia Inquirer*, February 24, 1898.
[4] Eugene Schuyler, *Turkistan*, p. 29.

means simply that a person has taken cold.[1]   In Mexico, also, it was formerly believed either that somebody was speaking evil of one who sneezed, or that he was being talked about by one or more persons.[2]

Sussex people are prejudiced against cats which develop sneezing proclivities, for they believe that, when a pet feline sneezes thrice, it augurs ill for the health of the household, and is premonitory of influenza and bronchial affections.[3]

In an interesting article in " Macmillan's Magazine," entitled " From the Note-book of a Country Doctor,"[4] a physician practicing in a remote part of Cornwall tells of a peculiar cure for deafness which recently came to his notice.

One of his patients, an elderly woman whose name was Grace Rickard, complained that she could no longer hear the grunting of her pigs, a sound which, from childhood, had roused her from sleep in the early morning.   The doctor was obliged to tell her that the difficulty was due to advancing years.

A short time after, on calling at her house, he found her sitting before the fire with a piece of board in her lap, and deeply absorbed in thought.   Just as the door opened, she exclaimed : " Lord, deliver me from my

---

[1] Griffis, *Japan*, p. 187.
[2] *Journal of American Folk-Lore*, vol. x. p. 272. 1897.
[3] Henderson, p. 206.
[4] Vol. 73, pp. 41, 42. 1896.

sins," and this petition was followed by a peculiar noise
which sounded like an abortive sneeze. "Don't be
frited, zur," she said, " 't es aunly a sneeze." "It's
the oddest sneeze I ever heard," said the doctor; "why
can't you sneeze in the ordinary way?" "So I do,
when I can," she explained; "but now 't es got up to
nine times running, and wherever to get nine sneezes
from is moor 'n I knaw."

It appeared that Grace was making trial of an infallible cure for deafness, the necessary apparatus for
which consisted of a piece of board and some stout
pins. One of the latter is stuck into the board every
morning, the patient's forefingers being crossed over
the pin, while the pious ejaculation above mentioned is
repeated simultaneously with a vigorous sneeze. On
the next morning two pins must be stuck in the board,
the petition and sneeze being once repeated; on the
following morning three pins, three prayers, and three
sneezes, and so on up to nine times.

IV. THE DOCTRINE OF DEMONIACAL POSSESSION

The natural instinct of the untutored savage is to
regard the act of sneezing as the manifestation of
an attack by a demon. Certain African tribes, for
instance, are said to believe that whoever sneezes is
possessed of an evil spirit, to whose malicious agency
is due the violence of the paroxysm and its utter disregard of times and seasons.

Dr. Edward B. Tylor, in his "Primitive Culture" (vol. i. p. 97), asserts that the Zulus have faith in the agency of kindly spirits as well, and says that, when one of these people sneezes, he is wont to exclaim: "I am now blessed; the ancestral spirit is with me. Let me hasten and praise it, for it is that which causes me to sneeze." Thereupon he praises the spirits of the dead, and asks for various blessings. But among most uncivilized peoples sneezing is placed in the category of paroxysmal diseases, and reckoned to be of demoniac origin.

Inasmuch as sneezing is often one symptom of an incipient cold, which is a physical ailment, and as among savage tribes every physical ailment is regarded as a case of demoniacal possession, the use of charms and exorcisms to counteract the efforts of the evil spirits seems a natural expedient.[1]

When an American Indian falls sick, he believes his illness to be the work of some spiteful demon. Therefore, when he gets well, he changes his name, so that the demon may not be able to recognize him again.[2]

The chief aim of the medicine-man, in treating a patient, is the expulsion of the evil spirit; and this is the prime object of the various superstitious cere-

[1] *Cornhill Magazine*, vol. 76.
[2] Lecture by Dr. D. G. Brinton, at the Lowell Institute, Boston, Mass., November 9. 1896.

monies and incantations which are a prominent feature in medical practice among savages.[1] The medicine-man strives to drive away the demon by frightful sounds and gesticulations, and by hideous grimaces and contortions. Sometimes he makes a small image typifying the spirit of sickness, and this image is then maliciously broken in pieces.[2]

The natives of West Africa believe that the mere mention of unpleasant names suffices to frighten away the demons who cause sickness; and these spirits may moreover be deceived by simply changing the name of a sick child. In the province of Tonquin, a French possession in southeastern Asia, hateful names given to ailing children are likewise thought to terrify the evil spirits; but when the little patients are convalescent, pleasanter names are substituted.[3]

The Indians of Nootka Sound, Vancouver Island, attribute physical ailments either to the absence or irregular conduct of the soul, or to the agency of spirits, and medical practice is governed accordingly; therefore the Okanogons of the State of Washington subject patients affected with serious illnesses to the magical treatment of the medicine-man.[4]

The islanders of the South Pacific have their own

[1] Elijah M. Haines, *The American Indian*, p. 416.
[2] D. G. Brinton, *Myths of the New World*, p. 307.
[3] Andree, *Ethnographische Parallelen*, p. 177.
[4] Herbert Spencer, *Principles of Sociology*, vol. iii. p. 186.

doctrine about the philosophy of sneezing. They
believe that, when the spirit goes traveling about, its
return naturally occasions some commotion, as is evident from the violent act of sneezing. They therefore
deem it proper to welcome back the wandering spirit,
the form of greeting varying in the different islands.
The phrase employed by the natives of Raratonga, for
example, means " Ha ! you have come back ! " [1]

The " Sadda," one of the sacred books of the
Parsees, counsels the faithful to have recourse to
prayer when they sneeze, because at that critical moment the demon is especially active.

The Parsees regard sneezing as a manifestation that
the evil spirits, who are constantly seeking to enter the
body, have been forcibly expelled by the interior fire
which, in their belief, animates every human being.
When, therefore, a Parsee hears any one sneeze, he
exclaims, " Blessed be Ormuzd ! " thus praising his
chief deity. The Parsees are forbidden to talk while
eating, because at such times demons are on the alert,
watching for opportunities to gain admission to the
body through the mouth while a person is engaged in
conversation.[2]

Pious Brahmins are careful to touch the right ear

[1] Rev. William Wyatt Gill, B. A., *Myths and Songs from the South Pacific.*

[2] L. Maria Child, *The Progress of Religious Ideas*, vol. i. p. 276.

when they happen to sneeze either during the performance of a religious ceremony or at certain other times specified in the "Shastra," or holy books of the Hindus. Evil spirits were believed to enter the body through the ears, as well as by the nose or mouth, and the object of touching the ear was to prevent their gaining admission there.

In reference to this subject, Gerald Massey says, in the "Natural Genesis" (vol. i. pp. 83–85):—

Sneezing is not only a vigorous form of breathing, but it is involuntary; hence inspired, or of extraordinary origin. A hearty sneeze, when one is ill and faint, would imply a sudden accession of the breathing power, which was inwardly inspiring and outwardly expelling. The good spirit enters and the bad spirit departs, cast out by the sudden impulsion. The expulsion and repudiation implied in sneezing is yet glanced at in the saying that such a thing is "not to be sneezed at."

The natives of Turkistan consider yawning to be a reprehensible act, originating from an evil place in one's heart, and indicative of a state of preparedness for the reception of demons. When, therefore, they yawn, the hand is placed, palm outwards, before the open mouth, thus barring out the demons.[1]

The once popular opinion, which is still met with to-day, that the efficacy of a medicine is proportionate to

[1] Schuyler, *Turkistan*, p. 29.

its harshness of flavor, is probably a relic of the ancient
theory which attributed illnesses to possession by evil
spirits. When one's body was believed to be the
abode of such a spirit, the natural desire was to drive
out the unwelcome visitor, and to force him to seek
some other habitation. Nowadays we have so far
abandoned this theory that, while we may have faith
in the virtues of bitter herbs, we are ready to welcome
also the palatable remedies of the modern pharmacopœia ; but until comparatively recent times the science
of therapeutics was dominated by superstition, and
physicians prescribed remedies composed of the most
repulsive and uncanny ingredients.

In Tibet antiseptics are employed in surgical operations, the rationale of their use in that country being
the preservation of the wound from evil spirits ; and
when smallpox rages in the neighborhood of the city
of Leh, capital of the province of Ladakh, the country
people seek to ward off the epidemic by placing
thorns on their bridges and at their boundary lines.[1]
This practice is strikingly analogous in principle to
some of the superstitious uses of iron and steel in the
form of sharp instruments, of which mention has been
made elsewhere in this volume.

The aboriginal Tibetans ascribe illnesses to the spite
of demons, and hence a chief object of their religious

[1] Isabella L. Bishop, *Among the Tibetans*, p. 104.

rites is the pacification of these malignant beings by the sacrifice of a cow, pig, goat, or other animal.[1]

Throughout Christendom it is customary for those present to invoke the divine blessing upon a person who sneezes, and the Moslem, under like circumstances, prays to Allah for aid against the powers of evil. In either case the underlying idea appears to be the same, namely, the doctrine of invading spirits.

In ancient Egypt illnesses were thought to be caused by demons who had somehow entered the patient's body and taken up their abode there; and the Chaldean physicians, actuated by the same belief, were wont to prescribe the most nauseating medicines in order to thoroughly disgust the demon in possession, and thus enforce his departure.[2]

This doctrine of spiritual possession was formerly even supposed to be warranted by Scripture, and especially by a verse of the 141st Psalm: "Set a watch, O Lord, before my mouth; keep the door of my lips." This passage was interpreted as an entreaty for preservation from evil spirits, who were likely to enter the body through the mouth,[3] especially during the acts of yawning, sneezing, talking, and eating. The Hindus consider yawning as dangerous for this reason, and

---

[1] Rev. J. A. Graham, M. A., *On the Threshold of Three Closed Lands*, p. 76.

[2] G. Maspero, *The Dawn of Civilization.* 1894.

[3] Professor E. P. Evans, *Popular Science Monthly*, November, 1895.

hence the practice of mouth-washing, which is a part
of their daily ritual. Hence also their custom of
cracking their fingers and exclaiming " Great God!"
after yawning, to intimidate the *Bhúts*, or malignant
spirits. Sneezing is usually accounted lucky in India,
except at the commencement of an undertaking, because it means the expulsion of a *Bhút*.[1]

Josephus relates having seen a Jew named Eleazar
exorcise devils from people who were possessed, in the
presence of the Emperor Vespasian and many of his
soldiers. His mode of procedure consisted in applying
to the demoniac's nose a ring containing a piece of the
root of a magical herb, and then withdrawing the evil
spirit through the nostrils, meanwhile repeating certain
incantations originally composed by Solomon.

V. SALUTATION AFTER SNEEZING

The origin of the benediction after sneezing, a custom well-nigh universal, is involved in obscurity. A
popular legend says that, before the time of Jacob, men
sneezed but once, as the shock proved fatal. The patriarch, however, obtained by intercession a relaxation
of this law, on condition that every sneeze should be
consecrated by an ejaculatory prayer.[2] According to
a well-known myth of classical antiquity, Prometheus

---

[1] W. Crooke, B. A., *Popular Religion and Folk-Lore of Northern India.*
[2] S. Baring Gould, *Legends of the Patriarchs and Prophets.*

formed of clay the model of a man, and desiring to animate the lifeless figure, was borne to heaven by the Goddess Minerva, where he filled a reed with celestial fire stolen from a wheel of the Sun's chariot. Returning then to earth, he applied the magical reed to the nostrils of the image, which thereupon became a living man, and began its existence by sneezing. Prometheus, delighted with his success, uttered a fervent wish for the welfare of his newly formed creature. The latter thenceforward always repeated aloud the same benediction whenever he heard any one sneeze, and enjoined upon his children the same practice, which was thus transmitted to succeeding generations.

Famianus Strada, the Italian Jesuit historian (1572–1649), in his "Prolusiones Academicæ," relates that one day, when Cicero was present at a performance of the Roman opera, he began to sneeze, whereupon the entire audience, irrespective of rank, arose and with one accord cried out, "God bless you!" or, as the common phrase was, "May Jupiter be with thee!" Whereat three young men named Fannius, Fabalus, and Lemniscus, who were lounging in one of the boxes, began an animated discussion in regard to the antiquity of this custom, which all believed to have originated with Prometheus.[1]

Even in the time of Aristotle, salutation after sneez-

[1] *The Catholic World.* vol. iii. 1866.

ing was considered an ancient custom;[1] and references
to it are to be found in the writings of Roman authors.
Pliny narrates in his "Natural History" that the
Emperor Tiberius Cæsar, who was known as one of
the most melancholy and unsociable of men, scrupu-
lously exacted a benediction from his attendants whenever he sneezed, whether in his palace or while driving
in his chariot; and Apuleius, the platonic philosopher
of the second century, alludes to the subject in his
story of "The Fuller's Wife."

Although the fact of the existence of this custom
centuries before the Christian era is beyond cavil, yet a
very general popular belief attributes its origin to a
much later period. The Italian historian, Carlo Sigonio,
voices this belief in his statement that the practice
began in the sixth century, during the pontificate of
Gregory the Great. At this period a virulent pestilence
raged in Italy, which proved fatal to those who sneezed.
The Pope, therefore, ordered prayers to be said against
it, accompanied by certain signs of the cross.[2] And
the people were wont also to say to those who sneezed,
"God help ye!"[3] a revival of a custom dating back to
prehistoric times.

Again, Jacobus de Voragine (1230–98) wrote as

[1] Brand's *Popular Antiquities of Great Britain.*
[2] *Encyclopædia of Arts and Sciences.* Philadelphia, 1798.
[3] Pedro Mexio, *The Treasurie of Auncient and Moderne Times.* 1613.

follows in the "Golden Legend," a popular religious
work of the Middle Ages:—

For a right grete and grevous maladye: for as the Romayns
had in the lenton lyved sobrely and in contynence, and after
at Ester had receyvd theyr Savyour; after they disordered
them in etyng, in drynkyng, in playes, and in lecherye. And
therefore our Lord was meuyed ayenst them and sent them
a grete pestelence, which was called the Botche of impedymye,
and that was cruell and sodayne, and caused peple to dye
in goyng by the waye, in pleying, in leeyng atte table, and
in spekyng one with another sodeynly they deyed. In this
manere somtyme snesyng they deyed; so that whan any per-
sone was herd snesyng, anone they that were by said to hym,
God helpe you, or *Cryst helpe*, and yet endureth the custome.
And also whan he sneseth or gapeth, he maketh to fore his
face the signe of the crosse and blessith hym. And yet
endureth this custome.

The Icelander, when he sneezes, says, "God help
me!" and to another person who sneezes he says,
"God help you!" In Icelandic tradition the custom
dates from a remote period, when the Black Pest raged
virulently in portions of the country, and the mortality
therefrom was great. At length the scourge reached a
certain farm where lived a brother and sister, and they
observed that the members of the household who suc-
cumbed to the disease were first attacked by a violent
paroxysm of sneezing; therefore they were wont to exclaim "God help me!" when they themselves sneezed.

Of all the inhabitants of that district, these two were the only ones who survived the pest, and hence the Icelanders, throughout succeeding generations, have continued the pious custom thus originated.[1]

In mediæval German poetry are to be found occasional references to this subject, as in the following passage quoted in Grimm's "Teutonic Mythology:" " The pagans durst not sneeze, even though one should say, ' God help thee.' " And in the same work allusion is made to a quaint bit of fairy - lore about enchanted sprites sneezing under a bridge, that some one may call out " God help," and undo the spell.

In the year 1542 the Spanish explorer, Hernando de Soto, received a visit in Florida from a native chief named Guachoya, and during their interview the latter sneezed. Immediately his attendants arose and saluted him with respectful gestures, at the same time saying: " May the Sun guard thee, be with thee, enlighten thee, magnify thee, protect thee, favor thee," and other similar good wishes. And the Spaniards who were present were impressed by the fact that, in connection with sneezing, even more elaborate ceremonies were observed by savage tribes than those which obtained among civilized nations. And hence they reasoned that such observances were natural and instinctive with all mankind.[2] We have the testimony of the earliest

[1] *Legends of Iceland*, collected by Jon Arnason, 2d series, p. 646.
[2] Edward B. Tylor, *Primitive Culture.*

English explorers that the custom of salutation after sneezing was common in the remotest portions of Africa and in the far East. Speke and Grant were unable to discover any trace of religion among the natives of equatorial Africa, except in their practice of uttering an Arabic ejaculation or prayer whenever a person sneezed.[1]

The Portuguese traveler, Godinho, wrote that whenever the emperor of Monomotapa sneezed, acclamations were universal throughout his realm; and in Guinea in the last century, whenever a person of rank sneezed, every one present knelt down, clapped their hands, and wished him every blessing. The courtiers of the king of Sennaar in Nubia are wont on the occasion of a royal sneeze to turn their backs on their sovereign while vigorously slapping the right hip.[2] Among the Zulu tribes, sneezing is viewed as a favorable symptom in a sick person, and the natives are accustomed to return thanks after it. In Madagascar, when a child sneezes, its mother invokes the divine blessing, conformably to European usage; and in Persia the sneezer is the recipient of congratulations and good wishes.

In the " Zend-Avesta," or sacred writings of the Persian religion, is the injunction: " And whensoever

---

[1] *Temple Bar*, vol. 43. 1875.
[2] *Dictionnaire des sciences occultes.*

it be that thou hearest a sneeze given by thy neighbor, thou shalt say unto him, *Ahunavar Ashim-Vuhu*, and so shall it be well with thee." [1] In Egypt, if a man sneeze, he says, " Praise be to God ! " and all present, with the exception of servants, rejoin, " God have mercy upon you ! " [2]

The Omahas, Dakotas, and other Sioux tribes of American Indians attach a peculiar importance to sneezing. Thus, if one of their number sneeze once, he believes that his name has been called either by his son, his wife, or some intimate friend. Hence he at once exclaims, " My son ! " But if he sneeze twice, he says, " My son and his mother ! " [3]

In France the rules of etiquette formerly required that a gentleman who sneezed in the presence of another should take off his hat, and on the subsidence of the paroxysm he was expected formally to return the salutes of all present. The salutation of sneezers by removal of the hat was customary in England also. Joseph Hall, who was Bishop of Exeter in 1627, wrote that when a superstitious man sneezed he did not reckon among his friends those present who failed to uncover.

The Italians are wont to salute the sneezer with the

[1] William S. Walsh, *Handy-Book of Literary Curiosities.*
[2] Edward William Lane, *The Modern Egyptians.*
[3] James Owen Dorsey, " A Study of Siouan Cults," *Eleventh Annual Report of the Bureau of Ethnology,* Washington, D. C.

ejaculation *Viva,* or *Felicità ;* and it has been reasoned that the latter expression may have been sometimes employed under like circumstances by the ancient Romans, because an advertisement on the walls of Pompeii concludes by wishing the people Godspeed with the single word *Felicitas !*

So, too, in Ireland the sneezer is greeted with fervent benedictions, such as, " The blessing of God and the holy Mary be upon you! " for such invocations are thought to counteract the machinations of evil-disposed fairies.[1]

The Siamese have a unique theory of their own on this subject. They believe that the Supreme Judge of the spiritual world is continually turning over the pages of a book containing an account of the life and doings of every human being; and when he comes to the page relating to any individual, the latter never fails to sneeze. In this way the Siamese endeavor to give a plausible reason for the prevalence of sneezing among men, and also for the accompanying salutation. In Siam and Laos the ordinary expression is, " May the judgment be favorable to you." [2]

In the Netherlands a person who sneezes is believed thereby to place himself in the power of a witch, unless some one invokes a divine blessing; and such notions

[1] Lady Wilde's *Ancient Cures, Charms, and Usages of Ireland.*
[2] M. l'Abbé Bertram, *Dictionnaire de toutes les religions.*

afford a plausible explanation of one theory of the origin of this custom.[1]

Grimm (vol. iv. p. 1637) refers to a passage in the "Avadanas," or Buddhist parables, in which the rat is represented as wishing the cat joy when she sneezes. And in the department of Finistere in northwest France, when a horse sneezes or coughs the people say, "May St. Eloy assist you!" St. Eloy was the guardian of farriers and the tutelar god of horses.[2]

The natives of the Fiji Islands exclaim after a sneeze, "*Mbula*," that is, "May you live!" or "Health to you!" And the sneezer politely responds with "*Mole*," "Thanks." Formerly Fijian etiquette was yet more exacting and required the sneezer to add, "May you club some one!" or "May your wife have twins!"[3]

A Spanish writer, Juan Cervera Bachiller, in his book "Creencias y superstitiones," Madrid, 1883, says that this widely diffused practice appears to have originated partly from religious motives and partly from gallantry, and that it is as obviously a relic of pagan times as are the various omens which have ever been associated with sneezing.

The apparently independent origin of the custom of

[1] *Cornhill Magazine*, vol. 76.
[2] Brand, vol. i. p. 361.
[3] C. F. Gordon-Cumming, *At Home in Fiji*, p. 105.

salutation after sneezing among nations remote from
each other, and its prevalence from time immemorial
alike in the most cultured communities and among
uncivilized races, have been thought to furnish striking
evidence of the essential similarity of human minds,
whatever their environment.

VI. LEGENDS RELATING TO SNEEZING

In the traditional lore of ancient Picardy is the following legend : —

In the vicinity of Englebelmer nocturnal wayfarers
were often surprised at hearing repeated sneezes by the
roadside, and the young people of the neighboring villages made frequent attempts to ascertain the origin of
the mysterious sounds, but without avail. The mischievous spirit or *lutin* took pleasure in seeing them
run about in a vain search while he himself remained
invisible. Finally people became accustomed to hearing these phantom sneezes, and, as no harm had ever
resulted to any one, with the contempt bred of familiarity they gave little heed to the spiritual manifestations,
and were content with merely crossing themselves devoutly.

One fine moonlight evening in summer a peasant
returning from market heard the usual *Atchi, atchi,*
but pursued his way with equanimity. However, the
lutin pursued him for about a mile, sneezing repeat-

edly. At length the peasant impatiently exclaimed, "May the good Lord bless you and your cold in the head!" Scarcely had he spoken when there appeared before him the apparition of a man clad in a long white garment. "Thank you, my friend," said he; "you have just released me from the spell under which I have long rested. In consequence of my sins, God condemned me to wander about this village sneezing without rest from eve till morn, until some charitable person should deliver me by saying a benediction. For at least five hundred years I have thus roamed about, and you are the first one who has said to me 'God bless you.' Fortunately it occurred to me to follow you, and thus I have been set free. I thank you. Good-by."

Thereafter the mysterious sounds were no longer heard; and thus, in the belief of the peasants of Picardy, arose the custom of salutation after sneezing.[1]

Under a bridge near the town of Paderborn, in Prussia, there lives a poor soul who does nothing but sneeze at frequent intervals. If a wagon happens to pass over the bridge at the moment when a sneeze is heard, and the driver fails to say "God help thee," the vehicle will surely be overturned, and the driver will become poor and break his leg.

Tradition says that a godless fellow who died long

[1] E. Henry Carnay, *Litterature orale de la Picardie.* Paris, 1883.

ago of incessant sneezing, during an epidemic of the
plague at Wurmlingen in Würtemberg, was condemned
on account of his sins to wander about the neighborhood, still sneezing at intervals.   One day, while one
of the villagers was crossing a bridge over some mead-
ows near the town, he heard some one underneath
sneeze twice, and each time he piously responded, "God
help thee ! "   When, however, he heard a third sneeze,
the villager thought to himself, "That fellow may keep
on sneezing for a long time and make a fool of me."
So he cried out angrily, " May the Devil help you ! "
Thereupon a voice from under the bridge exclaimed
pitifully, "If you had only said, ' God help thee ! ' a
third time, I should have been freed from the spell
which binds me." [1]

[1] Ernst Meier, *Deutsche Sagen, Sitten und Gebräuche aus Schwaben.*
Stuttgart, 1852.

DAYS OF GOOD AND EVIL OMEN

Friday's moon,
Come when it will, it comes too soon.
Proverb.

I. EGYPTIAN DAYS

THE belief in lucky and unlucky days appears to have been first taught by the magicians of ancient Chaldea, and we learn from history that similar notions affected every detail of primitive Babylonian life, thousands of years before Christ. Reference to an " unlucky month " is to be found in a list of deprecatory incantations contained in a document from the library of the royal palace at Nineveh. This document is written in the Accadian dialect of the Turanian language, which was akin to that spoken in the region of the lower Euphrates ; a language already obsolete and unintelligible to the Assyrians of the seventh century B. C.[1] Certain days were called *Dies Egyptiaci*, because they were thought to have been pronounced unlucky by the astrologers of ancient Egypt.

In that country the unlucky days were, however,

[1] François Lenormant, *Chaldean Magic.*

fewer in number than the fortunate ones, and they also
differed in the degree of their ill-luck. Thus, while
some were markedly ominous, others merely threatened
misfortune, and still others were of mixed augury,
partly good and partly evil. There were certain days
upon which absolute idleness was enjoined upon the
people, when they were expected to sit quietly at home,
indulging in *dolce far niente*.[1]

The poet Hesiod, who is believed to have flourished
about one thousand years B. C., in the third book of
his poem, "Works and Days," which is indeed a kind
of metrical almanac, distinguishes lucky days from
others, and gives advice to farmers regarding the most
favorable days for the various operations of agriculture.
Thus he recommends the eleventh of the month as
excellent for reaping corn, and the twelfth for shearing
sheep. But the thirteenth was an unlucky day for
sowing, though favorable for planting. The fifth of
each month was an especially unfortunate day, while
the thirtieth was the most propitious of all.

Some of the most intelligent and learned Greeks
were very punctilious in their observance of Egyptian
days. The philosopher Proclus (A. D. 412–485) was
said to be even more scrupulous in this regard than the
Egyptians themselves. And Plotinus (A. D. 204–270),
another eminent Grecian philosopher, believed with the

---

[1] Adolf Erman, *Life in Ancient Egypt*, p. 351.

astrologers of a later day, that the positions of the
planets in the heavens exerted an influence over human
affairs.[1]

In an ancient calendar of the year 334, in the reign
of Constantine the Great, twenty-six Egyptian days
were designated.[2]   At an early period, however, the
church authorities forbade the superstitious observance
of these days.

Some of the most eminent early writers of the Christian Church, St. Ambrose, St. Augustine, and St. Chry-
sostom, were earnest in their denunciation of the prevalent custom of regulating the affairs of life by reference
to the supposed omens of the calendar.   The fourth
council of Carthage, in 398, censured such practices;
and the synod of Rouen, in the reign of Clovis,
anathematized those who placed faith in such relics of
paganism.[3]

We learn on the authority of Marco Polo that the
Brahmins of the province of Laristan, in southern
Persia, in the thirteenth century, were extremely punctilious in their choice of suitable days for the performance of any business matters.   This famous traveler
wrote that a Brahmin who contemplated making a
purchase, for example, would measure the length of his

[1] F. Chabas, *le calendrier des jours fastes et néfastes et de l'année egyp-
tienne,* p. 124.

[2] M. Court de Gebelin, *Monde primitif,* vol. iv.   Paris, 1776.

[3] Jean Baptiste Thiers, *Traité des superstitions.*   Paris, 1679.

own shadow in the early morning sunlight, and if the
shadow were of the proper length, as officially prescribed for that day, he would proceed to make the
purchase; otherwise he would wait until the shadow
conformed in length to a predetermined standard for
that day of the week.

The Latin historian, Rolandino (1200–76), in the
third book of his "Chronicle," describes an undertaking which resulted disastrously because, as was alleged,
it was rashly begun on an "Egyptian day." There is
frequent mention of these days in many ancient manuscripts in the Ambrosian Library at Milan.[1]

In a so-called "Book of Precedents," printed in
1616, fifty-three days are specified as being "such as
the Egyptians noted to be dangerous to begin or take
anything in hand, or to take a journey or any such
thing." An ancient manuscript mentions twenty-eight
days in the year "which were revealed by the Angel
Gabriel to good Joseph, which ever have been remarked to be very fortunayte dayes either to let blood,
cure wounds, use marchandizes, sow seed, build houses,
or take journees."

Astrologers formerly specified particular days when
it was dangerous for physicians to bleed patients; and
especially to be avoided were the first Monday in April,
on which day Cain was born and his brother Abel slain;

[1] *Historia litteraria*, vol. ii. London. 1731.

the first Monday in August, the alleged anniversary of the destruction of Sodom and Gomorrah; and the last Monday in December, which was the reputed birthday of Judas Iscariot.

In Mason's "Anatomie of Sorcerie" (1612), the prevailing notions on this subject were characterized as vain speculations of the astrologers, having neither foundation in God's word nor yet natural reason to support them, but being grounded only upon the superstitious imagination of men. A work of 1620, entitled "Melton's Astrologaster," says that the Christian faith is violated when, like a pagan and apostate, any man "doth observe those days which are called *Egyptiaci*, or the calends of January, or any month, day, time, or year, either to travel, marry or do anything in." And the learned Sir Thomas Browne, in his "Pseudodoxia Epidemica," published in 1658, declaimed in quaint but forcible language against the frivolity of such doctrines.

II. ROMAN SUPERSTITION CONCERNING DAYS

The Romans had their *dies fasti*, corresponding to the modern court days in England. On such days, of which there were thirty-eight in the year, it was lawful for the prætor to administer justice and to pronounce the three words, *Do, dico, addico,* "I give laws, declare right, and adjudge losses."

The days on which the courts were not held were called *nefasti* (from *ne* and *fari*), because the three words could not then be legally spoken by the prætor. But these days came to be regarded as unlucky, a fact rendered evident by an expression of Horace. The Romans also classed as unfortunate the days immediately following the calends, nones, and ides of each month. Unlucky days were termed *dies atri*, because they were marked in the calendar with black charcoal, the lucky ones being indicated by means of white chalk. There were also days which were thought especially favorable for martial operations, but the anniversary of a national misfortune was considered very inauspicious. Thus after the defeat of the Romans by the Gauls under Brennus on the banks of the river Allia, July 16, 390 B. C., that date was given a prominent place among the black days of the calendar. But not every general was influenced by such superstitions. Lucullus, when an attempt was made to dissuade him from attacking Tigranes, king of Armenia (whom he defeated B. C. 69), because upon that date the Cimbri had vanquished a Roman army, replied, "*I* will make it a day of *good* omen for the Romans." [1] The Roman ladies, we are told, gave less heed to the unlucky days of their own calendar than to the works

[1] Monsieur Danet, *A Dictionary of Greek and Roman Antiquities.* London, 1700.

of Egyptian astrologers, among whom Petosiris was
their favorite authority, when they wished to ascertain
the proper day, and even the hour, for the performance
of household and other duties.[1]

Horace (book ii. ode xiii.) thus apostrophizes a tree,
by whose fall he narrowly escaped being crushed at
Sabinum: "Thou cursed tree! whoever he was that
first planted thee did it surely on an unlucky day, and
with a sacrilegious hand."

The Latin writer, Macrobius, stated that when one of
the *nundinæ* or market days fell upon New Year's, it
was considered very unfortunate. In such an event the
Emperor Augustus, who was very superstitious, adopted
the method of inserting an extra day in the previous
year and subtracting one from that ensuing, thus pre-
serving the regularity of the Julian style of reckoning
time. Ordinarily, however, New Year's Day was deemed
auspicious, and on that day, as now, people were accustomed to wish each other happiness and good fortune.

III. MEDIÆVAL BELIEF IN DAY-FATALITY

The early Saxons in England were extremely credulous in regard to the luck or misfortune of particular
days of the month, and derived a legion of prognostics,
both good and evil, from the age of the moon. Thus,
they considered the twelfth day of the lunar month a

[1] Chabas, p. 124.

profitable one for sowing, getting married, traveling, and blood-letting, but the thirteenth day was in bad repute among the Saxons, an evil day for undertaking any work. The fourteenth was good for all purposes, for buying serfs, marrying, and putting children to school; whereas the sixteenth was profitable for nothing but thieving. The twenty-second was a proper time for buying villains, or agricultural bondmen, and a boy born on that day would become a physician. The twenty-fifth was good for hunting, and a girl then born would be of a greedy disposition and a " wool-teaser." [1]

In an English manuscript of the twelfth century mentioned in Chambers's " Book of Days," and known as the " Exeter Calendar," New Year's is set down as a *Dies mala.* As an illustration of the credulity prevalent in England in the fifteenth century regarding the influences, meteorological and moral, of the occurrence of important church festivals on particular days of the week, a few lines from a manuscript of the Harleian Collection in the British Museum are here quoted : —

> Lordlings all of you I warn,
> If the day that Christ was born
> Fell upon a Sunday,
> The winter shall be good, I say,
> But great winds aloft shall be ;
> The summer shall be fair and dry,

[1] Rev. Edward Cockayne, M. A., *Leechdoms, Wortcunning, and Starcraft of Early England.*

By kind skill and without loss.
Through all lands there shall be peace.
Good time for all things to be done,
But he that stealeth shall be found soon.
What child that day born may be
A great lord he shall live to be.

Not alone in Britain, but throughout the world, men have esteemed one day above another. This universal tendency of the human mind is tersely expressed in a translation by Barnaby Googe of some verses accredited to the Bavarian theologian, Thomas Kirch maier (1511–78), whose literary pseudonym was Naogeorgus :—

And first, betwixt the dayes they make no little difference,
For all be not of vertue like, nor like preheminence,
But some of them Egyptian are and full of jeopardee,
And some againe, beside the rest, both good and luckie bee,
Like difference of the nights they make, as if the Almightie King,
That made them all, not gracious were to them in everything.[1]

John Gaule, in his " Magastromancer " (1652), remarks that, according to the teachings of the astrologers,

Times can give a certain fortune to our business. The magicians likewise have observed, and all the antient verse men consent in this, that it is of very great concernment in what moment of time and disposition of the heavens everything, whether naturall or artificial, hath received its being in this world : for they have delivered that the first moment hath so great power that all the course of fortune dependeth thereon and may be foretold thereby.

[1] Brand's *Popular Antiquities.*

In the dark ages, and also in early modern times, the
false doctrines of astrology, an inheritance from the
ancients, dominated the actions of men. In all important enterprises, as well as in every-day labors, it was
deemed essential to make a beginning under the influence of a favorable planet. Nor did these beliefs prevail exclusively among ignorant people, but were as
well a part of the creed of scholars, and of the nobility and gentry. Modern astronomical discoveries, and
especially the Copernican system, availed to banish a
vast amount of superstition regarding the malevolent
character of certain days. But neither science nor
religion have yet been able wholly to eradicate it, as is
evident from the ill-repute associated with the sixth day
of the week even at the present time, a subject to be
considered later.

In the "Loseley Manuscripts," edited by Alfred John
Kempe, London, 1836, is to be found a letter, some
extracts from which may serve to illustrate the para-
mount influence of astrology in England in the sixteenth century. The letter is addressed to Mr. George
More, at Thorpe : —

As for my comming to you upon Wensday next . . . I
cannot possibly be wth you till Thursday.

On Fryday and Saterday the signe will be in the heart, on
Sunday, Monday and Tuesday in the stomake, during w^{ch}
tyme it wil be no good dealing wth your ordinary phisicke

until Wensday come Sevenight at the nearest, and from that tyme forwards for 15 or 16 days passing good.   In w'ch time yf it will please you to let me understand of your convenient opportunity and season, I will not faill to come along presently wth your messenger.

Your worship's assured
lovinge fr(ie)nd
SIMON TRIPPE, M. D.

WINTON. Septemb. 18. 1581.

The influence of the position of the moon in determining the proper seasons for surgical operations, and for the administration of medicines, may be best illustrated by a few extracts from ancient almanacs.

An antique illustrated manuscript almanac for the year 1386 contains the following advice to physicians:

In a new mone sal not be layting of blode, for yan are mennys bodyes voyed of blode and humos, and yan by layting of blode sal yay more be anoyded.

And again : —

It es to know generally, yt ye tyme electe to gyve a medcyn in es whan ye mone and ye Lord ascendyng ar free from all ille and not let by it, . . . and it es hyely to be ware to a medcyn whyles ye mone es in an ill aspect, wt Satne or Mars.

An almanac for the year 1568, published by John Securis, London, contains a list of days in that year favorable or otherwise for the preservation of man's health.

The second day of January was therein declared to be wholly propitious. The twelfth was unfavorable, owing to the furious aspect of Mars to the Sun, which was not, however, likely to cause bodily sickness, but rather to incline the hearts of some people to imagine evil of their rulers. The fifteenth of April was especially to be dreaded. On that day, says the writer, " God keep us from the fury of Mars."

In June evil passions were to stir men's hearts, anger, hatred, and strife ; for in that month were no less than six quartile aspects of the planets, one to another.

Many propitious days are also mentioned, and in conclusion *all* days are declared to be favorable to a good man.

" A New Almanacke and Prognostication for the Yeare of our Lord God 1569 " (London) says that surgical operations must be performed only when " the Moone or Lorde of the firste house " is in the zodiacal sign governing the particular member or organ which is to be operated upon.

And in an English almanac for the year 1571 we find the following passage : —

No part of man's body ought to be touched with the Chirurgicall instruments, or cauterie actuall or potencial, when the Sunne or Moone, or the Lord of the Ascendent, is in the same signe that ruleth that part of man's body.

Also *Gemini*, *Leo*, the last halfe of *Libra*, and the first 12 degrees of *Scorpio*: with *Taurus*, *Virgo*, and *Capricorne*, are not good for the letting of bloud. Two days before the change of the Moone, and a day after, is yll to let bloud. . . .

If the same be for the Pestilence, the Phrensie, the Pluresie, the Squincie, or for a Continuall headach, proceeding of choler or bloud; or for any burning Ague, or extreme paine of partes, a man may not so carefully stay for a chosen day by the *Almanack*: for that in the meane tyme the pacient perhaps may dye. For which cause let the skilfull Chirurgeon open a veine, unless he finde the pacient verie weake, or that the Moone be in the Same Syne that governeth that part of man's body.

The persistence of similar beliefs is shown by the following extract from " A Briefe Prognosticon or rather Diagnosticon for this Year of Grace " (1615), by John Keene, London:—

Seeing that these inferiour and sublunary mixt bodies are governed of the superiour and simple bodies, and especially by the motion of our neighbour Planet, the Moone, diseases vary and differ, and not for that she exceedes the rest in vertue and power, but because she is neerer us and swifter in motion; for wee see, the Moone increasing, humours increase; and when she decreaseth, humours decrease: for the bones in the full of the Moone are full of marrow, all living creatures both on sea and land, are then augmented in humiditie, as the Crab, Lobster, Oyster, etc. Also humours in man's bodie and in Plants are then increased: for when the Sunne and Moone are in hot signes, heate is increased, in

cold signes, cold exceedes heate; therefore have we just cause
in purging of humours to consider the motion of the Moone
through every signe of the Zodiacke, not only in purging of
humours, but also in curing diseases and in strengthening
the faculties and vertues.

In the "Dialogue of Dives and Pauper," printed
by Richard Pynson in 1493, this subject is referred to
as follows: —

Alle that take hede to dysmal dayes, or use nyce observances in the newe moone, or in the newe yeere, as setting of
mete or drynke by night on the benche to fede alholde (or
gobelyn).

The French traveler, Jean Chardin (1643–1713),
stated that in the year 1668 Cossacks invaded the
northern provinces of Persia; and when the inhabitants
appealed to the Persian government for aid, they
received only the reply that no assistance could be sent
them until the moon had passed out of the sign of the
Scorpion. The Persians formerly divided all the days
of the year into three classes, — preferable or lucky, mid-
dling or indifferent, and unlucky or detested ones;[1] and
the Emperor Frederick the Great of Prussia (1712–
86) was governed in his military operations by the
advice of astrologers, and always waited until they had
indicated the fortunate moment for a start.

[1] Dr. C. Edward Sachau, *The Chronology of Ancient Nations*. London,
1879.

The "English Apollo, by Richard Saunders, student in the divine, laudable, and celestial sciences, London, 1656," in giving advice to mariners, says that the good or bad position of the planets at the time of sailing has much influence over the fortunes of a voyage. The ancient sages, moreover, declared that the chief means of averting evil were, first, the devout invocation of Providence; and, secondly, the careful choice of a proper time for sailing by observation of the rules of astrology.

In William Jones's "Credulities Past and Present" (1525), St. Augustine is quoted as follows:—

No man shall observe by the days on what day he travel, or on what he return; because God created all the seven days which run in the week to the end of this world. But whithersoever he desires to go, let him sing and say his *Paternoster*, if he know it, and call upon his Lord, and bless himself, and travel free from care, under the protection of God, without the sorceries of the Devil.

IV. PREVALENCE OF SIMILAR BELIEFS IN MODERN TIMES

Among the Chinese of to-day, as with the inhabitants of ancient Babylon, the days which are deemed favorable or otherwise for business transactions, farming operations, or for traveling are still determined by astrologers, and are indicated in an official almanac published annually at Pekin by the Imperial Board of Astronomers. The various tribes of the island of Madagascar also are exceedingly superstitious in regard to the luck or ill-luck attending certain days, and the lives of children born at an unlucky time are sometimes sacrificed to save them from anticipated misfortune.

Natives of the Gold Coast of West Africa, in their divisions of the year, observe a "long time" consisting of nineteen lucky days, and a "short time" of seven equally propitious days. The seven days intervening between these two periods are considered unlucky, and during this time they undertake no voyages nor warlike enterprises. Somewhat similar ideas prevail in Java and Sumatra, and in many of the smaller islands of the Malay Archipelago. The Cossacks of western Siberia, the natives of the Baltic provinces of the Russian Empire, and the Laplanders of the far North, all adapt their lives to the black and white days of their calendar. The peasantry of West Sussex in England will not permit their children to go blackberrying on the tenth day of October, on account of a belief that the Devil goes afield on that day, and bad luck would surely befall any one rash enough to eat fruit gathered under such circumstances. The same people believe that all cats born in the month of May are hypochondriacs, and have an unpleasant habit of bringing snakes and vipers into the house.

Among the Moslems of India there are in each month seven evil days, on which no enterprise is to be undertaken on any consideration. Some of the peculiar superstitions of these people with regard to traveling on the different week-days are shown in " Zanoon-E-Islam, or the Customs of the Mussulmans of India," by Jaffur Shurreef. Thus, if any one proposes journeying on Saturday, he should eat fish before starting, in order that his plan may be successfully accomplished, but on Sunday betel-leaf is preferable for this purpose. In like manner, on Monday he should look into a mirror in order to obtain wealth. On Tuesday he should eat coriander-seed, and on Wednesday should partake of curdled milk before starting. On Thursday, if he eat raw sugar, he may confidently anticipate returning with plenty of merchandise; and on Friday, if he eat dressed meat, he will bring back pearls and jewels galore.

Some idea of the beliefs current in the mother country during the last century may be obtained by a study of the advertisements of astrologers and medical charlatans in the public press of that period. For example, in the year 1773 one Sylvester Partridge, proprietor and vendor of antidotes, elixirs, washes for freckles, plumpers for rounding the cheeks, glass eyes, calves and noses, ivory jaws, and a new receipt for changing the color of the hair, offered for a consideration to furnish advice as to the proper times and seasons for letting blood, and to indicate the most favorable aspect of the moon for drawing teeth and cutting corns. He proffered counsel, moreover, as to the avoidance of unlucky days for paring the nails, and the kindest zodiacal sign for grafting, inoculation, and opening of bee-hives.

In enlightened England there are still to be found many people who believe that the relative positions of the sun, moon, and planets are prime factors in determining the proper times and seasons for undertaking terrestrial enterprises. Zadkiel's Almanac for 1898 states that natural astrology is making good progress towards becoming once more a recognized science. To quote from the preface of this publication: —

As the whole body of the ocean is not able to keep down one single particle of free air, which must assuredly force its way to the surface to unite with the atmosphere, so cannot the combined forces of the prejudice and studied contempt of all the *soi-disant* " really scientific men " of the end of the century prevent the truth of *astrologia sana* from soaring above their futile efforts to crush it down, to join the great atmosphere of natural science, to enlighten the human mind in its onward course and effort, — " to soar through Nature up to Nature's God."

One example may suffice to exhibit the character of the predictions given in this same work. Under the caption, " Voice of the Stars," August, 1898, the writer says that the stationary positions of Saturn and Uranus are likely to shake Spain (and perhaps Tuscany) physically and politically about the 10th or 11th insts. There will be strained diplomatic relations between the United States and Spain; for Mars in the sign Gemini, and Saturn in Sagittarius, must create friction and disturbances in both countries.

The Jewish current beliefs in the influence of certain days and seasons appear to have been mostly derived from the Romans of old. Even nowadays among the Jews no marriages are solemnized during the interval of fifty days between the Feast of the Passover and Pentecost; and formerly the favorite wedding-days were those of the new or full moon.[1] In Siam the eighth and fifteenth days of the moon are observed as sacred, and devoted to worship and rest from ordinary labor. Sportsmen are forbidden to hunt or fish on these days. The Siamese astrologers indicate the probable character of any year by associating it with some animal, upon whose back the New Year is represented as being mounted.[2]

[1] Israel Abrahams, M. A., *Jewish Life in the Middle Ages*, p. 184.
[2] Bowring, *Siam*, vol. i. p. 158.

V. THE SIXTH DAY OF THE WEEK

Let us now consider the subject of Friday as an alleged *dies mala*. The seven week-days were originally named after Saturn, Jupiter, Mars, the Sun, Mercury, Venus, and the Moon, in the order given, and these names are found in the early Christian calendars. The Teutonic nations, however, adopted corresponding names in the Northern mythology, — the Sun and Moon, Tyr, the Norse God of War, Wodan, Thor, Freyja, and Saturn; and our early Saxon ancestors worshiped images representing all these deities until Christianity supplanted paganism in Britain. It has been suggested that our Friday may have been named after Frigga, the wife of Odin and the principal goddess of the ancient Scandinavians. But it is much more probable that the day derives its name from Freyja, the Goddess of Love, a deity corresponding to the Roman Venus and the Grecian Aphrodite. Freyja, the most easily propitiated of the goddesses, was wont to listen favorably to all who invoked her aid, and was especially tender-hearted to disconsolate lovers. She dwelt in a magnificent palace, and journeyed about in a car drawn by two cats.[1]

It has been hinted that Freyja's character was not irreproachable, and that thence arose Friday's ill-repute, but such an hypothesis is wholly untenable.

[1] Mallet's *Northern Antiquities.*

From the prose "Edda" we learn that this goddess was the wife of one Odur, and had a daughter named Hnossa, who was wonderfully beautiful. Sad to relate, Freyja was abandoned by her husband, who went away to visit foreign lands, and she has since spent much time in weeping, her tears being turned into drops of pure gold.[1]

The fish was an emblem of Freyja, and as such was offered by the Scandinavians to their goddess on the sixth day of the week.[2] The fish was also held sacred by the Babylonians and Assyrians, and by the ancient Romans as a symbol of Venus.

The generally accepted theory is that the crucifixion of our Lord on Good Friday was the origin of the widespread superstitions regarding the sixth day of the week. It is highly probable, however, that these beliefs originated at a much earlier epoch; for similar ideas are current among the inhabitants of heathen countries, as in Hindostan, for example. According to an ancient monkish legend, Adam and Eve partook of the forbidden fruit on a Friday; and in the Middle Ages many inauspicious occurrences of history or tradition were thought to have happened on that day.

In a French manuscript of the year 1285, preserved in the Bibliotheque Nationale in Paris, entitled "Re-

[1] Mallet, p. 426.
[2] Clifford Howard, *Sex Worship*, p. 119.

commandation du Vendredi," the following events are alleged to have occurred on a Friday : Adam's creation, his sin and expulsion from Eden, the murder of Abel, Christ's crucifixion, the stoning of Stephen, the massacre of the Innocents by Herod, the crucifixion of Peter, the beheading of Paul and that of John the Baptist, and the flight of the children of Israel through the Red Sea ; also the Deluge, the Confusion of Tongues at the Tower of Babel, and the infliction of the Plagues upon the land of Egypt.[1]

The following extract from a translation of a Saxon manuscript of about the year 1120 may serve to illustrate the credulity of that epoch in England, and the odium attaching to Friday : —

Whoever is born on Sunday or its night, shall live without anxiety and be handsome. If he is born on Monday or its night, he shall be killed of men, be he laic or be he cleric. If on Tuesday or its night, he shall be corrupt in his life, and sinful and perverse. If he be born on Wednesday or its night, he shall be very peaceable and easy and shall grow up well and be a lover of good. . . . If he be born on Friday or its night, he shall be accursed of men, silly and crafty and loathsome to all men and shall ever be thinking evil in his heart, and shall be a thief and a great coward, and shall not live longer than to mid-age. If he is born on Saturday or its night, his deeds shall be renowned, he shall be an alderman, whether he be man or woman ; many things shall happen unto him, and he shall live long.[2]

[1] Mélusine, tome iv. 1888–89.   [2] Cockayne, vol. iii. p. 163.

Although the superstitions of the dark ages may seem to us so childish, it may yet be affirmed with reason that, in proportion to the enlightenment of the times, the beliefs then current regarding day-fatality were no more absurd than those of our own era. In the "Reliques of Ancient English Poetry," by Thomas Percy, D. D., is to be found the following "excellent way to get a fayrie:" —

First, get a broad square christall or Venice glasse, in length and breadth three inches. Then lay that glasse or christall in the blood of a white hen, three Wednesdayes or three Fridayes. Then take it out and wash it with holy aq; and fumigate it. Then take three hazle sticks or wands of an yeare groth; pill them fayre and white; and make them so longe as you write the spiritt's name, or fayrie's name, which you call three times on every stick being made flatt on one side. Then bury them under some hill, whereat you suppose fayries haunt, the Wednesday before you call her; and the Fridaye followinge take them uppe and at eight, or three or ten of the clocke which be good planetts and houres for that turne; but when you call be in cleane life and turn thy face towards the east, and when you have her bind her in that stone and glasse.[1]

Whiston, the translator of Josephus, publicly proclaimed in London that the comet of 1712 would be visible on October 14 of that year, and that on the Friday morning ensuing the world would be destroyed

---

[1] "Popular Superstitions," *Gentleman's Magazine Library*, vol. i.

by fire. In the resulting panic, many people embarked in boats on the Thames, believing the water to be the safer element, on that particular Friday at least.

Mr. Charles Godfrey Leland, in his "Etruscan Roman Remains," says that in certain mediæval manuscripts the Goddess Venus was represented as the Queen of Hearts and a dealer of lucky cards. Therefore Friday, the *Dies Veneris*, was sometimes considered a lucky day, especially for matrimony. This opinion finds favor in Glasgow, where a large proportion of marriages take place on this day; whereas, in the midland counties of England, less than two per cent. of the weddings occur on the sixth day of the week.[1]

References to the popular sentiment regarding Friday are frequent in the works of English writers. Sir Thomas Overbury, in his description of "a faire and happy Milk-mayd," says: "Her dreams are so chaste that shee dare tell them; only a Fridaie's dream is all her superstition: that she conceales for feare of anger." Again, in the play of "Sir John Oldcastle" is this passage: "Friday, quotha, a dismal day, Candlemas Day this year was Friday."[2] And in Scott's "Marmion" is the following: —

> The Highlander, whose red claymore
> The battle turned on Maldas' shore,

[1] William Jones, *Credulities Past and Present.*
[2] T. F. Thiselton Dyer, *British Popular Customs.*

Will on a Friday morn look pale
If asked to tell a fairy tale.
He fears the vengeful Elfin King,
Who leaves that day his grassy ring ;
Invisible to human ken,
He walks among the sons of men.

As a refreshing instance of independence of thought
in a credulous age, we may quote from a letter written
by Sir Winston Churchill, father of the Duke of Marl-
borough, and printed in a tract of 1687. The letter,
though ungrammatical, is given verbatim : —

I have made great experience of the truth of it, and have
set down Friday as my own lucky day, the day on which I was
born, christened, married, and which, I believe, will be the
day of my death. The day on which I have had sundry
deliverances from perils by sea and land, perils by false
brethren, perils of law-suits, etc. I was knighted (by chance
unexpected of myself) on the same day and have several good
accidents happened to me on that day ; and am so superstitious in the belief of its good omen, that I choose to begin
any considerable action that concerns me, on the same day. [1]

VI. FRIDAY IN MODERN TIMES

Friday is the Sabbath of the Moslems, corresponding
to the Sunday of the Christians and the Saturday of
the Jews. In Egypt Friday is therefore blessed above
all other days, while Saturday is the most unfortunate.

However, although Friday was the day selected by

---

[1] Isaac Disraeli, *Curiosities of Literature*, vol. i. p. 280.

Mahomet for the holding of the Moslem Assembly, it was not wholly devoted to religious worship, and at the conclusion of public prayers business was transacted as on any other week-day.[1] Among Mohammedans Friday is considered the most lucky of days; and it is also the most popular for commencing any enterprise of importance, whether building a house, planting a garden, embarking on a voyage, contracting a marriage, or making a garment.[2]

One reason for Mahomet's choice of Friday as the day for public prayers was probably because this day was consecrated by the people of many nations to Ali-lat, the celestial Venus or Urania, whom the ancient Arabs worshiped.[3] Mahomet said that whoever bathed on Friday and walked to the public religious service, taking a seat near the *Imam* or *Khalifah* (the leader of a Moslem tribe), and listened attentively to the sermon, avoiding meanwhile frivolous conversation, would obtain the reward of a whole year's prayers at night for every step which he took between his home and the place of this assembly.[4]

The Moslems among the peasants inhabiting the frontier region between Afghanistan and Hindostan have a special reverence for Friday; for they believe

[1] Sir William Muir, K. C. S. I., *The Life of Mahomet.*
[2] John J. Pool, *Studies in Mohammedanism*, p. 103.
[3] M. l'Abbé Bertrand, *Dictionnaire universel de toutes les religions.*
[4] Thomas Patrick Hughes, B. D., M. R. A. S., *A Dictionary of Islam.*

that on that day God rested, after having created the world. On Friday eve, according to their belief, the spirits of the departed are wont to revisit their former abodes, and hence the custom prevails of sending delicacies to the mosque at such times.[1]

Friday was the most popular day for weddings among the Jews in mediæval times, and its selection appears to have been due to expediency, because of its nearness to the Jewish Sabbath, and the convenience of associating the marriage ceremony with the services in the synagogue on the latter day. The bridal pair fasted on the morning of the wedding, and ashes were sprinkled over their heads during the ceremony.[2]

According to the teachings of the Talmud, a second soul was believed to enter men's bodies every Friday evening and to remain throughout the following day, its presence being indicated by an increased appetite for food.[3]

On Friday, says an old tradition, is held the Witches' Sabbath or Assembly, and one should be careful not to speak of these creatures on that day, for their hearing is then especially acute, and disrespectful remarks will render one liable to incur their spite.

In the popular belief of the Swabians, Friday is the

---

[1] S. S. Thorburn, *Bannú.*
[2] Israel Abrahams, M. A., *Jewish Life in the Middle Ages*, p. 186.
[3] Gerald Massey, *The Natural Genesis*, vol. ii. p. 298.

day when the witches celebrate their joint festival
with the Devil on the Heuberg, near Rotenburg,
and afterward scour the country, intent on working
all manner of mischief upon the people and their
cattle.[1]

According to a Scotch superstition, however, witches
were supposed to hold their weekly meetings on Satur-
days, in unfrequented places. The formal proceedings
on these occasions included an address by the Devil,
and the holding of a court, wherein each witch was
expected to give a detailed statement of her doings;
and those who had been idle were given a beating with
their own broomsticks, the diligent being rewarded by
gifts of enchanted bones. A dance followed, the Devil
playing on the bag-pipes, and leading the music.[2]

The Irish are careful not to mention fairies by name
either on Wednesdays or Fridays, for these invisible
creatures are unusually alert on these two days.

On Fridays especially, their power for evil is very
strong. On that day, therefore, a careful watch is kept
over the children and cattle; a lighted wisp of straw is
waved about the baby's head, and a quenched coal is
placed under the cradle and churn. And if the horses
are more than usually restive in their stalls, it is a sure
sign that the fairies are riding them; therefore the

---

[1] Moritz Busch, *Deutscher Volksglaube.*
[2] Rogers, vol. iii. p. 278.

people spit three times at the animals, and the fairies thereupon immediately take their departure.[1]

In Ireland Friday is *facile princeps* among unlucky days, and especial care should be taken not to open the door of one's dwelling to any stranger on that day. Neither butter nor milk should be given away, nor should a cat be taken from one house to another on a Friday. To undo a sorcerer's spell, one should eat barley cakes over which an incantation has been said; but the cakes must be eaten on a Monday or Thursday, and never on Friday.[2]

In Welsh tradition the water-sprites are thought to keep an especially watchful eye over the sea on Fridays, making it rough and tempestuous.

On a Friday morning in the year 1600, says an old legend, a ship set sail from a Northern port, having on board a young man and a maiden of rare beauty, whose strange actions and demeanor seemed to betoken that they were supernatural beings. The vessel never reached port, but one stormy night a phantom ship was seen, enveloped in an uncanny light; and on its deck stood the youth and his sweetheart, a weird vision, as the spectral craft moved along over the stormy sea against the wind.[3]

[1] Lady Wilde, *Ancient Legends, Mystic Charms, and Superstitions of Ireland*, p. 136.

[2] Lady Wilde, *Ancient Cures, Charms, and Usages of Ireland.*

[3] P. G. Heims, *Seespuk*, p. 135.

In Hesse Frau Hölle, the modern Freyja, is the special guardian and protectress of newly married people, and so tenacious has been this old belief in the minds of the Hessian peasants that the day of Venus is still in high favor among them as the most propitious for weddings.[1]

In some places it is unlucky to receive any news, whether good or bad, on a Friday; and, according to a Shropshire saying, "if you hear anything new on a Friday, it gives you another wrinkle on your face, and adds another year to your age."[2] Indeed, the term "Friday-faced" was used to denote a gloomy or dejected visage, as in the following quotation: —

Marry, out upon him! what a friday-fac'd slave it is! I think in my conscience his face never keeps holiday.[3]

In Servia children born on Friday are thought to be invulnerable to the assaults of the whole army of hags and sorcerers. In Germany Friday is reckoned the most fateful of all the week-days, whether for good or evil. The beliefs vary in different portions of the empire, but there is a universal prejudice against setting out on a journey, moving into a new house, or changing servants on this day. In eastern Prussia, whoever bakes on a Friday will get but little bread; but Sunday

---

[1] Wilhelm Kolbe, *Hessische Volks-Sitten und Gebräuche.*
[2] *Shropshire Folk-Lore,* p. 260.
[3] "Wily Beguiled," Hawkins's *English Drama,* vol. iii. p. 356.

baptisms are thought to offset the unlucky auspices of
children born on Friday. The North German farmers
consider Friday the best day on which to begin gathering the harvest.[1]

In olden times Friday was the most favorable day
for courtship and weddings in Germany, and, unless a
bride first entered her new home on that day, domestic
strife was likely to ensue.

If she wished to tame a bad-tempered husband, her
first care was to prepare for him a soup made with the
rain-water of a Friday's shower. The magic charm of
words wherewith cattle were freed from the mange was
spoken on a Friday morning; and a hare which had
been shot on the first Friday in March was of great
therapeutic value, especially its eyes, which were dried
and carried about as a sovereign remedy for defective
vision.

Only on a Friday did the church-bells strike the hour
for the release of bewitched spirits, and the delivery of
enchanted souls from their spells.[2]

Doctor M. Höfler, in his "Volksmedizin und Aberglauben in Oberbayern" (p. 208), says that Bavarian
peasants still cherish many superstitions about the sixth
day of the week, the day sacred to Freyja, the old German Goddess of Love. Moreover, wonderful amuletic

---

[1] Dr. Adolf Wuttke, *Der deutsche Volksaberglaube*. Berlin, 1869.
[2] E. L. Rochholz, *Altdeutsches Bürgerleben*, pp. 52, 53.

virtues are attributed to hens' eggs laid during Good
Friday night, and whoever eats these eggs is thought
to be thereby insured against bodily harm. How long
this immunity holds good does not appear; but probably until another Good Friday night egg is eaten. In
farmers' households these precious eggs are therefore
eagerly sought by the house-mistress, who is wont to
give them to her husband and the farm-hands; or else
she uses them as an ingredient of the dough figures
which ornament the Easter bread.

In some districts of Hungary the following peculiar
custom is in vogue : —

Whenever any one's name-day happens on a Friday,
that person selects a piece of one of his cast-off garments, rubs thereon a few drops of his own blood and
saliva, and then burns the fragment of clothing. By
so doing he burns up also all the ill luck which else
might have befallen him during the next year. In
southeastern Transylvania a rag mystically dealt with
as above is hung on a tree before sunrise on the day
in question; if it disappear before dawn of the next
day, the person who thus superstitiously celebrates the
occurrence of his name-day on a Friday may laugh
at ill luck for a year.[1]

The Magyars begin no work on a Friday, for it is
bound to miscarry; neither do they give any milk out

[1] Wlislocki, *Aus dem Volksleben der Magyaren*, p. 68.

of the house on that day, for by so doing they imagine
the usefulness of the cow to be impaired. In Bihar
County, Hungary, a loaf of bread baked on Friday
and impaled upon a stick is accounted a safeguard
against the spread of fire. The natives of this district
likewise entertain various curious fancies which are
decidedly unique. For example, when a newly born
child is knock-kneed, the mother regards it as a changeling. She therefore seats herself on the threshold
on a Tuesday or Friday, when witches are abroad, and
peremptorily addresses those creatures, demanding the
restoration of her own child, whom she believes they
have stolen away. "Pfui! Pfui! you scoundrels!"
she exclaims, "give it back!" [1]

The Sicilians have a host of superstitions on this
subject. The following are among the more interesting items of their folk-lore relating to Friday. On
this day the owner of a rented house will not hand
over the keys to a new tenant, neither would the latter
receive them. In the southern part of the province of
Palermo no thief dares steal on a Friday, and the
accuracy of this statement is corroborated by the
criminal statistics. Indeed, on this day the most timid
householder may journey in safety anywhere in the
province, a fact which the sagacious traveler in a land
notorious for brigandage will not fail to note. This

---

[1] *Zeitschrift des Vereins für Volkskunde,* vol. iv. p. 307. 1894.

immunity is not attributable to any special veneration for Freyja's day, but rather to a popular belief that thefts and other misdemeanors then committed are sure of speedy detection. Laughter is thought to offend the goddess, and the proverb runs, "He who laughs on Friday weeps on Saturday." In an anonymous manuscript in the municipal library of Palermo appears a statement that whoever cuts out garments on a Tuesday or a Friday runs the risk of making them too short and of losing the cloth. Such clothing has little wear in it, for nothing begun on these days has any durability.[1]

The inhabitants of ancient Gascony are no less credulous, as is apparent from the following bits of Friday lore. Any one rash enough to start on a journey on horseback runs especial risk of falling off his horse, and of being drowned in attempting to ford a stream. It has even happened that newly baked loaves have been found tinged with blood in the oven. However, Friday is a good day for making vinegar, and the casks filled at three o'clock in the afternoon of that day are found to be superior to others. This is because our Lord, while on the cross, was given vinegar to drink, mingled with gall, at three o'clock on the afternoon of Good Friday.[2]

---

[1] Giuseppe Pitré, *Usi e costumi, credenze e pregiudizi del popolo Siciliano.* 1889.

[2] M. Jean-François Bladé, *Contes populaires de la Gascogne.* Paris, 1886.

In Normandy, also, Friday is the favorite day for putting water in wine or cider, for the people believe that on any other day the mixture would become sour.[1]

According to a quaint Italian belief, whoever is born on a Friday will be of sanguine temperament, passionate, light-hearted, and handsome. He will delight in music, both vocal and instrumental, and will have a liking for fine clothes. Moreover, he will be voluble in speech, though of unstable character.[2]

The Tyrolese have a saying, " Whoever is born on a Friday must experience trouble," and they regard it as folly to marry on that day.[3]

The French people share fully the general distrust of the sixth day of the week. This is shown by statistics of the Parisian theatres, where there are produced on an average nearly two hundred new pieces annually, and for many years not one of these has had its first performance on a Friday.[4]

In Alsace Wednesday and Friday are unlucky days, and the former is never chosen for a wedding or baptism. But of the two, Friday is the more undesirable, and no business of importance is done thereon, nor any journey undertaken. It is foremost among witch days, for evil spirits are then abroad, and their activity on a

---

[1] M. l'Abbé Migne, *Dictionnaire des superstitions populaires.*

[2] Giuseppe Pitré, *Il venerdì nelle tradizioni popolari italiane.*

[3] Busch, *op. cit.*

[4] *A World of Wonders,* edited by Albany Poyntz.

Friday is proverbial. These sentiments prevail in other German districts, and are entertained by people of cultivation and learning. Indeed, it may be affirmed truly that the possession of intellectual force is by no means incompatible with a superstitious belief in the luck or misfortune of particular days. The credulousness of the great Napoleon in this regard is well known. Bismarck is said to have once written to his wife from Letzlingen, a village of Prussian Saxony: "I have not had such good luck in hunting to-day as I had three years ago; but then — it is a Friday."[1] The French statesman, Gambetta, is reported to have arranged his journeyings and business affairs with reference to auspicious hours, as determined by a professional reader of cards; and President Felix Faure, we are told, is similarly credulous. Indeed, so prevalent are notions of this kind in the French capital that tastefully ornamented cards with a list of "hours to be avoided" find a ready sale in the streets.[2]

Among the Slavonians St. Prascovia, the modern successor of Venus and Freyja, is believed to visit the peasants' houses every Friday, and woe to the luckless woman whom she then finds engaged in certain occupations. Local tradition says that sewing, spinning, and weaving on that day are sinful, and are

[1] *Zeitschrift für deutsche Mythologie*, iv. 147.
[2] *Boston Herald*, May 1, 1898.

especially distasteful to St. Prascovia, familiarly known
as "Mother Friday," because the dust so produced gets
into her eyes. She is very apt to take revenge by
inflicting upon the offenders divers physical ailments,
such as sore eyes, whitlows, or hang-nails. In some
districts the peasants retire earlier than usual on
Friday evenings, under the impression that Mother
Friday will punish those whom she may find awake
when she makes her evening visits. These popular
beliefs are exemplified in the following tradition: —

There was once a certain woman who did not pay
due reverence to Mother Friday, but set to work on a
distaff full of flax, combing it and whirling it. She
spun away until dinner-time, then sleep fell upon her.
Suddenly the door opened, and in came Mother Friday,
before the eyes of all who were there, clad in a white
dress, and in such a rage! And she went straight up
to the woman who had been spinning, and scooped up
from the floor a handful of the dust that had fallen
out of the flax, and began stuffing and stuffing that
woman's eyes full of it! After she had stuffed them
full, she went off in a rage, — disappeared without
saying a word.

When the woman awoke, she began squalling, at the
top of her voice, about her eyes, but could not tell what
was the matter with them. The other women, who
had been much frightened, began to cry out: "Oh,

you wretch, you! you've brought a terrible punishment on yourself from Mother Friday." Then they told her all that had taken place. She listened to it all, and then began imploring: " Mother Friday, forgive me! Pardon me, the guilty one! I'll offer thee a taper, and I'll never let friend or foe dishonor thee, mother!"

"Well, what do you think? During the night, back came Mother Friday, and took the dust out of that woman's eyes, so that she was able to get about again. It's a great sin to dishonor Mother Friday, combing and spinning flax, forsooth!"[1]

Professor Max Müller, in his " Contributions to the Science of Mythology" (New York and Bombay, 1897), cites a tradition of the as yet little known mythology of the Mordvinians, a Finnish race inhabiting the middle Volga provinces of Russia. A woman who had been working all day long on a Friday, baking bread for some orphan children, was taken up in a dream to the sun, and when she was nearly exhausted, owing to the effects of the heat, and to the rapidly increasing size of a piece of dough which she had put into her mouth, she was accosted by Chkaï, the large-eyed Mordvine sun-god, who told her that she was being punished because she had baked bread for the orphans on a Friday. She was charged, moreover, to tell all

[1] W. R. S. Ralston, M. A., *Russian Folk-Tales.*

the people so. "But who will be such a fool as to believe me?" asked the woman most disrespectfully. Thereupon Chkaï placed his mark in scarlet and blue upon her forehead, — an emblem which is thought to bring luck. And after that the Mordvine women were careful to bake no bread, nor to do any other work, on a Friday.

It was a very early custom in England to appoint Friday as the day for the execution of criminals, and until recently the same was true in this country, but through the persistent efforts of the "Thirteen Club," of New York, whose object is the discouragement of certain popular superstitions, the sixth day of the week has been partially relieved of the odium of being "hangman's day" in the United States.

A writer of an inventive turn of mind has suggested that Friday's unpopularity is partly owing to its being late in the week and money runs short to the poor. Saturday being the close of the week, and pay-day as well, there is no time then to be superstitious.

Some modern writers have displayed a misguided zeal in the collection of statistical evidence that Friday has been a most auspicious day in American history, and have cited among other events the surrender of Burgoyne at Saratoga, and that of Cornwallis at York-town, as occurring on that day. But will such an argument appeal with success to English readers? If

by general consent we should teach our children that
Friday was the luckiest day of the week, evidence in
favor of this theory would no doubt rapidly accumu-
late, and the new belief would soon be worth just as
much as the old one.

SUPERSTITIOUS DEALINGS WITH ANIMALS

I. RATS AND MICE AS AVENGERS

WHEN in ancient times fields were overrun and crops destroyed by swarms of pestiferous animals or insects, these creatures were regarded either as agents of the Devil, or as being themselves veritable demons. We learn, moreover, that rats and mice were formerly especial objects of superstition, and that their actions were carefully noted as auguries of good or evil.[1] A rabbinical myth says that the rat and the hog were created by Noah as scavengers of the Ark; but the rat becoming a nuisance, the patriarch evoked a cat from the lion's nose.[2] In the "Horapollon," the only ancient work now known which attempted to explain Egyptian hieroglyphics, the rat is represented as a symbol of destruction. But the Egyptians also regarded this animal as a type of good judgment, because, when afforded the

[1] Larousse, *Grand dictionnaire universel.*
[2] M. D. Conway, *Demonology and Devil-Lore.*

choice of several pieces of bread, he always selects the best.[1]

According to an early legend, the Teucri, or founders of the Trojan race, on leaving the island of Crete to found a colony elsewhere, were instructed by an oracle to choose as a residence that place where they should first be attacked by the aborigines of the country. On encamping for the night, a swarm of mice appeared and gnawed the leathern thongs of their armor, and accordingly they made that spot their home and erected a temple to Apollo Smintheus,[2] this title being derived from the word meaning "a rat" in the Æolic dialect. In ancient Troas mice were objects of worship; and the Greek writer, Heraclides Ponticus, said that they were held especially sacred at Chrysa, a town famous for its temple of Apollo. At Hamaxitus, too, mice were fed at the public expense.[3] Herodotus relates, on the authority of certain priests, that when in the year B. C. 699 Egypt was invaded by an Assyrian army under Sennacherib, it was revealed in a vision to the Egyptian king, Sethon, that he should receive assistance from the gods. And on the eve of an expected battle the camp of the Assyrians was attacked by a legion of field-mice, who destroyed their quivers and bows, so that, being

[1] Fr. Noel, *Dictionnaire de la fable.*
[2] Danet's *Dictionary of Greek and Roman Antiquities.* London, 1700.
[3] Andrew Lang, *Custom and Myth.*

without serviceable weapons, the invaders fled in dismay on the ensuing morning. And in memory of this fabulous event a stone statue of King Sethon, bearing a mouse in his hand, was erected in the temple of Vulcan at Memphis, with this inscription : " Whoever looks on me, let him revere the Gods."

Cicero, in his treatise on Divination, while commenting on the absurdity of the prevalent belief in prodigies, remarked that, if reliance were to be placed in omens of this kind, he ought naturally to tremble for the safety of the Commonwealth, because mice had recently nibbled a copy of Plato's " Republic " in his library. Pliny wrote that rats foretold the Marsian war, B. C. 89, by destroying silver shields and bucklers at Lavinium, an ancient city near Rome; and that they also prognosticated the death of the Roman general, Carbo, by eating his hose-garters and shoe-strings at Clusium, the modern Chiusi, in Etruria. The same writer, in the eighth book of his " Natural History," devotes a short chapter to an enumeration of instances, fabulous or historical, in which the inhabitants of several cities of the Roman Empire were driven from their homes by noxious animals, reptiles, and insects. He states, on the authority of the Greek moralist, Theophrastus (B. C. 372–287), that the natives of the island of Gyaros, one of the Cyclades, were forced to abandon their homes owing to the ravages of rats and mice, which devoured everything they could find, even including iron substances.

When the Philistines took the ark of the Lord from the camp of the Israelites, as recorded in 1 Samuel iv., a plague of mice was sent to devastate their lands; whereupon the Philistines returned the ark, together with a trespass-offering, which included five golden mice, as an atonement for their sacrilegious act.

In mediæval legendary lore rats figure not unfrequently as avengers. The Polish king, Popiel II., who ascended the throne in the year 820, rendered himself obnoxious to his subjects by his immorality and tyranny, and, according to tradition, Heaven sent against him a multitude of rats, which pursued him constantly. The king and his family sought refuge in a castle situated on an island in the middle of Lake Goplo, on the Prussian frontier. But the rats finally invaded this stronghold and devoured the king and all belonging to him.

Again, in the year 970, so runs the legend, Hatto II., Archbishop of Mayence, who had made himself hateful to his people on account of his avarice and cruelty during a season of famine, was informed by one of his servants that a vast multitude of rats were advancing along the roads leading to the palace. The bishop betook himself at once to a tower in the middle of the Rhine, near Bingen, still known as the "Mouse Tower," where he sought safety from his pursuers. But the rats swam out to the tower, gnawed through its walls, and devoured him. We read also in "A Chronicle of the Kings of England" that, in the reign of William the Conqueror, a great lord was attacked by mice at a banquet, and "though he were removed from land to sea and from sea to land again," the mice pursued him to his death.

Rats and mice were not, however, the only agents employed as avengers. In the year 350, during a long siege of the Roman stronghold, Nisibis, in Mesopotamia, by the Persian king, Sapor II., the inhabitants besought their bishop, St. James, to utter a malediction against the enemy. Accordingly the prelate, standing on one of the wall towers, prayed God that a host of flies might be sent to attack the Persians, and tradition has it that the prayer was answered at once. A multitude of the insects descended upon the besiegers, their horses, and elephants; and men and animals, thus goaded to frenzy, were compelled to retreat, and so the siege was raised. The Philistines of old worshiped a special deity, Beelzebub, to whom they attributed the power of destroying flies.[1] This same region is still infested with insect plagues; but the modern traveler, who has no faith in Beelzebub, is more likely to employ fly-traps and energetic practical measures.

Such are a few instances of the supernatural employ-

[1] Ermete Pierotti, *Customs and Traditions of Palestine.*

ment of vermin and insects as instruments of ven-
geance; and we need hardly wonder that, conversely,
people in olden times should avail themselves of supernatural methods in order to protect themselves or their
property from the ravages of these noxious creatures.

In Mexico rats were anciently the objects of superstitious regard, for they were credited with possessing
a keen insight into the characters of all members of a
household, and were wont publicly to announce fla-
grant breaches of morality on the part of such members
by gnawing various articles of domestic furniture, such
as mats and baskets. It does not appear, however,
that the rodents were sagacious enough to indicate
the individual whose conduct had aroused their displeasure.

The Mexicans had also a superstition that whoever
partook of food which had been gnawed by rats would
be falsely accused of some wrong-doing.[1]

II. SPIRITS ASSUME THE FORMS OF BLACK ANIMALS

The belief in the demoniacal possession of animals
was prevalent in Europe for several centuries, and in
order to drive away the evil spirits it was customary to
employ various exorcisms and incantations, which were
supposed to be infallible after approval by ecclesiastical
authority. Reginald Scot, in his "Discovery of Witch-

[1] *Journal of American Folk-Lore*, vol. x. No. 39, p. 274. 1897.

craft," says that, according to the testimony of reliable authors, spirits were wont to take the forms of animals, and especially of horses, dogs, swine, goats, and hares. They also appeared in the guise of crows and owls, but took the most delight in the likenesses of snakes and dragons. Bewitched animals were usually of a black color. A black cat is the traditional companion or familiar of witches the world over, and the black dog is also associated with sorcery in the folk-lore of some lands. Among the Slavs the black demon Cernabog has this form, and the black hen is a common devil-symbol in mediæval witch-lore. The gypsies believe, moreover, that black horses are gifted with a supernatural sight, which enables them to see beings invisible to the eye of man.[1] Black animals figure prominently in many legends of the dark ages. Thus the Devil, in the form of a black horse, disturbed a congregation which had gathered to listen to a sermon delivered by St. Peter of Verona in the thirteenth century, but was put to flight by the sign of the cross.[2] Among birds the crow is considered an ominous creature in some countries, and in northeast Scotland is always associated with the " black airt." [3] The raven, too, is traditionally portentous, and is sometimes called the Devil's

[1] Leland's *Gypsy Sorcery.*

[2] Brewer's *Dictionary of Miracles.*

[3] Rev. Walter Gregor, M. A., *Notes on the Folk-Lore of the Northeast of Scotland.*

bird; its plumage is said to have been changed from white to black on account of its disobedience.[1] In Swedish legend the magpie shares the evil reputation of the raven and crow, and is characterized as "a mystic bird, a downright witches' bird, belonging to the Devil and the other powers of the night." [2]

The Kirghis, a nomadic people of Turkestan, are very superstitious in regard to the magpie, and note with care the direction whence the sound of its cry is heard. If from the north, it portends evil; from the south, a remarkable occurrence; from the east, it denotes the coming of guests; and from the west, a journey.[3]

The Rev. Alexander Stewart, in his "Nether Lochaber," deprecates as unreasonable the universal distrust of the magpie. It seems probably that this is due less to its color than to certain other characteristics; for the magpie is a confirmed mimic and kleptomaniac, and of exceeding slyness withal.

Apropos of crows as foreboders, whether of good or evil, an amusing story is told of a man who wished to test for himself the truth or falsity of a popular belief that seeing a couple of crows in the early morning is a sign of good luck. He therefore directed his servant

---

[1] Hulme, *Natural History Lore and Legend*, p. 241.
[2] Thorpe, ii. p. 84.
[3] Schuyler, *Turkestan*, p. 30.

to awaken him at daybreak whenever two crows were to be seen. Accordingly one morning the servant called him, but in the mean time one of the birds had flown away. Thereupon the master became angry and gave his servant a sound beating, upbraiding him with having delayed until but one crow remained. The servant, however, nothing daunted, replied: " Lo, sir, have you not seen the luck which is come to me from seeing two crows?"[1]

Superstition has been defined as " a belief not in accordance with the facts," but this is manifestly incorrect. An ignorant person, who thinks that black cats are more evil-minded than white ones, thereby cherishes a mistaken idea, but is not necessarily superstitious. If, however, he believes that a black cat or any other animal is endowed with a supernatural faculty of exerting evil influences over human beings, then he is not only ignorant, but also superstitious.

III. EXORCISM AND CONJURATION OF VERMIN

The Grecian husbandmen were accustomed to drive away mice by writing them a message on a piece of paper and sticking it on a stone in the infested field. A specimen of such a message, beginning with an adjuration and concluding with a threat, is to be found in the " Geoponica," a Grecian agricultural treatise.

[1] Edward Jewitt Robinson, *Tales and Poems of South India*, p. 378.

In the endeavor to justify the employment of radical measures against vermin, some curious questions of casuistry were involved. Rats and mice being God's creatures, one ought not to take their lives. But it was considered entirely proper to drive them off one's own domain, while recommending as preferable the well-stocked cellar of a neighbor. Formulæ of exorcism, or sentences containing warnings to depart, were written on scraps of paper, which were then well greased and rolled into little balls, or wrapped about poisoned edibles, and placed in the rat-holes.[1]

Conjurations of vermin were usually in the name of St. Gertrude, the first abbess of Nivelle in Belgium, and also the patron saint of travelers and cats, and protectress against the ravages of the smaller rodents.

The Spanish ecclesiastic, Martin Azpilcueta, surnamed Navarre, stated that when rats were exorcised, it was customary to banish them formally from the territory of Spain; and the creatures would then proceed to the seashore and swim to some remote island, where they made their home.

The public records of Hameln, in the kingdom of Hannover, state that in the year 1284 a stranger, in gay and fantastic attire, visited the town and proclaimed himself a professional rat-catcher, offering for a consideration to rid the place of the vermin which

[1] E. Rolland, *Faune populaire de la France.* Paris, 1877.

infested it. The townsfolk having agreed to his proposal, the stranger began to play a tune upon his pipe, whereupon the rats emerged in swarms from their hiding-places and followed him to the river Weser, where they were all drowned. The people of Hameln now repented of their bargain and refused to pay the full amount agreed upon, for the alleged reason that the rats had been driven away by the aid of sorcery. In revenge for this, the piper played the same tune on the next day, and immediately all the children of the town followed him to a cavern in the side of a neighboring hill, called the Koppenberg. The piper and the children entered the cavern, which closed after them; and in remembrance of this tragic event several memorials are to be seen in Hameln. Indeed, some writers maintain that the legend has an historical foundation, and such appears to have been the opinion of the townspeople, inasmuch as for years afterwards public and legal documents were dated from the mournful occurrence.

An old tradition says that mice originally fell upon the earth from the clouds during a thunder-storm, and hence these animals are emblematic of storms; they are also mystical creatures, and have a relationship with Donar, Wodan, and Frigg. In Bavaria profanity is thought to increase the number of mice in a dwelling, and their appearance in the fields in large numbers indi-

cates war, pestilence, or famine.[1] Bohemian peasants
are wont to make a certain provision for these elfish
rodents; on Christmas Eve and on the first holiday
of the year, whatever food remains from the midday
meal is thrown upon the barn floor, and the following sentence is repeated: "O mice, eat these rem-
nants and leave the grain in peace!" On Christmas
Eve, also, peas are placed in heaps, shaped like a cross,
in the four corners of a mouse-infested room, lest
the vermin get the upper hand and the premises be
overrun. In eastern Prussia, when the harvest is
gathered, the last sheaf of corn is left standing in the
field, while the peasants surround it and sing a hymn
as an incantation against future devastation of their
lands by rats or mice. Or, when the corn is harvested,
three inverted sheaves are fixed upon the barn floor for
a like purpose.[2]

According to a Bohemian legend, the mouse was
originally a creation of the Devil, at the time when
Noah entered the Ark, attended by the members of his
family and followed by a numerous retinue of animals.
The Devil, so runs the tale, hated the patriarch for his
piety, and with evil intent created the mouse, whom he
sent to gnaw a hole in the side of the Ark, through
which the water might enter. But God then created

[1] Wuttke, p. 118.
[2] Wuttke, p. 276.

the cat, who pursued and devoured the mouse, thus frustrating the design of the Evil One.[1]

At the siege of Angers, the ancient capital of Anjou, in the year 845, during the reign of King Charles the Bald, the French were much annoyed by swarms of grasshoppers of unusual size. They were duly exorcised according to the custom of the times, and having been put to flight, are reported to have precipitated themselves into a river.[2]

The French writer, St. Foix, in his "Essais historiques sur Paris," has recorded that in the year 1120, the Bishop of Laon, in the Department of Aisne, pronounced an injunction against field-mice, on account of their ravages; and St. Bernard, a contemporary of that prelate, while preaching at Foigny in the same diocese, in order to relieve his congregation of the annoyance caused by a multitude of flies, repeated a formula of excommunication against them, whereat, according to monkish records, the flies fell dead in heaps and were gathered up with shovels.

The early Anglo-Saxons not only made use of amulets of wood or other material, on which were engraven Runic characters, to secure protection from elves and demons,[3] but they carried about with them the herb

---

[1] Dr. Joseph Virgil Grohmann, *Aberglauben und Gebräuche aus Böhmen und Mähren*, p. 232.

[2] *Encyclopédie theologique*, tome, "Sciences occultes."

[3] John Thrupp, *The Anglo-Saxon Home*. London, 1852.

called periwinkle, of the botanical genus *Vinca*, as a
charm against snakes and wild animals.[1]

IV. CHARMS AGAINST ANIMALS

As illustrative of the superstitious use of charms and
exorcisms against animals and reptiles in different epochs
and countries, we have examples from many and varied
sources.

The Egyptians used, as charms against venomous
serpents, various magic formulæ inscribed upon strips
of papyrus, which were rolled up and worn as talismans. A specimen of such an one is to be seen among
the Egyptian manuscripts in the Louvre collection.
The following is a translation of a portion of one of
these incantations, which invokes the aid of a god to
protect the bearer against wild animals and reptiles : —

Come to me, O Lord of Gods, drive far from me the lions
coming from the earth, the crocodiles issuing from the river,
the mouth of all biting reptiles coming out of their holes.[2]

Pliny recommended a particular herb as an amulet
against serpents and vipers. This herb, to which he
gives no less than five Latin names, appears to be identical with the *Anchusa officinalis* of modern pharma-
copœias, the bugloss or ox-tongue of southern Europe, a
plant now seldom used in therapeutics.

---

[1] *Leechdoms, Wortcunning, and Starcraft*, edited by the Rev. Oswald
Cockayne.
[2] Francis Lenormant, *Chaldean Magic and Sorcery*.

The Grecians also were doubtless addicted to the superstitious use of charms against animals, although there is good authority for the statement that the citizens of ancient Athens did not hesitate on occasion to accelerate the flight of " ominous creatures, as cats and the like," by throwing stones or other handy missiles at them in the night, a method wholly mundane and natural.[1] And in this connection we may quote the opinion of the Rev. Father Pierre Le Brun, in his "Histoire critique des pratiques superstitieuses" (Amsterdam, 1733). The learned writer remarks that, if it were desired to drive a strange dog out of one's room, it would be quite unsuitable to *begin* with prayer and the use of holy water. One should rather first open the door and take hold of a stick, or throw some food outside ; and if these and other practical measures fail, then recourse may be had to supernatural expedients, provided these have ecclesiastical sanction.

In a treatise against superstition by a French *savant*, Martin of Arles, published in 1650, it was stated that the friars of the monastery of Ardennes were wont to boast that no rats could thrive in their neighborhood, and that this fact was due to the merits of St. Ulric, Bishop of Augsburg, some of whose relics were deposited in their church. In this monastery also it had been formerly customary to scatter crumbs of bread

[1] Francis Rous, *Archæologiæ Atticæ.* London, 1635.

which had been blessed, in places infested by vermin, and the monks believed that this procedure either caused the death of the animals or frightened them away.

Thuringian houses are sometimes cleared of rats in the following manner: Before sunrise on Good Friday morning, the master of the house, barefooted and in his shirt-sleeves, goes through every room blowing on a tiny whistle made out of the thigh bone of a rat's hind leg.[1] Another curious method of expelling vermin from a dwelling is in vogue in some portions of the Austrian Empire. Before the dawn of a principal feast day, one must take an old shoe which has not been recently cleaned, and lay it on the ground at a place where two roads cross. No word must meanwhile be spoken aloud, but a *Paternoster* is to be silently repeated. The direction in which the shoe points indicates the course to be taken by the rats in their flight.[2] In the village of Bechlin, a few miles north of Prague, troublesome mice are thus dealt with: Very early on an Easter Sunday morning, before the bells have rung for the first Mass, the peasant matron collects and fastens together all the house-keys. Then she waits until the first stroke of the bell for High Mass at noon, whereupon she proceeds to the cellar, meanwhile jin-

---

[1] Grohmann, *Apollo Smintheus*, p. 60.
[2] Grohmann, *Aberglauben*, vol. i. p. 59.

gling the keys vigorously so long as the church-bells
ring; when they cease she retraces her steps, still rat-
tling the keys; and these measures are believed to
permanently frighten away the mice.[1]

Towards the middle of the seventeenth century a
great army of locusts invaded the fields in the neighborhood of the town of Mixco, in Guatemala. So
numerous were they as for a time to obscure the light
of the sun, and to break the branches of the trees
whereon they clung; and they speedily devoured the
corn and other crops. Moreover, they covered the
highways and startled the traveling mules by their
fluttering movements. By order of the magistrates,
the people of the country assembled in the fields with
trumpets and other instruments in order to scare
away the unwelcome visitors. Idols were brought out,
especially pictures of the Virgin and of St. Nicholas
Tolentine. From the country regions near and far
came the Spanish farmers to the town of Mixco, with
propitiatory offerings for the saint, and all brought
with them loaves of bread to be blessed. These loaves
they carried back to their farms, and either threw into
their cornfields or buried beneath their hedges, hop-
ing by this method to protect their crops from the
locusts.[2]

[1] Grohmann, *Aberglauben*, vol. i. p. 61.
[2] Thomas Gage, *A New Survey of the West Indies*. London, 1677.

The mountain ash, or rowan-tree (the Scotch *roun-tree*), is thought to have derived its name from the Latin word *runa*, an incantation, because of its employment in magical arts. Woe to the witch who is touched by a branch of this tree in the hand of a christened man![1]

Much has been written concerning the folk-lore of the mountain ash, and it is indeed a powerful rival of the horse-shoe in its talismanic virtues, though not as a luck-bringer.

But for the protection of cattle from the incursions of witches, not even the horse-shoe may assume to usurp the rowan's prestige. Branches of this favorite tree, when hung over the stalls of cows or wreathed about their horns, are potent to avert the evil glances or contact, whether of witches or malicious fairies. And their efficacy is enhanced if the farmer is careful to repeat at regular intervals the following fervent petition : —

From Witches and Wizards, and long-tailed Buzzards, and creeping things that run in hedge-bottoms, good Lord, deliver us!

Jamieson, in his "Scottish Dictionary," remarks that this practice of twining the rowan about the horns of cows bears a certain resemblance to an ancient custom of the Romans in their *Palilia*, or feast celebrated at

[1] Rev. Hilderic Friend, *Flowers and Flower-Lore*, p. 554.

the end of April, whose object was the preservation of the flocks. He says : —

The Shepherd, in order to purify his sheep, was in the dusk of the evening to bedew the ground around them with a wet branch, then to adorn the fold with leaves and *green branches* and to cover the door with garlands.

In China it is customary for the Taouist priests to perform certain magical rites on the completion of a new pigsty, and before the admission of the animals to their new quarters. An altar is erected in honor of the Chu-Lan-Too-Tee, or genii of pigsties, and the walls of the compartments of the sty are adorned with strips of red paper, upon which are Chinese characters, signifying, "Let the enemies of horses, cows, sheep, fowls, dogs, and pigs be appeased." [1]

V. IMAGES OF ANIMALS AND BIRDS USED AS CHARMS

The belief that cities or towns may be protected from the incursions of noxious animals, birds, or insects, by an image or figure representing one of these creatures, is of great antiquity. This seems to be on the principle of the homœopathic doctrine, "Like cures like." A homely illustration of the same idea is afforded by the shrewd farmer who hangs up a dead crow in his cornfield to protect the crops. On the other hand, the eccentric French writer, Antoine Mizauld, recommended

[1] John Henry Gray, M. A., LL. D., *China*, p. 169.

the following as an effective charm for attracting a
large number of crows to one spot: As soon as the
constellation of the Virgin rises above the horizon, the
figure of a half crow is to be painted on a piece of
cloth, while these words are repeated : " Let no crow
in all this district move away without coming to this
image, in whatever spot it may be buried." The piece
of cloth, with its magical figure, is then interred and
the charm is complete.[1]

Apollonius of Tyana in Cappadocia, the philosopher
and pretended magician of the first century, is said to
have freed Antioch from scorpions and flies by means
of the brazen image of a scorpion. The French bishop,
Gregory of Tours, mentions an ancient popular belief
that no serpents or dormice were to be seen in Paris.
In his time, however, or toward the close of the sixth
century, while workmen were removing the mud which
covered one of the arches of the Bridge of Paris, they
found imbedded therein two brazen images of a serpent
and dormouse, which were taken away; and thence-
forth, he says, the city was infested by prodigious
numbers of dormice and snakes. In Jean Baptiste
Thiers's treatise on Superstitions (Paris, 1679), we find
allusion to a serpent of brass at Constantinople, which
long served as a talisman to bar the entrance of living
serpents. But when the city was captured by Maho-

[1] Martin Frederick Blumber, *A History of Amulets.*

met II. in 1453, that monarch broke the teeth of the image by the force of an arrow-shot; and immediately a legion of serpents attacked the inhabitants, but without doing them any harm, for the teeth of all were broken. In the reign of Charlemagne it was customary in Piedmont to use a formula for blessing holy water with which to drive away noxious animals from the crops, and with such success that not a single mole could be found in the whole town of Aosta, nor within three thousand paces beyond its boundaries.

Mr. Andrew Lang, in his volume entitled "Custom and Myth," says that, in a church of a certain old Saxon town, the verger is wont to exhibit to visitors a silver mouse dedicated to Our Lady; explaining that the town was infested with mice until this now precious relic was presented by some ladies as a propitiatory offering, whereupon the creatures disappeared at once.

According to the ancient Doctrine of Signatures, the therapeutic virtues of plants were indicated by certain peculiarities of their external appearance. Thus *Dracontium*, or great dragon, a plant which has a fancied resemblance to this mythical monster, was thought to be a preservative against serpents; and the scorpion-grass (*Myosotis*), whose flower-spike was not unlike a scorpion's tail, was deemed an antidote to the stings of noxious insects.

Indeed, the old herbalists of England claimed by the

sole use of herbs, not only to cure all fleshly ills, but to drive away or keep at a distance wolves, leopards, and all venomous wild beasts.[1]

In Tibet, according to L. Austine Waddell, M. B., ferocious mastiffs are permitted to roam at large in the night, a source of terror to wayfarers, who therefore carry about charms consisting of "the picture of a dog muzzled and fettered by a chain, terminated by the mystic and all-powerful thunderbolt sceptre," while along the dog's body are written certain Sanskrit magical sentences.[2]

VI. WORDS USED AS CHARMS

The English word "charm" is derived from the Latin *carmen*, a verse; and the magical potency of a sentence used as a charm was believed to rest in the words themselves, and not in the person who uttered them. In the opinion of the cabalistic magicians of the Middle Ages, the power of a charm of words depended upon its being unintelligible.

The Latin poet, Varius, wrote in the first century B. C. that old women, by the sole use of words as charms, were able not only to restrain and subjugate wild animals and serpents, but also to drive away noxious creatures and vermin. Few early writers allude to this

[1] Richard Folkard, Jr., *Plant-Lore*, p. 160.
[2] *The Buddhism of Tibet.*

practice, which appears, however, to have been much in vogue in different countries towards the close of the mediæval period. The Swiss theologian, Felix Hammerlein (1389–1457), wrote of a peasant living near Zurich who was able, by repeating a magic formula, to rid infested premises of adders, vipers, lizards, and other reptiles;[1] and in some parts of Normandy it was a custom formerly to place small rolls of hay under the fruit trees. The hay was then set on fire by means of torches carried by young children, who repeated meanwhile: "Mice, caterpillars, and moles, get out of my field; I will burn your beard and your bones; trees and shrubs, give me three bushels of apples." Hampson remarks that this incantation somewhat resembles one employed by the ancient Grecians against beetles, whom they held responsible for the destruction of their corn. These magical lines are thus translated: "Fly, beetles, the ravenous wolf pursues you."[2]

It was currently reported among the ancients that the famous philosopher, Pythagoras, not only possessed the faculty of predicting storms and earthquakes, but that he had by a magical word been enabled to tame a Daunian bear, and had also prevented an ox from eating beans by whispering in his ear.[3]

[1] The Nation. June 15, 1866.
[2] R. T. Hampson, Medii Ævi Kalendarium. See, also, article by W. W. Newell in Journal of American Folk-Lore, vol. v. No. 14.
[3] Anthon's Classical Dictionary.

Antoine Mizauld, the French physician and astrologer, affirmed that, according to Ptolemy, in order to drive away serpents, one should prepare a talisman by engraving the figure of two serpents upon a square piece of copper and pronouncing a charm of words as follows: "With this image I forbid serpents to harm any one, and command them to leave the place where it shall be buried." In like manner, says the same authority, to expel rats and mice, one has only to represent an image of one of these creatures upon a piece of tin or copper, and at the proper time, as determined by astrology, command them to depart.

In order to expel snakes, insects, and vermin from their dwellings, the Bulgarian women of Turkey, on the last day of February, endeavor to frighten the creatures by beating copper vessels all over the house, while shouting, "Out with you, snakes, scorpions, flies, bugs, and fleas!" One of the vessels is then taken into the court-yard, the pests being expected to follow it. And in Serfo, an island of the Grecian archipelago, at the commencement of the vintage a bunch of grapes is thrown into each house to expel the vermin, while this formula is repeated: "The black grape will sicken you; the black grape will poison you! Out with you, rats and fleas!"[1]

In Albania, when locusts or cockchafers devastate the

[1] Garnett, p. 340.

fields, a number of women, having caught some of the insects, form a mock funeral procession, and proceed to drown them in some convenient stream. And while on their way thither they chant in turn the following dirge, which all repeat in chorus : —

> O locusts, O cockchafers, parents kind,
> Orphaned you have left us all behind.

And this proceeding is thought to be destructive to the whole swarm of insects.[1]

The following charm against foxes was formerly used in France, and was to be repeated thrice a week : —

Foxes, both male and female, I conjure you in the name of the Holy Trinity, that ye neither touch nor carry off any of my fowls, whether roosters, hens or chickens ; nor eat their nests, nor suck their blood, nor break their eggs, nor do them any harm whatever.[2]

The Roman Catholic Church formerly sanctioned the use of certain sentences as charms against vipers, and the following may serve as a specimen : —

I conjure thee, O serpent, in this hour, by the five holy wounds of Our Lord, that thou remove not out of this place, as certainly as God was born of a pure Virgine. Otherwise, I conjure thee, serpent, by Our Lady St. Mary, that thou

[1] Lucy M. J. Garnett, *The Women of Turkey*, p. 286.
[2] Jean Frederic Bernard, *Superstitions anciennes et modernes*, tome i. p. 101. 1733.

obey me, as wax obeyeth the fire, and as fire obeyeth water, that thou neither hurt me nor any other Christian, as certainly as God was born of an immaculate Virgine, in which respect I take thee up. *In Nomine Patris et Filii et Spiritus Sancti.* . . . Otherwise, O vermine, thou must come as God came unto the Jews." [1]

When a Turk chances to encounter a serpent, he is wont to invoke the aid of Chah-Miran, the serpent-king, and in the name of this deity he bids the reptile depart. Now Chah-Miran has long been dead, but the astute Turk reasons that serpents are not aware of this fact, for, if they were, the human race would be helpless against their attacks. [2]

As preservatives from the stings of insects, and to prevent the croaking of frogs, the Moslems use scraps of paper containing magical formulæ, or sentences from the Koran engraved on stones or pieces of metal; [3] and a method formerly in vogue in France, to protect pigeons from the incursions of scorpions, consisted in writing the word " Adam " on each of the four walls of the pigeon-house. [4]

The natives of Mirzapur, in cases of scorpion-bite, recite a charm meaning as follows: " Black scorpion of the limestone, green thy tail and black thy mouth,

---

[1] Scot's *Discoverie of Witchcraft.*
[2] *The Folk-Lorist,* vol. i. July, 1893.
[3] William Jones, *Credulities Past and Present.*
[4] J. B. Thiers, *Traité des superstitions.*

God orders thee to go home. Come out, scorpion, at
the spell. Come out, come out!"[1]

The following charm against insects is in vogue in
Lesbos : In the evening a black-handled knife is stuck
in some spot where the insects congregate, and certain
Greek verses are repeated, of which the following is a
translation : —

> I got three naughty bairns together,
> One a wasp, one caterpillar,
> And a swarming ant the other.
> Whate'er ye eat, whate'er ye drink,
> Hence, hence avaunt,
> To the hills and mountains flee,
> And unto each fruitless tree.

The knife is to remain in the same spot until the
next morning, and is then to be removed. This com-
pletes the charm, and the insects are expected to
depart at once.[2]

In Great Britain there formerly prevailed a belief
that rats could be rhymed to death by anathematizing
them in metrical verse, a practice mentioned by Shakespeare and contemporary poets, and which is even
to-day not wholly obsolete.[3]

In southern Germany, during the campaigns of Napoleon I., mice with inked feet were placed upon the map

---

[1] W. Crooke, B. A., *North Indian Folk-Lore.*
[2] *Folk-Lore.* June, 1896.
[3] W. W. Newell, *Journal of American Folk-Lore*, No. 16. 1892.

of Europe, and their tracks were held to foretell the routes by which the French soldiers would advance.[1]

The Hindus consider the rat to be a sacred animal, and among the lower classes of the natives of western India it is thought unlucky to call a rat by his own name, so they speak of him as the " rat-uncle." [2]

VII. SUPERSTITIOUS DEALINGS WITH WILD ANIMALS

In encountering a wild animal, the ancients deemed it a matter of great importance that a man should see the beast before the latter was aware of a human presence. If a wolf, for example, first perceived the man, the brute was master of the situation, and the man was bereft alike of speech and strength; whereas the wolf, if first seen by the man, became an easy prey. The side from which a wild beast approached was also of moment. Thus the "Geoponica" warned its readers not to allow a hyena to approach from the right side, lest one be rendered motionless by the fascination of its presence; but if it appeared on the left side, the animal might be attacked with confidence.

Various wonderful tales are current among the natives of Senegambia, and other districts of western Africa, regarding the lion. This noble animal, it is said, forbears to attack a man who salutes him with a

[1] M. D. Conway, *Demonology and Devil-Lore.*
[2] James M. Campbell, *Notes on the Spirit Basis of Belief and Custom.*

respectful gesture, and the same gallant instinct re-
strains the beast from harming a woman.[1] In most
lion-haunted regions, however, the natives do not have
such implicit confidence in the courtesy and forbear-
ance of wild animals, but trust rather to the efficacy of
various amulets. The Kaffirs of southeastern Africa,
for example, on encountering a lion or leopard in the
forest, proceed at once to nibble a so-called lion-charm,
which is merely a small bit of wood or root. And if
the animal moves away without molesting him, the
Kaffir attributes his security to the magic power of
the charm, not realizing that his escape is due to the
natural dread of man which is characteristic of animals
generally.[2]

So, too, the priests of Mexico were accustomed to
rub their bodies with a certain ointment which they believed to be an efficient protection against wild beasts,
its pungent odor acting as a charm, so that they were
enabled to wander unmolested amid the wildest soli-
tudes.[3] The skilled hunter, however, confident in his
own prowess, depends neither upon the alleged gallantry of lions nor the potency of amulets, but rather
on his trusty rifle.

The belief in charms against noxious animals is wide-

---

[1] *Bulletin de la societé d'ethnographie.* July, 1887.
[2] Rev. J. G. Wood, M. A., *The Uncivilized Races of Men.*
[3] *The Occult Sciences,* from the French of Eusebe Salverte.

spread; for not alone in African jungles does this form of superstition prevail: it is found among civilized people as well, and more particularly in southern lands; indeed, wherever venomous creatures abound. In a collection of amulets belonging to Professor Joseph Belucci, of Perugia, Italy, which was exhibited at the Paris Exposition, 1891, were a number of perforated stones and other objects used by Italians as charms to protect the bearer against the bite of serpents and reptiles.[1]

VIII. LEGAL PROSECUTION OF ANIMALS

Legal proceedings were formerly instituted against vermin, who were thus treated as if they were human beings endowed with consciences and responsible for their actions. Prosecutions of animals were common in France and Switzerland, with a view to protect communities from their depredations. Thus rats and mice, and also bulls, oxen, cows, and mares; sheep, goats, pigs, and dogs; moles, leeches, caterpillars, and various reptiles, were liable to punishment by legal process.[2] The Roman Catholic Church claimed full power to anathematize all animate and inanimate things, founding its authority on the Scriptural precedents of the malediction pronounced on the serpent in the garden

---

[1] *Journal of American Folk-Lore*, No. 13. 1891.
[2] L. Lalanne. *Curiosités des traditions.* Paris. 1847.

of Eden, and the cursing of the barren fig-tree by our Lord.[1] The belief in the moral responsibility of animals was also thought to be warranted by the old Mosaic law as declared in Genesis ix. 5 : —

And surely your blood of your lives will I require; at the hand of every beast will I require it, and at the hand of man.

Also in Exodus xxi. 28 : —

If an ox gore a man or a woman, that they die: then the ox shall be surely stoned, and his flesh shall not be eaten; but the owner of the ox shall be quit.

In the Code of the Spartan lawgiver, Lycurgus, and in that of the Athenian legislator, Draco, provision was made for the formal trial of animals for misdemeanors.[2] A vestige of the unreasonable belief that brutes and even inanimate objects were accountable for their actions is to be found in that now obsolete term of English law, *deodand*, meaning, according to Blackstone, " a personal chattel which was the immediate cause of the death of a rational creature, and for that reason given to God; that is, forfeited to the Crown to be applied to pious uses." The *deodand* was of Grecian ancestry, as appears from the ceremonies connected with the offering of a sacrifice by the Athenians. When the animal or victim had been dispatched by an axe in the

---

[1] E. P. Evans, *Atlantic Monthly*, vol. 54. 1884.
[2] W. Lander Lindsay, M. D., *Mind in the Lower Animals*.

hands of the officiating priest, the latter immediately
fled, and to evade arrest he threw away the axe. This
instrument was then seized by his pursuers, and an
action entered against it. The advocate for the axe
pleaded that it was less guilty than the grinder who
sharpened it; the grinder laid the blame on the grind-
stone which he had used; and thus the whole process
became a farce and a mockery of justice.[1]

We learn from the writings of the Benedictine monk,
Leonard Vair, that in certain districts of Spain, in the
fifteenth century, when the inhabitants wished to drive
away grasshoppers or noxious vermin, they chose a
conjurer as judge and appointed counsel for the de-
fendants, with a prosecuting attorney, who demanded
justice in behalf of the aggrieved community. The
mischief-makers were finally declared guilty, and either
duly anathematized or formally excommunicated,[2] the
technical distinction between the two sentences being
doubtless to them a matter of profound indifference.
At this period, also, prosecutions of pigs or sows guilty
of devouring young infants were not uncommon.

Barthélémy Chassaneux, a famous French advocate
of the sixteenth century, first won distinction by the
originality of his pleas in defense of some rats in a
notable trial at Autun. He represented to the judge

---

[1] Banier's *Mythology*.
[2] J. B. Thiers, *Traité des superstitions*.

that his clients found it extremely difficult to obey the summons issued to them by the court, owing to their being obliged to traverse a region abounding in cats, who were, moreover, especially alert on account of the notoriety of the legal proceedings.[1]

Chassaneux wrote that the people of Autun had long agitated the question how best to rid the province of Burgundy of locusts, and he expressed the belief that a sure method of accomplishing so desirable a result was by the scrupulous payment of all tithes and ecclesiastical dues, and by causing a woman to walk barefoot round the infested fields.[2]

After the seventeenth century, prosecutions of animals and the use of incantations for their expulsion became less common. The Ritual of Séez in 1743 forbade such practices without the special permission of the church, but the same volume contains a formula for driving away grasshoppers, maybugs, and other insects. Mr. C. G. Leland states, in his "Gypsy Sorcery," that exorcism has been vigorously applied in the United States, not only against the Colorado beetle and army worm, but also for the suppression of blizzards and the grape disease. It has not had much success hitherto, probably owing, as he naively remarks, to the uncongenial climate.

[1] Louis Duval, *Rôle des croyances populaires dans la protection des animaux*. 1889.

[2] *The Student and Intellectual Observer*. vol. iii. 1869.

THE LUCK OF ODD NUMBERS

"For there's luck in odd numbers," says Rory O'More.
                                        SAMUEL LOVER.

I. EARLY SIGNIFICANCE OF NUMBERS

In the "Cabala," or ancient mystic philosophy of
the Jews, much importance is attributed to the com-
bination of certain numbers, letters, and words. According to one tradition, the earliest Cabala was given
by the angel Raziel to Adam, and orally transmitted
through generations until the time of Solomon, by
whom it was first embodied in written form. Another
report alleges that the cabalistic secrets of nature were
received from God by Moses in the Mount, and afterwards taught to Joshua, who communicated them to the
seventy elders, and they have since been treasured by
the initiated among the Jews.

According to the doctrine of the Pythagoreans, the
unit or monad was regarded as the father of Numbers,
while the duad, or two, was its mother; and thus is
explained one source of the general predilection for
odd numbers, the father being esteemed worthy of
greater honor than the mother, and the odd numbers

being masculine, while the even numbers were feminine. Moreover, the unit, being the origin of all numbers, represented Divinity, as God was the creator and originator of all things.[1] It was also the symbol of Harmony and Order, whereas the duad signified Confusion and Disorder, and represented the Devil.

Plutarch remarks in his "Roman Questions" that the beginning of number, or unity, is a divine thing; whereas the first of the even numbers, Deuz or Deuce, is directly opposite in character. As for the even number, said this writer, it is defective, imperfect, and indefinite; whereas the uneven or odd number is finite, complete, and absolute.

The belief in the lucky significance of odd numbers is of great antiquity, and reference to it is made by Virgil in the eighth Eclogue, and by Pliny, who comments on its prevalence in his time, but offers no explanation therefor. The Roman king, Numa Pompilius, is said to have added days to certain months in order to make an odd number.

It is related, moreover, that the Emperor Julius Cæsar (B. C. 100-44), having once been thrown out of his chariot through some mishap, refused thereafter to set out upon a drive or journey until he had thrice repeated a magic formula; and this practice appears to have been commonly in vogue in those days.[2]

[1] Rev. G. Oliver, D. D., *The Pythagorean Triangle*.
[2] Pliny, *Natural History*, book xxviii.

The persistency of a traditional belief is exemplified by the modern association of luck with uneven numbers; and probably the Goddess Fortune herself preferred a three-legged stool. However this may be, it is evident that the legions of her worshipers to-day are firmly convinced of the mystic charm inherent in triplets. The Chinese pagodas, or sacred towers, built by devout persons with the object of improving the luck of a neighborhood, have always an odd number of stories, being from three to thirteen floors high.[1] In Siam, also, this superstition holds universal sway, and its influence in the construction of buildings is especially noticeable; for the Siamese religiously adhere to odd numbers in architecture, and every house must have an uneven number of rooms, windows, and doors; each staircase must have an uneven number of steps.[2]

In the early literature and mythology of the Northern nations much importance was attached to the numbers three and nine, which were held especially sacred and dear to the gods. This fact is shown in their religious ceremonies, and more particularly in their sacrifices, which occurred every ninth month. Each sacrifice, moreover, lasted nine days, and each day nine victims, whether men or animals, were offered up.[3]

[1] *Century Dictionary.*
[2] Sir John Bowring, F. R. S., *The Kingdom and People of Siam*, vol. i. p. 139.
[3] Mallet's *Northern Antiquities*, p. 112.

II. THE NUMBER THREE

Three, as emblematic of the Trinity, has always been considered a sacred number, and long before the Christian era God was worshiped as a triple Deity. This is true not only of the Assyrians, Phœnicians, Greeks, and Romans, but also of the ancient Scandinavians, the Druids, the inhabitants of Mexico and Peru, as well as the Chinese and Japanese.

So from earliest times the Hindus have worshiped their triad of Brahma, Vishnu, and Siva. In Holy Writ we find three sister virtues, Faith, Hope, and Charity; and in classic mythology are trios of Graces, Fates, and Furies, the three-forked lightning of Jupiter, the three-headed dog, Cerberus, and the trident of Neptune. The tripod was anciently a symbol of prophecy and of divine authority, and the triangle was originally the pagan emblem of a holy triad.

The peculiar significance of the number three was due partly to the fact of its being the first uneven number containing an even one; and from the importance formerly attributed to it may have originated the familiar saying, " The third time never fails."

In the several codes of ancient Welsh laws are numerous so-called triads, of which the following are curious examples : —

Three things which a villain is not at liberty to sell without permission of his lord; a horse, swine, and honey. Three things not to be paid for though lost in a lodging-house; a knife, a sword, and trousers. There are three animals whose tails, eyes, and lives are of the same worth; a calf, a filly for common worth, and a cat, excepting the cat that shall watch the king's barn.

Among the ancient Irish, also, considerable importance was attached to the number three. Thus we read that among the household officials of the High King of Erin were three royal jugglers, three jesters, three head charioteers, three equerries, three swineherds, three janitors, and three drink-bearers.

Multiples of the mystic number three were much employed by witches in their incantations, and they are even now favorites with the Chinese, who have a saying that one produced two and two produced three, while three produced all things. This partiality is illustrated in the dimensions of the Temple of Heaven in Pekin, where three and nine constantly recur.

In a book entitled " Varieties," by David Person (London, 1635), being "a surveigh of rare and excellent matters, necessary and delectable for all sorts of persons," the author comments at some length on the significance of certain triads. Among others he mentions three things incident to man, — to fall into sin, which is human; to rise out of it again, which is angelical;

and to lie in sin, which is diabolical. Again, three powerful enemies, the world, the flesh, and the Devil, which constantly assail man, should be opposed by three efficient weapons, fasting, prayer, and almsgiving. Thomas Vaughan, in his " Anthroposophia Theomagica," has much to say concerning the virtues of numbers. "Every compound whatsoever," he says, "is three in one and one in three." In speaking of a natural triplicity, however, he does not wish to be understood as referring to " kitchen-stuff, those three pet principles, water, oil, and the earth, but to celestial hidden natures, known only to absolute magicians."

In Northumberland smooth holly leaves, gathered late on a Friday, are collected in a three-cornered handkerchief and carried home. Then nine of the leaves are tied into a handkerchief with nine knots, and placed under the would-be diviner's pillow, and, as a result, interesting revelations from dreamland are confidently anticipated. In another magical ceremony, a maiden before retiring sets three pails of water on the floor of her bedroom, and pins three holly leaves on her left breast. She will then, conformably to the popular belief, be awakened from her first nap by three loud yells, followed by three horse-laughs, whereupon the form of her future husband will be revealed to her.[1]

The supposed efficacy of these rites doubtless de-

---

[1] Folkard, p. 377.

pends chiefly upon the use of the magical holly, but
the repetition of odd numbers is also characteristic of
charms, incantations, and mystic procedures in all ages
and throughout the world.

III. THE NUMBER SEVEN

The number seven has ever been regarded as having
a peculiar mystic significance, and its manifold virtues
have been the theme of elaborate monographs.   Alike
in Holy Writ and among the earliest historic peoples,
in classic antiquity and in the mythologies of many
nations, this number has been most prominent, and to
this fact may reasonably be attributed a portion of the
luck associated with odd numbers in general.   A complete enumeration of familiar examples of the use of
this favorite number, although germane to our subject,
would be beyond the scope of this sketch, but a few
instances may be appropriately given.

The origin of the respect accorded this number by
the nations of antiquity was probably astronomical, or
more properly astrological, and arose from their observation of the seven great planets and of the lunar
phases, changing every seventh day.

> *Saturn* is first, next *Jove*, *Mars* third in place ;
> The *Sun* in midst, fifth *Venus* runs her race,
> *Mercury* sixth, *Moon* lowest and last in band,
> The Planets in this rank and manner stand.[1]

[1] Robert Vilvain, of Excester, *Enchiridium Epigrammatum*, p. 148. 1654.

It was a saying of Hippocrates that the number seven, by reason of its mystic virtues, tended to the accomplishment of all things, and was the dispenser of life and the fountain of all its changes; for as the moon changes its phases every seven days, so this number influences all sublunary beings.[1] The phrase "to be in the seventh heaven" was derived from the seven planets, which were believed by the Babylonians to be carried around upon as many globes of crystal, the seventh being the highest.[2] In the writings of the Cabalists of old are likewise portrayed seven heavens, one above another, and the seventh or highest was the abode of God and the higher angels. The ultimate source of the sanctity of the number seven has, however, been ascribed to the *septentriones*, the seven ploughing oxen, stars of the constellation of the Great Bear.

An ingenious but not especially plausible reason alleged for the popularity of this number is the fact of its being composed of *three*, the number of sides in a triangle, and *four*, the number of sides in a square, thus representing two of the simplest geometric figures.[3]

Certain Biblical critics of a speculative turn of mind

---

[1] T. Wain, *The Wonderful Number Seven.*
[2] Charles De B. Mills, *The Tree of Mythology.*
[3] *The International Cyclopædia*, vol. xiii. p. 360.

have concluded that its prominence as a symbol is due
to the emblematic significance of its component parts,
three and four; the former representing Divinity, and
the latter Humanity: in other words, "the union between God and man, as affected by the manifestations
of the Divinity in creation and revelation."[1]

In some portions of a great work on magic, discovered by Mr. A. H. Layard among fragments of clay
tablets in the ruins of a palace in ancient Nineveh, are
many incantations, formulæ, and conjurations, in which
the number seven occurs repeatedly.[2]

As familiar instances of the prominence of this number in former times may be cited the seven wise men
of Greece, the seven gates of Thebes, and the legend
of the seven sleepers of Ephesus.

Other examples are given in the following "seven
heroic verses" sent by a certain Mr. Michelburn to one
Mr. Crisp, who owed the former seven shillings: —

> Friend Crisp, I send you verses only sev'n,
> The number's od, God numbers lovs unev'n;
> Sev'n Hills at Rome, sev'n mouths of *Nilus* are,
> Sev'n sacred Arts, the World's sev'n Wonders rare,
> The week sev'n dais, the Heav'ns sev'n Trions show.
> But one thing rests, sev'n shillings you me ow,
> Which that you'l pay, sev'n Verses I bestow.[3]

In ancient Ireland every well-to-do farmer had seven

---

[1] Smith's *Dictionary of the Bible*, art. "Seven."
[2] F. Lenormant, *Chaldean Magic and Sorcery*.
[3] *Enchiridium Epigrammatum*, p. 141. 1654.

prime possessions, — a house, a mill or a share in it, a kiln, barn, sheep-pen, calf-house, and pigsty.

The number seven appears more than three hundred times in the Scriptures. God created the world in six days and rested on the seventh, and throughout the Old Testament, as well as in the Apocalypse, the constant recurrence of this sacred number is noteworthy. Thus we read of the seven fat and seven lean kine of Pharaoh's dream, and also, in the account of the Fall of Jericho (Joshua vi. 4): "And seven priests shall bear before the ark seven trumpets of rams' horns: and the seventh day ye shall compass the city seven times, and the priests shall blow with the trumpets."

According to a popular mediæval tradition, Adam and Eve remained but seven hours in Eden.

Seven archangels are mentioned in the Bible and in Jewish writings, — *Michael*, who was the special guardian and protector of the Jews, and in whose honor the Festival of Michaelmas is celebrated on the twenty-ninth day of September by the Anglican and Roman Catholic churches; *Gabriel*, the messenger who appeared to the Virgin Mary and to Zacharias; *Raphael*, spoken of in the Book of Tobit as the companion and guardian of Tobias, and conqueror of the demon Asmodeus; *Uriel*, an angel mentioned in the Book of Esdras; *Chamuel*, who, according to Jewish tradition, wrestled with Jacob; *Jophiel*, who expelled Adam and

Eve from Eden, and who was the guardian of the "tree of the knowledge of good and evil;" and *Zadkiel*, the angel who is supposed to have stayed the hand of Abraham when the latter was about to sacrifice his son Isaac.[1]

Samson's strength resided in seven locks of his hair, representing the seven rays of Light, the source of Strength. And the shearing of these seven locks by Delilah, a woman of low character, has been described as a triumph of Evil in suppressing Light.[2]

According to Herodotus, the Arabs of the desert had a peculiar method of confirming a vow of friendship. Two men stood on either side of a third, who made incisions with a sharp stone on the palms of their hands, and, having dipped in the blood therefrom some portion of a garment of each, he proceeded to moisten with it seven stones lying on the ground.[3]

The age of the world, in the opinion of learned men of former times, was properly divided into seven great epochs; namely, the *first*, from the creation of Adam to the Deluge; *second*, from the latter event to the time of Abraham; *third*, from Abraham to the Exodus of the children of Israel; *fourth*, from that time to the building of Solomon's Temple; *fifth*, from

[1] T. Wain, *The Wonderful Number Seven.*
[2] S. Pancoast, M.D., *The Kabbala*, p. 247.
[3] *The National Review*, vol. xxi. p. 199. 1893.

then to the Babylonish Captivity; *sixth*, the period between that and the coming of our Lord; and *seventh*,
from the beginning of the Christian era to the end of
the world.

According to astrologers, man's age was divided into
seven parts, governed by seven planets. The first
part, *Infancy*, comprised four years, and was ruled by
the Moon, a weak, moist, and changeable body. Next
came *Childhood*, a period of ten years governed by
Mercury, a planet indifferently good or bad, according
to the character of the planets with whom he was associated. Following this came *Youthhead*, from fourteen
to twenty-two, over which Venus presided. Next was
Adolescence, lasting twenty years and ruled by the
Sun, and in this age man attained his full strength and
vigor. The fifth, from forty-two to fifty-six, was called
Manhood, and was under the dominion of Mars, a bad
star. At this time men began to wax angry, impatient,
and avaricious, but were more temperate in their diet,
and more discreet. The next period of twelve years
was called *Old Age*, governed by Jupiter, a noble
planet, whose influence rendered men religious, chaste,
and just. The seventh was *Decrepit Old Age*, ruled
by Saturn, and comprising the years from seventy-eight
to ninety-eight.[1]

In the Lambeth Palace Library there is a manuscript

[1] D. Person. *Varieties.*

of the fifteenth century in which the seven canonical hours are compared with the seven periods of human life, as follows : —

Morning,	Infancy.
Midmorrow,	Childhood.
Undern,	School Age.
Mid-day,	the Knightly Age.
Nones, or	
High Noon,	the Kingly Age.
Midovernoon,	Elderly Age.
Evenson,	Declining Age.[1]

In the "Secrets of Numbers," by William Ingpen, Gent. (London, 1624), the number seven is described as the most excellent of all for several notable and curious reasons, and prominent among these was the alleged fact that the Soul consists of seven parts, namely, Acuminie, Wit, Diligence, Counsel, Reason, Wisdom, and Experience.

IV. ODD NUMBERS IN WITCHCRAFT

Odd numbers are intimately associated with the black art, for witches' incantations are commonly repeated three or nine times. Who ever heard of a witch performing any of her mystic rites exactly four or six times? Apropos of this may be quoted the following story, taken from the advance sheets of a work entitled

[1] *All the Year Round*, vol. iii. 1870.

" Golspie," edited by Edward W. B. Nicholson, M. A.,
Bodley's Librarian in the University of Oxford, England, and loaned by him to the writer. The book contains much interesting folk-lore of the extreme north of
Scotland : —

A woman who lived near Golspie was always telling her
neighbors that a woman whom they all believed to be a
witch had cast an evil eye upon the cow and herself. " Her
milk and butter were spoiled," she said; and she also told
them that in a dream she saw the witch in the shape of a hare
come into her milk-house and drink the milk. One day when
she was in the wood for sticks, her neighbors went into her
byre, and seeing a petticoat on a nail, cut a number of crosses
on it and put it in the cow's stall. Then they tied nine rusty
nails to a cord with nine knots on it. This cord they tied to
the chain on the cow's neck, and then went away. Shortly
after the woman came home, she went into the byre, and seeing the petticoat, nails, etc., ran out to her neighbors scream-
ing, and calling to them to go and see what the witch had
done on her. To make sure that it was the witch's work,
she showed them the *unequal number* of nails and knots.
Then she took everything that she thought the witch had
handled, and made a fire of them, saying that she could no
longer harm any person, because her power was destroyed
by fire.

The employment of odd numbers in magical formulæ
is exemplified in the following recipe for a drink against
all temptations of the Devil, used by the Saxons in
England : —

Take betony, bishopwort, lupins, githrife, attorlothe, wolfs-comb, yarrow; lay them under the altar, sing nine masses over them, scrape the worts into holy water, give the man to drink at night, fasting, a cup-full, and put the holy water into all the meat which the man taketh. Work thus a good salve against the temptations of the fiend.[1]

A Hindu woman, on returning with her young child from a strange village, is careful, before entering her own dwelling, to pass seven small stones seven times around the baby's head, and throw them away in different directions, in order thus to disperse any evil which may have been contracted during her trip.[2]

And as a preliminary to other mystic procedures, in order to avert the Evil Eye, the Hindus wave around the patient's face seven pebbles taken from a spot where three roads meet, seven leaves of the date-palm, and seven bunches of leaves of the *bor* tree.[3] It may not be surprising that such mysterious rites, whose efficacy depends chiefly on the magical potency of certain odd numbers, should be popular among the natives of India, but it is noteworthy that these numbers are equally influential in Christian lands. A multiplication of examples might serve to emphasize this fact, but would occupy too much space. Charms and for-

---

[1] Cockayne, vol. ii. p. 335.
[2] Crooke, p. 199.
[3] Campbell, *Spirit Basis of Custom and Belief*, p. 208.

mulas are commonly thrice repeated, probably in reference to the Holy Trinity.

> Of all the numbers arithmeticall,
> The number three is heald for principall,
> As well in naturall philosophy,
> As supernaturall theologie.[1]

The Bavarian peasant, in passing through a haunted place, considers himself amply fortified against evil if he takes the precaution to carry three things; namely, (1) a new knife which has never cut anything, marked on the blade with three crosses; (2) a loaf of bread baked on Epiphany Eve; (3) a black cat.[2]

V. ODD NUMBERS IN FOLK-MEDICINE

In a volume containing a great variety of ancient charms and magical cures, collected by Marcellus Empiricus, a Latin writer of the fourth century A. D., in which volume various remedial measures are described with great minuteness, the even numbers seldom appear. Thus, for the removal of a foreign substance from the eye, one should rub the affected organ with the five fingers of the hand of the same side, and repeat thrice a charm of words. Again, for the cure of a sty on the eyelid, take nine grains of barley and poke the sty with each one separately, meanwhile repeating a magic formula in Greek. Then throw away the nine and do

---

[1] *Times' Whistle.*
[1] Fräulein Helene Raff.

the same with seven, throw away the seven and do the same with five, and so with three and one.

The early Saxon physicians in England seem also to have had faith in the peculiar virtues of the number nine, as is evident from many of their prescriptions, of which the following prefix to a lengthy Latin charm is a fair specimen : —

For flying venom and every venomous swelling, on a Friday churn butter which has been milked from a neat or hind all of one colour, and let it not be mingled with water. Sing over it nine times a litany and nine times the *Paternoster*, and nine times this incantation.[1]

In an ancient English manuscript (Harleian Collection, No. 585), frequent examples are given of the employment of odd numbers in therapeutics. Thus, for dropsical affections, a beverage containing alexander, betony, and fennel is to be drunk daily for seven days. "To expel venom," centaury is to be taken for fifteen days, and a potion prepared from the seed of cress is extolled for its curative qualities if taken faithfully during three days.[2]

Indeed, the odd numbers are prominent in the annals of folk-medicine throughout Great Britain. The three chief duties of a physician were declared to be as fol-

---

[1] *Leechdoms, Wortcunning, and Starcraft,* edited by the Rev. Oswald Cockayne.

[2] *Archæologia,* vol. xxx. p. 427. 1844.

lows: the restoration of health when lost, its ameliora-
tion when weak, and its preservation when recovered.
So also three qualities were requisite in a surgeon;
namely, an eagle's eye, a lion's heart, and a lady's
hand, attributes equally essential to the skillful operator
of the present day.

The natives of the Hebrides inherit the old Scandinavian and Celtic partiality for certain odd numbers.
Thus in Tiree a favorite cure for jaundice consists in
wearing a shirt previously dipped in water taken from
the tops of nine waves, and in which nine stones have
been boiled. These same people formerly employed a
peculiar method of treating sick cattle. The veterinary,
holding in his hands a cup of cream and an oat-cake,
takes his seat upon the animal, and repeats a Celtic
charm of words " nine times nine times," taking " a bit
and a sip " before each repetition.[1]

In Cornwall, for the cure of inflammatory affections,
the invocation of three angels is thrice repeated to each
one of nine bramble leaves; and a popular remedy for
whooping cough is to pass a child nine times under and
over a three-year-old donkey.[2] In the south of England, for intermittent fever, the patient is recommended
to eat seven sage leaves on seven successive mornings,
fasting meanwhile; and in northern Scotland scrofu-

---

[1] *Celtic Magazine*, vol. viii. p. 252.
[2] William G. Black, *Folk-Medicine*.

lous affections are thought to yield to the touch of a
seventh son, when accompanied by an invocation of
the Trinity.[1]

The belief in the magical curative qualities of the
number nine was not limited to the northern nations.
Thus the inhabitant of ancient Apulia, when bitten by
a scorpion, proceeded to walk nine times around the
walls of his native town.

Dr. D. G. Brinton, in his "Nagualism, a Study of
Native American Folk-Lore and History," remarks that
the number nine recurs very often in the conjurations
of Mexican magicians

The women of Canton, China, attribute magical properties for the cure of cutaneous affections to water
drawn after midnight of the seventh day of the seventh
month.

When a gypsy child bumps its head, a knife-blade is
first pressed upon the swelling, after which an incantation is pronounced three, seven, or nine times, and the
knife is stuck into the earth a like number of times.
Many charms employed by gypsies could be mentioned
in illustration of the avoidance of even numbers in all
their mystic rites.[2]

[1] *Social Life in Scotland*, vol. iii. p. 227.
[2] C. G. Leland, *Gypsy Sorcery*.

VI. THE NUMBER THIRTEEN

In regard to the luck of odd numbers, the exception, which is commonly supposed to prove the rule, is the much maligned thirteen.

In the Scandinavian mythology Loki, the Principle of Evil and the chief author of human misfortunes, accompanied the twelve Æsir, or Demigods, and was reckoned the thirteenth among them. Moreover, the Valkyrs, or Virgins, who waited upon the heroes in Valhalla, were thirteen in number, and from these sources is believed to have sprung the very common superstition concerning the ill luck and fatality of the number thirteen, especially in connection with a party of guests at table.

The most generally received explanation of the origin of this popular belief refers it to the Last Supper of our Lord, where Judas is sometimes represented as the thirteenth guest. But why Judas rather than John, the beloved disciple? However, this is the generally accepted starting-point of this notable superstition. As with the Jews the thirteenth month, and with the Christians the thirteenth day of the year, which began with Christmas, were accounted ominous, so, with the inhabitants of India, the thirteenth year was considered to be of evil import. It is evident, therefore, that the source of this nearly world-wide belief cannot be attrib-

uted wholly either to the mythology of the north or
to the Paschal Supper.[1]

When the year was reckoned as thirteen lunar
months of twenty-eight days each, the number thirteen,
according to one view, was considered auspicious; but
when, under the present method of solar time, the
number of months was reduced to twelve, thirteen's
reputation was changed for the worse.[2]

In early times the Feast of the Epiphany, which is
the thirteenth day after Christmas Eve, was feared
because at that time the three goddesses, Berchta,
Holle, and Befana, with their ghostly companions,
were especially active; and, as a guard against their
machinations, the initial letters of the names of the
three kings, or wise men, were written on many a door.

Of the former trio, Berchta was represented as a
shaggy monster, whose name was used as a bugbear with
which to frighten children. She was intrusted with the
oversight of spinning, and on the eve of Epiphany she
visited the homes of the countryfolk, distributing
empty reels, which she required to be filled within a
specified time; if her demands were not complied with,
she retaliated by tangling and befouling the flax.

Holle, or Holda, was a benignant and merciful god-

[1] *Das Kloster*, Band xii. p. 771; Thorpe's *Northern Mythology*, vol. i.
p. 227; Grimm's *Teutonic Mythology*, vol. i. pp. 272 *et seq.*
[2] Gerald Massey, *Luniolatry*, p. 17.

dess, of an obliging disposition, who was usually most lenient, except when she noticed disorder in the affairs of a household. Her favorite resorts were the lakes and fountains, but she had also an oversight over domestic concerns, and shared with Berchta the supervision of spinning. Sometimes, however, she appeared as an old hag, with bristling, matted hair and long teeth.

Befana, the third goddess, was of Italian origin, and her name signifies Epiphany. On that day the women and children used to place a rag doll in the window in her honor. In personal appearance she was black and ugly, but her disposition was not unfriendly.

So universal has been the superstition regarding the number thirteen at table, that it has long been a matter of etiquette in France to avoid having exactly that number of guests at dinner-parties. The Parisian *pique-assiette*, a person whose title corresponds to the English " trencher friend " or " sponger," is also known as a *quatorzième*, his chief mission being to occupy the fourteenth seat at a banquet.

The ancients, we learn, had ideas of their own regarding the proper size of festive gatherings, their favorite number of *convives* being between three and nine, the number of the Graces and Muses respectively.[1]

Opinions have differed as to whether misfortune were

[1] J. B. Salgues, *Des erreurs et des préjuges.*

likely to befall the whole company of thirteen persons rash enough to dine together, or only the one leaving the room first after the repast. All evil, however, was supposed to be averted by the entire company rising to their feet together. It has been wittily remarked that the only occasion when thirteen plates at table should cause disquietude is when the food is only sufficient for twelve persons.

At the thirteenth annual dinner of that unique organization, the Thirteen Club, held in New York city, January 13, 1895, at 7.13 o'clock, P. M., the custodian delivered an address in which were recounted the circumstances of the club's formation. So prevalent was the apprehension of evil likely to result from the assembling together of thirteen persons that, when at length the requisite number were seated at table, it was found desirable to lock the doors of the banquet-room, lest some faint soul should retire abruptly.

Field-Marshal Lord Roberts, in his "Forty-One Years in India" (vol. i. p. 24), mentions a circumstance occurring in his own experience, which affords evidence, were any needed, of the falsity of the superstition in question. On New Year's Day, A. D. 1853, Lord Roberts was one of a party of thirteen who dined together at a staff-officers' mess at Peshawer, on the Afghan frontier. Eleven years later all these officers were alive, the greater number having participated in the suppression of the great Sepoy Mutiny of 1857, during which several of them were wounded.

In Italy shrewd theatrical managers have found it expedient to change the number of Box 13 to 12A, and in many streets of Rome and Florence one may search in vain for house-numbers between 12½ and 14. A gentleman of the writer's acquaintance, living in Washington, D. C., sent a formal petition to the authorities asking leave to change the number of his house, for the sole reason that it contained the ominous figures.

As an illustration of the popular distrust of the number thirteen among the villagers of the Department of Ille-et-Villaine, France, may be cited the following custom, which is in vogue in that district. Children are there usually taught the art of knitting by devout elderly women. The little ones are first seated in a circle, and, to facilitate the work, on the completion of the first round of knitting they are made to repeat the following words: " *One*, the Father; " at the close of the second round, " *Two*, the Son; " and so on, as follows: " *Three*, the Holy Spirit; the *four* Evangelists; the *five* wounds of our Lord; the *six* commandments of the church; *seven* sacraments; *eight* beatitudes; *nine* choirs of angels; *ten* commandments of God; *eleven* thousand virgins; *twelve* apostles; " and at the close of the *thirteenth* round, the children mention the name of Judas.[1]

---

[1] *Zeitschrift des Vereins für Volkskunde*, vol. iv. p. 250. 1894.

This remarkable and unreasonable prejudice against an innocent number seems to pervade all classes and communities. The possession of intelligence and culture is no effective barrier against it. Arguments and reasoning are alike vain. Even at this writing, an evening journal records that at a recent meeting of a newly elected board of aldermen in an enlightened city of eastern Massachusetts, one of the members objected to casting lots for seats because he did not relish the idea of drawing number thirteen. However, his scruples having been in a measure overcome, he was much relieved to find that the number eleven, which is both uneven and lucky, had fallen to his share.[1]

Brand quotes as follows from Fuller's "Mixt Contemplations" (1660) in reference to this subject: —

A covetous Courtier complained to King Edward the sixt of Christ Colledge in Cambridge, that it was a superstitious foundation, consisting of a Master and twelve Fellowes, in imitation of Christ and His twelve Apostles. He advised the King also to take away one or two Fellowships, so as to discompose that superstitious number. "Oh, no!" said the King, "I have a better way than that to mar their conceit; I will add a thirteenth Fellowship unto them;" which he did accordingly, and so it remaineth unto this day.

Persians regard the number thirteen as so unlucky that they refrain from naming it. When they wish

[1] *Boston Transcript*, December 30, 1897.

to allude to this number, instead of mentioning the proper term, they use words meaning " much more " or " nothing."[1]

The Moors, or Arabs, of northern Africa have similar prejudices, whereas the American negro, ordinarily a most credulous being, appears to be quite indifferent to the evil influences of the fateful number;[2] but in Turkey, so great is the popular dislike of it that the word for thirteen is seldom used.[3]

In Scotland this number is known as the " Deil's Dozen," a phrase which has been supposed to have some connection with card-playing, there being thirteen cards in each suit of the " Deil's Books." John Jamieson, in his Scottish Dictionary, avows his inability to trace the superstition to its source, but believes that it includes the idea of the thirteenth being the Devil's lot. The number thirteen is also sometimes known as a " baker's dozen," because it was formerly a common practice to give thirteen loaves for twelve, the extra piece being called the *in-bread* or *to-bread*. This custom is supposed to have originated at a time when heavy fines were imposed for short weights, the additional bread being given by bakers as a precautionary measure.[4]

[1] Surgeon-General Edward Balfour, *The Encyclopædia of India.*
[2] *Journal of American Folk-Lore,* No. 17. April, 1892.
[3] Brewers' *Dictionary of Phrase and Fable.*
[4] *The Century Dictionary.*

In certain cases, contrary to the general rule, thirteen is accounted a fortunate numeral, or even as one possessing extraordinary virtues.

Dr. Daniel G. Brinton, in "A Primer of Mayan Hieroglyphics" (p. 25), says that in the old language of the Mayas, an aboriginal tribe of Yucatan, the numbers nine and thirteen were used to denote indefinite greatness and supreme excellence. Thus a very fortunate man was possessed of nine souls, and the phrase, "thirteen generations old," conveyed the idea of perpetuity. The "Demon with thirteen powers" was a prominent figure in the mythology of the Tzentals, a Mayan tribe.

According to a widely prevalent popular impression, a brood is usually odd in number, and therefore it is folly to set an even number of eggs under a hen. In spite of the falsity of this idea, it is still quite customary to set thirteen eggs, an even number in this case being accounted unlucky.

Gerald Massey, in "The Natural Genesis," remarks that "there were thirteen kinds of spices set out in the Jewish religious service, along with the zodiacal number of twelve loaves of shew-bread. There are thirteen articles to the Hebrew faith, and the Cabalists have thirteen rules by which they are enabled to penetrate the mysteries of the Hebrew Scriptures. Thirteen are the dialectical canons of the Talmudical doctors for determining the sense of the law in all civil and ecclesiastical cases."

In England the day of twenty-four hours was formerly divided into thirteen parts, as follows : —

1. After midnight.
2. Cock-crow.
3. Between the first cock-crow and daybreak.
4. The dawn.
5. Morning.
6. Noon.
7. Afternoon.
8. Sunset.
9. Twilight.
10. Evening.
11. Candle-time.
12. Bed-time.
13. Dead of night.

Recurring now to the prevalent notions regarding the sinister and portentous character of this number, one may well inquire in all seriousness whether the harboring of this and other firmly rooted superstitious fancies is compatible with a deep and abiding Christian faith. The answer is plainly in the negative. Therefore it is doubtless true — and the truth should make us free — that the greater our indifference to the various alleged omens and auguries which so easily beset us, the more readily shall we acquire and retain a firm and enduring dependence on Divine Providence.

TOPICAL INDEX